TAKEN TO THE STARS

SANCTUARY'S END

J. N. CHANEY
RICK PARTLOW

Copyrighted Material

Sanctuary's End Copyright © 2024 by Variant Publications

Book design and layout copyright © 2024 by JN Chaney

This novel is a work of fiction. Names, characters, places, and incidents are either products of the author's imagination or used fictitiously. Any resemblance to actual events, locales, or persons, living, dead, or undead, is entirely coincidental.

All rights reserved

No part of this publication can be reproduced or transmitted in any form or by any means, electronic or mechanical, without permission in writing.

1st Edition

CONNECT WITH J.N. CHANEY

Don't miss out on these exclusive perks:

- Instant access to free short stories from series like *Backyard Starship*, *Sentenced to War*, and more.
- Receive email updates for new releases and other news.
- Get notified when we run special deals on books and audiobooks.

So, what are you waiting for? Enter your email address at the link below to stay in the loop.

https://www.jnchaney.com/taken-to-the-stars-subscribe

CONNECT WITH RICK PARTLOW

Check out his website
https://rickpartlow.com

Connect on Facebook
https://www.facebook.com/DutyHonorPlanet

Follow him on Amazon
https://www.amazon.com/Rick-Partlow/e/B00B1GNL4E/

JOIN THE CONVERSATION

Join the conversation and get updates on new and upcoming releases in the awesomely active **Facebook group**, "JN Chaney's Renegade Readers."

This is a hotspot where readers come together and share their lives and interests, discuss the series, and speak directly to J.N. Chaney and his co-authors.

facebook.com/groups/jnchaneyreaders

CONTENTS

Chapter 1	1
Chapter 2	11
Chapter 3	23
Chapter 4	35
Chapter 5	47
Chapter 6	63
Chapter 7	77
Chapter 8	87
Chapter 9	101
Chapter 10	113
Chapter 11	125
Chapter 12	135
Chapter 13	147
Chapter 14	159
Chapter 15	173
Chapter 16	189
Chapter 17	203
Chapter 18	211
Chapter 19	223
Chapter 20	233
Chapter 21	245
Chapter 22	257
Chapter 23	269
Chapter 24	279
Chapter 25	291
Chapter 26	303
Chapter 27	311
Chapter 28	323
Chapter 29	333
Chapter 30	345

Chapter 31	355
Epilogue	365
Connect with J.N. Chaney	373
Connect with Rick Partlow	375
About the Authors	377

1

"Get your stinking paws off me, you damned dirty cow!"

Yeah, I know, but that's exactly how the translation goo inside my head rendered the words. I didn't know which of the Strada had said it, but I knew who they were saying it *to*. The Gan-Shi bull was huge, seven feet tall and probably north of 300 pounds, wearing only a pair of homespun trousers that barely came down past his knees. His massive shoulders were knotted with muscle, and his powerful hands wrapped around the neck of a Strada warrior, dangerously close to throttling him.

Sanctuary was a small place, a city and a settlement and a planet where almost everyone knew each other, and normally, I would have expected the people watching wide-eyed from the sidewalks and street corners to intervene in the fight, to try to break it up. And maybe if it had been a Copperell brawling with the Gan-Shi, they might have, but Strada were supposed to be badass warriors, and if two of them couldn't handle the lone male, none of the Copperell shopkeepers and farmers were going to try.

We were lucky they'd come and warned us. I only wished we'd been *closer* when they told us about it because I hadn't gotten nearly enough cardio in lately and the sprint through nearly a mile of the dusty, midsummer streets had left me dripping with sweat even in my civilian clothes. The fact that Laranna never seemed to get out of breath when she sprinted had offended me on a moral level since I'd run track in high school and *should* have had the edge on her with respect to cardiovascular stuff. Not to mention that the Strada warrior garb she wore, tight cloth reinforced with leather, was a lot more practical for running than my Chicago concert T shirt and blue jeans.

But I was determined not to let her beat me to the fight, and if I didn't have the slightest idea what the hell I was going to do when I got there, well…first things first. The Strada who wasn't getting the life choked out of him kicked the Gan-Shi in the thigh over and over in what would have been a devastating attack on me or any other normal-sized humanoid, but the big bull ignored it and swatted backward with his free hand. The Strada's head snapped around, his eyes rolled up in his head, and he collapsed like a felled tree.

So, don't go for the legs. The arm was out, his neck was so thickly muscled I might have busted my hand hitting him there, and a torso strike was probably about as likely as me putting a hole through my punching bag. But for all that weight, he was tall and top-heavy. And facing away from me.

"Laranna!" I yelled over my shoulder. "I'll hit him low!"

"And I'll hit him high," she confirmed, her voice disgustingly calm and composed.

Not the leg, but the ankle. Not the Taekwondo I'd taken as a kid nor even the Strada martial arts Laranna had taught me but the baseball I'd played through middle school before I'd traded it in for track. A slide into home plate against a catcher I really didn't like—not that I'd ever spiked anyone, but I'd certainly thought about it. No spikes on the soles of my Nikes, but the full momentum of my 170 pounds moving as fast as I could run all focused on the edge of my heel right into the Gan-Shi's ankle…at the same time as Laranna's flying side kick into his face.

The Gan-Shi bull grunted at the double strikes, then squawked in a very un-Gan-Shi-like sound and fell backward, less the tree falling of the Strada's collapse and more a downtown skyscraper knocked over by Godzilla on a particularly nasty rampage. It wouldn't last long, but he'd dropped the Strada warrior he'd been strangling, and that had been the goal.

Jumping to my feet, I looked around the area, both to figure out what had started all this and to find any possible improvised weapons since I wasn't carrying a gun. An overturned cart with hearth-baked loaves of bread was the only clue as to the instigation and also the only possible weapons. Since an overdose of baked goods would only be deadly in the long run, I ignored the cart and helped the stunned Strada who'd been backhanded, pulling him to his feet and away from the Gan-Shi.

The bulls always looked angry, but this guy was a few degrees above that, and if this had been a Bugs Bunny cartoon, I would have expected steam to be coming out of his ears. He wasn't fast, and I had the time to get three or four more hits in before he made it to his feet, but I had the sense that wouldn't do a whole lot of good.

"Wait up, big fella," I told him, holding out a hand and putting on my best stern-teacher face, copied from my most feared martial arts instructors and ROTC cadre. "There's no point in hurting each other any more than we already have."

"You didn't hurt me," he grunted, which was depressing but also a good sign in that he was actually talking instead of throwing down.

"Then tell me why you were trying to hurt them," I said, gesturing at the Strada. One massaged his throat with a pained expression on his face, his breathing labored, while the other's eyes weren't quite focused and he seemed to be off-balance, leaning against Laranna for support. "We're supposed to be allies here, remember?"

"They got in my way," the bull said, his answer grudging, like he was reluctant to even explain that much rather than just wading back in, fists swinging. "Made me tip over the damned bread cart." His scowl deepened. "A male shouldn't be doing this sort of work…it's a female thing. And now I have to go back and reload the entire cart with more bread and get yelled at by the Elder!"

He surged toward the Strada warriors, and I stepped into the way, both hands raised in front of me now, strategies of how to jump out of the way before he hit me running through my head.

"How about if they say they're sorry?" I suggested quickly. "Maybe they could record the apology in a message to your Elder so she knows this wasn't your fault?"

"But we were just walking down the damn street!" The croaked protest came from the Strada who'd been choked, and the Gan-Shi snarled his opinion of the objection.

"Unless you want me to have Nareena assign you to cleaning the barracks toilets for the next two months," Laranna said tautly to the Strada, "you'll *apologize* and explain to the Gan-Shi Elder that this incident was entirely your fault. Am I clear?"

"Yes, ma'am!" the warrior rasped, hand still rubbing his throat.

"Then get on it," she snapped.

"Is everything all right here?"

I turned at the deep baritone and suddenly found myself in the shade of another seven-foot giant, the vestigial, stubby horns on his forehead a sign of his bovine Gan-Shi ancestry.

"Yeah, Shindo," I told him. "Just a little misunderstanding."

The older Gan-Shi male approaching behind him snorted derisively, shaking his head hard enough to send his jowly cheeks flapping.

"There have been *many* such misunderstandings lately," Warrin said. "Whenever your people and mine mingle, it seems like violence ensues."

"Perhaps that's because your people have sequestered themselves away from the rest of the population." Brandy had taken a while to catch up, mostly because she hadn't tried to run after us. Not that I blamed her for that since she was already six months pregnant. She'd always had a nurturing glow about her, like a grade-school teacher, and her current baby bump and long, matronly dress only accentuated it. "I think it would be best for your people and ours if the Gan-Shi made an effort to integrate into the population rather than maintain their own encampment outside the city."

"It is important that we learn to fit in if we're to live here long term," Shindo agreed, putting a hand on the shoulder of the young bull who'd been in the fight. "These people will be our neighbors for years." He guided the other Gan-Shi over to the cart and helped him turn it upright.

"I think you ask too much too fast," Warrin said, glaring at Brandy. "It was only a few months ago that we were on Wraith Anchorage, living in the Below with just our own people. For generations, only our males ventured out, and even those were exploited and abused. To expect us to trust you, to accept you as friends whose intentions are beneficent, is to expect a miracle."

"We'll discuss it later," I interjected, noticing a couple dozen onlookers staring at us, fascinated by the interplay. "Why don't you escort your buddy here back to the encampment," I said to Warrin and Shindo, "and we'll get these guys to a doctor."

I swear to God, half of the Gan-Shi vocabulary is grunts because that's the only response I got from Warrin before they took their younger friend down the road toward the encampment.

"I'll take them to the medic," Laranna volunteered, leaving me with Brandy and a pile of useless bread that was already drawing flies.

"Well, that was a load of fun," I said, cleaning dirt off the seat of my jeans...then moaning when I found a hole. These jeans weren't the reproduction ones Lenny fabricated for me from my original pair on the *Liberator*, they were brand new, bought back in Virginia, and they cost way too much. "How often do you get problems like this?"

"At least once a day," Brandy sighed. "Most not as violent as this, but all of them troubling. And I fear that oversized lunk Warrin is correct. There is no easy way to get this many people assimilated into our culture here. With the others"—she nodded toward the Copperell, Plantar, and other species pushing carts with food, homespun clothing, and various and sundry wares down the streets of the rustic town—"they were brought here in twos and threes, family groups. They had nowhere else to go, no one to turn to other than their neighbors. The Gan-Shi, as the big lunk said, came here en masse, tens of thousands of them. You've seen their encampment?"

I nodded. I could *almost* see it from here at the edge of town, the tops of their canvas tents standing twenty feet tall at the pinnacle and glowing white in the midday sun. They stretched across the open grasslands all the way from the outskirts of town to the foothills, spread out over several square miles. They'd even managed to get small crops planted in the short time they'd been here and had isolated herds of goats—well, goat-*like* animals that gave milk—and the stink from the Gan-Shi and the goats nearly reached to the street we were on.

"Well then," Brandy went on, "you should know we don't have the infrastructure to police that many people. We try to integrate them against their will, or even strongly suggest it, there's going to be more trouble than we can handle."

"The problem might solve itself," I suggested. At her curious glance, I elaborated. "We're scheduled to launch the invasion of Copperell in just a few weeks. I figure if we take it back, most of the Copperell people here are going to want to resettle there, right? Help rebuild things?"

"Most likely," she admitted with a shrug. "I know I would want to take Maxx there. I've never seen the world, but my grandparents used to tell me about it. Val promised he'd take me there someday."

"Copperell are like three quarters of the population here. The Strada troops'll be coming with us in the invasion, and everyone else..." I waved a hand. "Losing Copperell will force the Anguilar to pull back to their core worlds, which means they can all go home if they want. The Gan-Shi don't have a homeworld to go back to, so they can stay here and make one out of this place." I looked around at the mountains stretching green and brown into the sky. "It's nice here. They could do a lot worse."

"It's been home for Val and Maxx and me for years now, and I'll miss it. But I feel like you've ignored a possibility." She cocked an eyebrow as if challenging me to figure it out on my own. I shook my head, and Brandy let me in on the secret. "*If* we liberate Copperell, then the refugees will relocate there and everything will solve itself. But what if we don't? What if we can't force the Anguilar off my world?"

"That's simple," I told her. "We're not going to lose. Because if we did, this would all be over. And I'm not going to let that happen."

2

"Good to see you again, Chuck," I told Major Charles Barnaby, offering a hand when he tried to salute me.

Uniformed Secret Service moved into the Diplomatic Reception Room behind us and closed the door to the South Entrance. We'd flown down to Joint Base Andrews as per usual and been driven to the White House in a plain black SUV, which felt kind of tawdry, like they were ashamed to have us here, but I understood. The first time we'd come publicly to the White House, we'd been attacked by Russian assassins, and since then, they'd launched hypersonic missiles at an American spaceship that *I* happened to be on and then Laranna and I had blown the hell out of their missile launchers. Better safe than sorry.

"I keep forgetting you're not a colonel anymore, Charlie," he confessed, shaking my hand instead. "Why the hell did you resign your commission anyway? We never had time to discuss it before you headed out for Sanctuary."

"Well, for one thing," I admitted, motioning at his dress greens, "I didn't want to have to wear that monkey suit anymore. I know I was ready to do it for a career back in college, but I've been dressing down way too long." Not that I'd worn my concert T to a meeting at the White House, of course. We had standard gray field utilities for use by all the resistance soldiers, and they were a hell of a lot more comfortable than Army fatigues. "Plus," I added, "after what happened with Gib and Wraith Anchorage, I figured it would be better for everyone concerned if I wasn't bound to follow orders from someone who might tell me I couldn't go rescue one of my friends."

"Particularly," Laranna added, coming up beside me, "when they couldn't throw him into prison for disobeying orders because I'd blow up the planet to free him."

"I could see that," Chuck agreed, nodding to her. "I know of all the people I wouldn't want to piss off, you rank right up near the top. But you're missing all the fun! We just started the field testing period for the Onyx."

"You mean that powered armor stuff?" I asked, frowning as I tried to picture the readouts from the file he'd shown me weeks ago.

"Powered exoskeleton," he corrected with the didactic tone of a man who'd been giving the same lecture over and over in one meeting after another. "It's some badass gear. Wait'll you see it in action." He looked around. "No Gib this time?"

"He's back at Andrews with the lander." I shrugged. "He still has bad memories of Donovan trying to get him vivisected."

Chuck sneered at the mention of the National Security Advisor's name.

"I can't believe he still has a job. I thought sure the president was gonna fire him."

"If there's one thing Dani taught me about the twenty-first century," I told him, "it's that politics is even more corrupt now than it was when I left."

"This room," Laranna said, making a face, "is ugly."

I couldn't argue with that. The wallpaper in the Diplomatic Reception Room showed tree-lined landscapes, which wasn't too bad, but the furniture was yellow, like something out of the 1970s, which I remembered better than any of these people. Uncomfortable-looking chairs and sofas upholstered in mustard, and God knows why anyone would think it looked anything other than hideous.

If the Secret Service had an opinion about the décor, they kept it to themselves.

"How long are we supposed to wait here?" Laranna asked, looking around with an expression of disdain. "Where I come from, it's rude to keep guests waiting."

"They must not have politicians where you come from," Chuck said. "This is the leader of the free world we're talking about. Keeping people waiting is his way of showing he's more important than them."

"And yet he's not," Laranna countered. "He only has what we've given him. Without the cruisers and the Starblades, even this greatest country on Earth would barely be able to get off the surface of their world. Now they…" She shrugged apologetically and nodded to Chuck. "…*you* can reach the stars. Thanks to us. Thanks to Charlie, because without his fondness for this place, we'd never have come back after we found the beacon in Ohio."

"Yeah," Chuck agreed. "But President Louis can't see it that way. Admitting it even in private would make him look weak."

His mouth snapped shut about the same time as I heard the approaching footsteps. Secret Service came first, of course, then the functionaries, aides, whatever they were called. Easy to pick out because they were younger, their clothes less expensive but trying to *look* more expensive. Then General Gavin, Chairman of the Joint Chiefs, and Parker Donovan. Gavin was the older of the two, though Donovan wielded more political power. And shouldn't have.

Then came President John Louis, the most powerful man in the western world, perhaps *the* world. He looked young for his age, some dark hair still amidst the gray, tall, and rangy. He'd been elected on a platform of reform, though I'd yet to hear anything he'd actually reformed, but I'd personally guaranteed him reelection by making the United States the first starfaring nation and giving them more military power than any other.

Oh, people still protested America's involvement in an interstellar war—we'd driven by a few hundred demonstrators waving *No Blood for Aliens* signs on the way from Andrews—but the Russian attacks had galvanized public opinion for the most part. If Louis had any reelection worries on his mind, they weren't obvious from the confident grin he offered me along with a handshake.

"I trust you had a good flight, Commander Travers," he said.

I'd resigned my commission in the US Army, yet he still insisted on calling me *commander* because it fit with the Earth idea of rank structures. Hell, the Vanguard and Liberator crews had started calling me that as well just out of habit, even though the Strada and Copperell organized their military forces according to position rather than rank. I imagined that it would catch on because we'd be fighting alongside Earth troops for the foreseeable future.

"Well, it's more comfortable than an airliner, Mr. President," I told him, forcing a civil smile, "but I do start to miss open skies and fresh air after a while."

"I feel like all I see are the inside of offices sometimes," Louis returned with a sigh, gesturing around us. "Or the inside of a plane or a limo. I used to go hiking, back in the days before I stepped onto the stage of national politics."

"Well, you're always welcome to visit Strada or Sanctuary, sir," I invited, and General Gavin barked a laugh.

"Oh, I can just see your Secret Service detail having an aneurysm at the very thought of you leaving the planet, sir. Even in one of our own cruisers."

"I'm doing it," Louis insisted, pointing a finger at the older general. "I fully intend to be the first president to go to space, even if it's only to orbit."

"I feel like we've stepped into an ongoing argument," Laranna said, arms crossed as if impatient for the human politicians to stop dithering and get to the point. To Louis's credit, he took the hint.

"And not one we need to retread right now." Louis plopped down onto one of the sofas and waved at the other chairs. "Everyone, have a seat."

I'd rather have stood, not least because the chairs didn't look very comfortable, but they surprised me. Somehow, despite their awkward appearance, they were expertly crafted for support. Louis must have noticed my reaction because he laughed softly.

"Yeah, it's weird, isn't it? I have a theory that this is all part of a diplomatic mind game, to get visitors thinking about how shocked they are by the chairs and keep them from thinking about why they actually came."

"Well, *I* haven't forgotten why we're here," Parker Donovan declared.

The National Security Advisor's broad, stocky shoulders strained against a dark-gray herringbone suit that seemed to be perfectly color-coordinated to both his tie and his café-aux-lait skin tone. He wasn't much past forty, and there wasn't a trace of gray in his short, tightly curled hair. Nor was there any doubt in those dark, piercing eyes, the sort of all-noticing gaze I'd seen from sergeants-major, the better colonels I'd met, and maybe my third-grade homeroom teacher.

"We're *all* here," General Gavin put in, sounding as if he wanted to head off Donovan's rant, "to discuss our plans with regard to the offensive against the Anguilar."

"What's to discuss?" Laranna wondered, absolutely no give to the woman. "We agreed to the plan, and our forces will be prepared. Are yours?"

"We've been training and prepping ever since you left," Chuck put in confidently. "I've been supervising the tacs lanes the Rangers are going through, getting them used to the new weapons."

"And the cruisers have been drilling almost round the clock," Gavin added. "The fighters, too. Exchanging crews and shifts, making sure they're ready."

"We're still having some issues synchronizing the combined arms," Chuck admitted. "It's a lot easier to outfit a few thousand infantry with the new armor and weapons than it is to scale that up to tanks, APCs and the like."

"Which is one of the reasons I think we need to push the launch date of this operation back a few months, minimum," Donovan interjected, hands shaping his point like a sculptor. "I don't see the need to rush this. The longer we wait, the longer we have to train, to rearm with the new weapons and armor, to get more infantry, armor, air assets involved in this."

"The perfect is the enemy of the good enough," Gavin insisted. "If we try to pull an Operation Desert Storm here and take months to build up our forces, well…I have a feeling this Zan-Tar asshole isn't quite as incompetent as Saddam Hussein."

"But we've already built up our offensive capabilities by waiting," President Louis said, and having known the man for a few months now, I had the sense that he was trying to play devil's advocate and force us all to examine our positions. "We didn't have the two cruisers before the attack here. Maybe we should concentrate on seizing more ships, building up our forces."

I didn't roll my eyes. I know, that doesn't sound like much of an accomplishment, but it was, given how badly I wanted to.

"Sir," I said, choosing my words carefully, "if this were two or three years ago, I might agree with you. Back then, the Anguilar were overconfident, arrogant, thinking none of the backward, unorganized power blocs left over after the Centennial War could oppose them. And they were right. The resistance wasn't a threat, they had no unified leadership, everything was smooth sailing."

"Then we came along," Laranna cut in, sounding uncharacteristically smug. I knew it wasn't a reflection of overconfidence as much as it was a dig at the politicians, reminding them who was boss.

"Exactly," I agreed, though my first instinct was to downplay any suggestion that the situation was because of anything I did, personally. "And we've had a lot of success because of the fact that they didn't expect us. But the Anguilar are like cockroaches. They're survivors. They made it here all the way from another galaxy, if Lenny is right. This Zan-Tar is a reflection of that. They didn't have any use for him when they were winning, but now that they've taken some hits, they're willing to take a chance on him."

"Maybe there's your answer, then," Donovan suggested, his expression brightening as if he thought he'd come up with a brilliant idea. "This Tarzan…"

"Zan-Tar," I corrected him.

"Right," he acknowledged, waving it away with a dismissive

gesture. "This Zan-Tar is a product of their desperation. But that means if he loses a few more times, the Anguilar are just as likely to get rid of him, too. Maybe we should avoid taking the risk of this kind of big swing, and stick with an island-hopping sort of campaign, like you did with…what the hell was the name of that planet you freed?"

"Thalassia," I supplied, already forming my reply but holding it back, giving him some more rope.

"Thalassia, exactly!" Donovan beamed now, ever more enthusiastic with each word. "We can help you, send maybe one of our cruisers and half the Starblades and as many ground troops as you'd like. We take all those little colony worlds that they haven't fortified, give them a bloody nose, and maybe their Emperor will fire General Zan-Tar and appoint someone less competent."

"There's a fatal flaw in that line of argument, Parker," Gavin said, shaking his head.

"No," I cut in. "There are *two* fatal flaws. Maybe three." I counted them off on my fingers, speaking quickly before Donovan could flap his lips again. "One, you're making the assumption that even if Zan-Tar is removed from his position, his replacement will be less daring instead of more. If they're actually getting desperate, that's not likely. Two…if we do manage to take a bunch more small colonies, how the hell do we defend them?"

"We already went through this line of thinking," Laranna added, "after Thalassia. We took it, and the Anguilar immediately hit back and came very close to reconquering it. We lost some good people in that fight, and that was with basically only two targets to defend—Thalassia and Strada, and Strada has their own defenses."

"Two?" the President cut in. "What about Sanctuary?"

"We generally leave one of the Liberty ships there," I replied, "but Sanctuary's main defense is secrecy. There are a *lot* of habitable worlds in the galaxy, and the way the hyperdrive works, you can't just head out blindly and hope you find something. You have to know the coordinates of where you're heading, so there's little danger of the Anguilar stumbling across the place by accident."

"Lucky you," Gavin muttered.

"What's the third thing, Commander?" President Louis asked, frowning. "You said there were three fatal flaws in Parker's argument. What was the third?"

"Oh, that one's easy," I told him. "And predictable, from what I've read about the recent military conflicts America's been involved in. You've been fighting counterinsurgencies in Third-World countries for decades. What the big-brain types like Chuck here call *asymmetric warfare*. Your main problem has been finding the right place to hit them, making sure you don't hurt too many civilians in the process, right?"

"Pretty much," Gavin agreed. "Vietnam, Iraq, Afghanistan…"

"Well, this ain't that," I declared flatly, aiming the words at Parker Donovan, totally unconcerned whether it offended him or not. "The Anguilar Empire is the most powerful political and military entity in the galaxy. They have shipyards that can build cruisers, and no one else has had that since the end of the Centennial War. This is asymmetric warfare in the other direction."

"In that case," Donovan interrupted, "doesn't the old saying apply? The conventional army loses if it does not win. The guerrilla wins if he does not lose."

"Kissinger," Gavin snorted. "Not sure if I want to be taking advice from that guy."

"I'll take advice from whoever offers it," Louis said. "But isn't Parker right about that? If we're on the weaker side, shouldn't we try to keep racking up small wins?"

Deep breath. Let it out. I shouldn't have had to explain this sort of thing to the damned President of the United States and the National Security Advisor, but here we were.

"You know what else guerillas have to do in order to win, sir? They have to be willing to accept horrendous losses without blinking. I don't know about you, but that's not the kind of war I'm looking to fight. But speaking of military quotes, you're all ignoring the one that applies the most to us here."

"And what's that?" Louis asked, the keen look in his eye hinting that he knew already, that his previous question had been more of his famous devil's-advocate act.

"Someone after my time, but Chuck told me about him. A Marine general named Mattis. He said 'in my line of work, the enemy gets a vote.' That's the thing about your idea of racking up small victories, Mr. Donovan. You make it sound like Zan-Tar is going to just sit there and take it, running from defeat to defeat until he gets fired. That's not the kind of general this guy is. The enemy always gets a vote, and when the enemy is as smart and ruthless as Zan-Tar, you can bet he already has plans in motion to hit us again before we get the chance to hit him back." I shook my head. "I'm worried we might have waited too long as it is."

Donovan looked like he still wanted to argue, but Louis nodded, though from the look on his face, his agreement was reluctant.

"All right. It still feels like we're rushing into this, and if we take this swing and miss, we're pretty much screwed, if you'll pardon my crude language. But you're right, we can't count on the Anguilar not to attack Earth again in order to prevent us doing exactly what you're planning. General Gavin, the operation is a go." Louis offered us a politician's insincere smile. "Now that we've settled that, could I offer you some lunch? My chef has prepared some of the best bacon burgers you'll ever taste."

"Of course, sir," Chuck said before I could tell him no. He offered me a glare, a warning to behave. "We'd be very grateful."

Chuck knew we had plans to go see his father before we headed back to orbit, but I suppose he also knew how impolitic it would be to refuse a lunch invitation from the President of the United States.

Good thing I liked bacon burgers.

3

"Is this even legal?" Chuck wondered, pitching his voice to carry over the scream of the shuttle's landing jets. Leaning over in his seat, he jerked a thumb outside at the green fields and the rustic farmhouse growing closer with every second. "I mean, sure, it's rural Virginia, but we're kind of violating air traffic control laws, aren't we?"

"Don't know," Giblet said absently, concentrating on the lander controls. "Don't care."

"The only sensors controlled by your country that could pick up this shuttle," Laranna told Chuck, "are on board the cruisers, facing the other direction."

"In other words," I added, "what they don't know won't hurt them. And there's no way I was gonna spend hours sitting in a car waiting on the Beltway traffic jams when I could fly here in ten minutes."

Dust and debris fountained from the gravel parking lot as the shuttle got closer to the ground, and Chuck shot Gib an aggrieved look.

"Try not to take out any of the farmhouse windows this time, okay?"

"I make no promises," he said. "If you Earthlings built sensibly with landing zones at a safe distance, we wouldn't have to worry about it."

Before Chuck or I could point out to Giblet that we hadn't had shuttles until a few months ago and didn't *need* landing zones, the little spacecraft settled onto its landing gear hard enough to toss us all forward against our restraint harnesses, and the engines whirred down to nothing. Gib offered Chuck a grin and flicked the switch to open the side hatch.

"Figured the faster we got down, the less chance I'd send a rock through your daddy's windows."

"Thanks," Chuck said dryly, pushing through the airlock before it was all the way open. "Appreciate the consideration."

Laranna smacked Gib on the back of the head as she passed, and he yelped, but I was grateful since it saved me the trouble of yelling at him. Midsummer in Virginia was miserable, worse than central Florida, and sweat trickled down the small of my back halfway to the house. I felt bad for Chuck, since he still wore his dress greens, but I suppose he'd gotten used to it since he'd grown up here.

I did notice George stayed in the doorway of the farmhouse, waving and smiling but unwilling to surrender his proximity to the benefits of the running air conditioning. General George

Barnaby, US Army (retired) and former deputy National Security Advisor, was just past sixty and might have looked younger if he'd shaved the gray-shot beard. The fact that we'd been in the same year of college together was a testament to how badly suspended animation could screw up a guy's life.

"Hey, Dad," Chuck said, hugging the older man, then slipping past him into the climate control of the heavily renovated farmhouse and tugging off his tie. "Glad you got the air cranked up. I'm dying in this monkey suit."

"Cry me a river, son," George told him, chuckling. "You had to wear it one afternoon. I wore it to work every day for five years. In that swamp they call the capitol."

"Well, it might have been uncomfortable, buddy," I told him, "but it sure was more dignified than cargo shorts." I made a face at his clothes. "You look like a professional skateboarder."

"It's not like I have anybody to impress out here," he said, showing no shame whatsoever. "You want to keep criticizing my fashion choices or come in out of this damned heat?"

I squinted at the Sun through the afternoon haze and shrugged.

"I can do both, right?"

He laughed and wrapped me up in a hug. I loved George like a brother, but hugging him felt more like hugging my grandfather than my old friend from college.

"Glad to see you made it back from that last fiasco," he said, eyeing Giblet sidelong. "I wouldn't know anything at all about having to pull my best friend's ass out of the fire when he gets into more trouble than he can handle."

"Ooh, that hurts," Gib said, miming clutching at a chest wound. "I'd feel bad if you weren't dressed like a teenaged boy."

"Hey now," George objected, "is that any way to talk to the guy who kept you from being cut open for scientific study?"

"Oh, great," Gib moaned. "Now I owe *everybody* my life. I don't like owing anyone anything."

"Come on in and you can owe me a beer, too."

The interior of the farmhouse had changed since the first time I'd seen it. Since George had retired and moved into the place full time, he'd put his own stamp on the place—new flooring, new paneling, new art hanging on the wall.

"Nice photography," I said, running a hand down the frame of a sixteen-by-twenty picture of a bear cub standing up on a tree limb, a sliver of bark held in its teeth like a cigar. "Who took these?"

"I did," George told me, grinning. "New hobby now that I've got a lot of time on my hands. I got that one in Yellowstone back in spring."

"Wow, Dad," Chuck said, raising an eyebrow. "That's some National Geographic shit. You didn't tell me you were chasing down grizzlies."

"It's a black bear," George corrected him over his shoulder from the kitchen, half inside the refrigerator. Refrigerators, I'd only recently noticed, were a hell of a lot snazzier now than in my time. Stainless steel, side by side, lots of computer controls and display screens, like they were the control panel to fly a house into hyperspace. "Grizzly cubs don't generally climb trees."

"I hope I never find out," I said, taking a beer from the

handful of bottles he'd tucked against his chest. It wasn't a brand I preferred, but it wasn't bad compared to the stuff my translator called beer that the Strada and Copperell produced.

"What?" George asked, handing off the rest of the bottles. "You spend all your time fighting murderous aliens, and you're scared of a bear?"

"I don't feel guilty shooting Anguilar," I clarified. "Bears are just animals doing what comes naturally. I don't want to hurt them."

"Don't worry, Charlie," Laranna teased, bumping her shoulder against mine. "I'll protect you from the mean bears."

"I've seen the predators on your planet," Gib told her after taking a swallow of Heineken. "I'll take the bears."

"What brings you four here all together?" George wondered, motioning toward the kitchen table. "I expected you, son," he said to Chuck, then looked back at the rest of us as he took a seat, "but if you're all here…"

"We're going to be leaving soon," Chuck confirmed. He frowned, tapping the bottom of his bottle against the table thoughtfully, as if considering how much he could reveal to his father.

Laranna rolled her eyes.

"The time has come for the attack on Copperell," she said, and Chuck gritted his teeth, hand halfway up in a quelling gesture. "Oh, come on, Chuck. If the Anguilar have spies on this world, they're a hell of a lot more likely to be in Washington than on your father's farm."

"The Anguilar aren't the only enemy we have to worry

about," George reminded her. He twisted off the cap of his beer slowly and methodically, as if using it as a focus of his thoughts. "Remember what happened when we relaunched the crashed cruiser a few months back."

"You mean the Russians," I assumed, my eyes flickering around the interior of the house. "You really think they're bugging the place?"

"You know all about hyperdrives and blasters," he replied with a knowing grin, "but you don't have a clue how sophisticated surveillance technology is nowadays. It's positively Orwellian. Luckily, I still have connections in the DoD who hooked me up with the latest in *counter*surveillance technology when I remodeled this house."

Chuck shaped a silent whistle, then chased it with a long pull on his beer.

"Damn. I'd call you paranoid, but it's not really paranoia if they're out to get you."

"Look, I know you're impatient with the president and particularly that asshat Donovan for dragging their feet on this operation, but you have to understand, they're not used to thinking about galactic-level threats. Everything they've faced up till now has been easy to understand. Russia is desperate for former glory and wants to expand. China is desperate for continued relevance and wants to distract its people from the fact that their economy is in a death spiral. The entire Middle East is imploding because they're all used to being the center of attention in world politics and can't handle nobody caring anymore."

George shrugged, stretching his legs out in front of his chair.

"Honestly," he went on, "it was sort of a nice change from when we were kids and everyone thought it was just a matter of time before the USSR either conquered the world or got into a nuclear war with the US. Of course, then *you* guys came along and overturned the apple cart for everyone."

"You think things are worse now?" Chuck asked, eyebrow shooting up. "I mean, yeah, there's an existential threat from the Anguilar, but we have fusion power and starships and space travel…" He shook his head. "In another couple years, we'll have power plants that can provide energy for the entire continent without polluting, and we'll be able to bring in minerals from the asteroid belt and the moons of Jupiter. We'll have colonies on other planets."

"In another couple years," George emphasized. "*If* we survive the next couple years."

"I thought you were on our side on this, George," I said, surprised and a little troubled. I respected George Barnaby's opinion a lot more than Parker Donovan's or even the president's.

"I am." He spread his hands. "Looking at the big picture, the Anguilar were going to make their way here eventually, and if they'd done it on their own, we would never have had a chance against them. You moved the schedule up, but you also gave us the tech and the weapons to put up a fight. And yeah, in the long run, this is a huge deal. We aren't an Earthbound species anymore. We have a chance to take our place among other interstellar civilizations. And the experience could bring the entire world together like nothing else ever has. In the long run." George sighed and took a drink, staring at the wall unfocused like he saw something light-years away. "If we have a long run."

"We'll do everything we can to protect your people, George," Laranna assured him.

"If I thought," I said slowly and carefully, "that our best chance to win this war was to keep nibbling at the Anguilar Empire's flanks, playing it safe, I'd do that. No question. But I don't. Zan-Tar is going to go on the offensive and say to hell with defending the peripheral systems. He'll let us waste time and resources freeing places like Thalassia and just aim everything they have here, the center of our resistance. The only way to stop that is to keep them busy fighting for something they actually need to defend."

"This guy seems to have made quite the impression on you," George surmised.

"Yeah, you could say that," Gib muttered, his expression darkening.

"I'm sorry, Gib." George leaned across the table, put a hand on the Varnell's arm, and squeezed tightly. "I haven't had the chance to say it since…you know. But I really am sorry. I wish you'd had the chance to take this bastard out."

"War's not over yet." Gib didn't pull away, but neither did he acknowledge the gesture. "I promised Charlie I wouldn't go rogue again, but if I have the chance to kill Zan-Tar in battle, I'm taking it."

"I hope you get it. But as someone who lost a loved one long before her time, I did want to tell you…it gets better. But only if you let it. Only if you don't shut out your friends and family."

Laranna scooted her chair closer to Gib and slipped an arm around his shoulder.

"And we're both of those," she reminded him, kissing him on the cheek. " Don't you ever forget it."

Giblet squirmed, clearly uncomfortable with both the attention and the affection. I knew him well enough to know he appreciated it, but he'd spent most of his life not getting either without conning people into it.

"So, you're here in the *Liberator*?" George asked, showing a keen awareness of when to change the subject.

"The whole fleet is here," I corrected him. "Out beyond lunar orbit. We left one Liberator at Sanctuary and a few squadrons of Starblades at Thalassia and Strada, but the other four Liberators, the cruisers, the Vanguards…all here, ready for the Copperell invasion. All we're really waiting on is the refitted tanks and Strykers to get through testing and load up on the shuttles. Should only be a couple more weeks." I knocked on the wooden tabletop.

"Even though I know you have this place surveillance-proofed," Chuck confessed with a grimace, "I feel really uncomfortable even hearing you guys talk about it. Like I'm going to walk outside and find the MPs waiting to haul me away for treason."

"Shit, dude," I scoffed, "you had a much better chance of being arrested when you helped me go AWOL to rescue Gib from Wraith Anchorage."

"Don't remind me," he said, raising a hand to block out the memory. "You wouldn't believe the chewing-out I got from

General Gavin once we were in private. He pretty much told me that the only reason I didn't get an official reprimand and a court-martial was that they needed you and your ships on their side."

"You're welcome," I told him, grinning broadly. "And that's another reason why I resigned my commission. Now they can't chew me out or order me around. If they want what I have, they need to ask nicely."

"Well, aren't you special?"

"Charlie, do you copy?"

I blinked at the interruption. I hadn't expected anyone upstairs to be radioing me, but I suppose I should have, considering this stop hadn't been official or scheduled. The voice was small and tinny on the comlink at my belt, but I still recognized it.

"Yeah, Lenny," I said, grabbing the device and holding it up to my mouth. I could have worn an earplug, what they called an ear*bud* in the here and now, but it felt weird, and I couldn't bring myself to walk around with one of the things stuck into my ear canal. "What's up?"

"Charlie…"

Now I *really* blinked, as if someone had slapped me in the face. Lenny was a very sentient artificial intelligence and could emulate the speech patterns of a humanoid very well, but one thing he never did was waste time. For instance, by hesitating. If he did that now, it was purposeful, to give me fair warning that he was about to say something I wouldn't like. From their concerned frowns, I could tell Laranna and Gib had noticed it, too.

"What is it, Lenny?" I demanded.

"We've received a relay message from Liberator Four."

Lenny had resisted giving the other zoo ships individual names because, to his way of thinking, every one of the robots controlling those ships was really another version of him, which made the ships just part of a larger whole. Instead, we'd given the others numerical designators, and Four was…

"The Liberator we left back at Sanctuary?" I asked, already knowing the answer. "What did they say?"

"The early warning web was tripped," he said, a hanging judge bringing the gavel down on a death sentence. "Imperial cruisers jumped into the system."

No one at the table said a word, all of them staring in open-mouthed disbelief at the comlink in my hand as Lenny finished the dirge.

"The Anguilar have found Sanctuary."

4

Too late. We were going to be too late.

The words echoed through my thoughts the way they had the entire journey, the week-long claustrophobic trek in the sightless, soundless hell of hyperspace. I'd never thought of it that way before. Hyperspace had just been a trick, a way of getting from here to there fast. The closest I'd come to an existential realization of the dimension was when I'd walked through the open area of an Anguilar ship while we'd been inside. I'd tried not to look at it then, but if I had the chance now, I would have stared into that utter nothingness with rage and impatience.

If being stuck incommunicado, unable to send or receive word of what was happening to my friends, my fellow warriors, the people I was responsible for, who looked to me for leadership, unable to see a single star, with only a vague idea of where we were wasn't hell, then it was close enough.

I didn't think anyone had said two words to each other the entire trip that didn't involve military prepping and planning. Talking about anything else hurt too much, and everyone who even opened their mouth for casual conversation got stared down. In the ship's gym, Strada and Copperell worked out in silence, the clank of weights and the slap of bodies tumbling on the sparring mats obscenely loud. No music this time. I usually played a mix from the database of songs Lenny had helped me upload into the ship's system, but that didn't feel right, either.

The closest I'd come to talking about it was when Laranna and I had fallen into bed at the end of every day, exhausted by maintenance on our Vanguards, target practice on the ship's range, running the track around the perimeter, and endless drilling. Just a few sentence fragments strung together, most of the thoughts left unsaid.

"Brandy is…" I'd begun, letting the question hang there.

"Six months," Laranna had finished for me, intuiting what I had asked. "A boy."

They'd had to have Lenny facilitate the pregnancy with some genetic manipulation since there was a slight difference in DNA between humans and Copperell. Not much, but enough to make a successful pregnancy difficult without technological aid. Laranna and I had the same problem, and we'd talked about having the same procedure once the war ended, but Val and Brandy hadn't been willing to wait that long.

"If anything happens to them…" Again, I hadn't finished. This time, Laranna hadn't either. There'd been no need.

It had been a very long week, and now, only seconds from the jump back to realspace, all those scenarios I'd worked so hard to avoid thinking about during the trip ran through my head at a hundred miles an hour. If hyperspace had seemed newly claustrophobic, the interior of the Vanguard starfighter was a coffin ready for the burial. And the worst part, the part I hadn't experienced since the battle in Earth orbit, was that Dani wasn't my gunner.

"Thirty seconds," Chuck told me. I'd intended to recruit one of the Copperell ship crew for a right-seater, but Chuck had insisted.

"I'm your liaison to the US military," he'd said when I tried to talk him out of it. "And General Gavin made it very clear to me that means I'm supposed to make sure you don't get yourself killed before all these plans for invading Copperell and making the United States a major player in the galaxy."

"And you think you can protect me by running the pulse cannon from the right seat?" I'd asked, shaking my head. "That didn't work out so well for my last gunner."

"Probably not," he'd admitted. "But at least if I screw up and you wind up dead, I'll be dead right beside you and won't have to fly home with my tail between my legs."

"Ten seconds," Chuck intoned, eyes fixed on the countdown.

"You really don't have to do that," I told him. "I can see the clock, too."

"Sorry," he said sheepishly. "I think I've seen too many movies."

Normally, I would have laughed at that, even if we'd been facing a battle. But the prospect of what we were about to see wouldn't even allow for the usual dark humor I used to cut the pre-fight tensions. I just nodded and watched the numbers get smaller.

Not that I needed them to know when we jumped. The lurch was unmistakable, the fabric of reality pushing its way through every atom of my body.

"Launch! Launch! Launch!" The order came out automatically, like a curse, but I hit the throttle for the maneuvering jets before the last iteration of the command, and the thrust pushed me into my seat until the inertial dampeners took effect.

We didn't know what was on the other side, but there wasn't time to wait, and before Lenny and the bridge crew could give us a heads-up, the dull gray of the hangar bay gave way to the star-dotted black of open space. Sanctuary was on the other side of the ship, along with the system's sun, and for just a fraction of a second, I could pretend that everything was cool, that nothing had happened and it was a false alarm.

Right up until the threat sensors lit up with the alert that three Anguilar cruisers hung only a few miles off our right side.

"Goddammit!" I hissed, knowing what their mere presence meant. Then aloud. "Vanguard Wing, this is Vanguard One. I designate the targets Alpha, Bravo, and Charlie."

This was the part we'd had to drill over and over before everyone accepted the new system...me, as well. I had limited experience as an Army grunt and none at all as a fighter pilot before the whole Vanguard Wing experience, so everything I'd learned and passed on to the rest of the squadron had come from lessons given to us by the fighter jocks at Joint Base Andrews. It turned out that for all the advanced tech in the Kamerian starfighters, the targeting software in American F-22s and F-35s could run circles around the original equipment.

I'd developed a theory about why that was. The Kamerians, much like the Strada, had been a warrior culture and didn't much like substituting technology for individual prowess, whether it be on the ground with a gun in their hand or sitting in the cockpit of a fighter. Not to mention all the societies out here were paranoid about sentient computers for some reason. Whatever the original reason, the problem had been solved by a joint venture between Lenny and DARPA, and each of the Starfighters came equipped with the latest in cutting-edge American targeting systems, married with exquisite care to the Kamerian sensors.

All it took was a tap on each of the cruiser icons to designate the different targets and transmit that not just to the Vanguards but to the Liberators and the cruiser as well.

"First Squadron," I continued once the designations had uploaded, "form on me, and we're taking Alpha. Second, you have Bravo, and Third, you have Charlie." Second was Gib, and Third was Laranna, and once upon a time, we'd had six squadrons of four planes each, but that was before we'd lost a couple birds in combat and reorganized into three squadrons of seven and one bird in reserve.

There was so much I wanted to know, wanted to ask the bridge crew of the *Liberator*, wanted to clear the ship and check the sensor readings for the planet. But one of the shitty parts about being a commander was that I didn't get to indulge in that kind of thing. The mission, the men and me, that was how I'd been taught, and if it was just college ROTC, well, it was still all I had to go on, and it had worked so far.

We had a job to do, and if we didn't take out these cruisers, it wouldn't matter what else had happened.

"Charlie," Lenny called, "do you need the *Liberator*'s support?"

"No," I snapped. "Get our infantry on the ground and get into low orbit to provide them fire support. We got this."

"Wish we could have brought the whole gang along," Chuck murmured.

"We couldn't take the chance." I didn't elaborate. We'd had the conversation before, the first time sitting in Earth orbit waiting for the Vanguards to dock.

Chuck and Gib had been all for bringing the cruisers and Liberty ships with us, but that was another thing about being the commander—I had to think about more than the bone Zan-Tar dangled in front of me. He'd found Sanctuary, but there was always the possibility that he was using it to draw us out, to get us to send all our forces there to leave Earth and Strada and Thalassia unguarded.

So, the America-flagged cruisers and Starblade squadrons stayed in the Solar System, while our cruisers had been sent to Strada to supplement their fighters and ground defenses. The other two Liberty ships had gone to Thalassia, and I could only hope that I hadn't screwed up and spread us too thin, because maybe *that* had been Zan-Tar's plan, and I was playing into it. I could go down that rabbit hole until I wound up coming behind myself and biting my own ass, but I had to make a decision, and this was the one I'd made.

I had more immediate problems now. The cruisers turned with the ponderous grace of a blue whale, spotting the jump signature of the *Liberator* and turning her way.

"They've seen us," Chuck said. "Or at least they've seen Lenny."

"They'll notice the Vanguards in a minute and split up their forces," I said. Maybe I wasn't a veteran fighter pilot, but I knew how Anguilar ship captains thought. "They know about the Vanguards so they'll send two our way and one for the *Liberator*."

And then they proved me wrong. All three of the cruisers burned straight for the *Liberator* at maximum acceleration, ignoring us completely.

"All squadrons, don't let them get to the *Liberator*!" I yelled the order—not because it was necessary to get their attention but more to fight the strain of the sudden rush of acceleration pushing briefly past the limits of the dampeners.

The fighter leapt across the gap, our acceleration mated with theirs, sacrificing control for speed. Decelerating would take a painful burn minutes long, and I'd only have time for one shot before we passed by, but with the entire squadron at my heels, maybe it would be enough.

"Why are they going after the ship?" Chuck wondered, his fingers twitching just above the control stick for the pulse turret, as if they longed to put a barrage into the cruiser. "Don't they know the Vanguards are more dangerous?"

It was a good question but not one I had the luxury of

thinking about. The red line showing the range of the particle cannon edged closer and closer to the nearest of the cruisers, and I had to concentrate on aligning the nose and the particle cannon mounted there with the forward particle battery on the Anguilar ship. Just another five seconds and...

All three of the cruisers jumped.

"Shit!" I blurted, grabbing the controls and pulling the Vanguard up and away from the event horizon of the wormhole through the fabric of space. "We're too close! Everyone pull up!"

The holes a hyperdrive tore through space were, Lenny had explained to me, basically a singularity, the core of a black hole. Not a long-lived one since they evaporated a second or so after the ship passed through, lacking the input of energy needed to keep them open, and not a large one. But larger corresponding to the size of the ship and the cruisers were pretty damned big, especially compared to our Vanguards.

The gravitational pull only lasted a few seconds, just long enough to yank the entire wing off course and send us tumbling planetward, straight toward the *Liberator*'s hull. The Vanguard's drives were on gimbals, and thank God because it saved us all the time it would have taken to spin end for end before we hit the brakes.

Inertial dampeners were magical tech as far as I or any of the scientists we'd dealt with back home were concerned, something none of us could begin to understand, but they had their limits, and if they could keep us from being crushed to a fine paste even when boosting at dozens of gravities, it still wasn't painless.

The seats spun with the gimbals, and they barely had time to lock into place before the hand of God slammed us into their padding hard enough to fill my vision with stars. I shook my head to clear it before the dampeners caught up, and a sharp pain in my neck reminded me why that was a bad idea, but the good news was, none of the fighters had collided with the *Liberator*.

"What the hell?" Gib squawked, as usual not giving a damn about radio discipline. Most of the aliens didn't, since intercepting signals was nearly unheard of out here. "Why did they jump?"

"Maybe because they knew about us," Laranna suggested, voice breathless in the aftermath of the braking burn. "They knew we could take them."

"That's never stopped them from skirmishing with us before," Gib pointed out.

"Later," I told them. "The landers are launching…we need to cover their descent."

And hope there was still something down there for them to save.

"Bandits!" Chuck announced, pointing at the tactical display. "We got bandits in the upper atmosphere! Four squadrons!"

And there they were, a constellation of white stars on the screen, growing bigger as they ascended. They had to have been in the air when we jumped into the system, but the cruisers leaving them behind didn't make any sense, even for the Anguilar. A left hook, a right uppercut, rope-a-dope. This was like boxing Muhammad Ali except we were blindfolded and there were three of him.

"Vanguard Three," I transmitted, "head low, run interference for the landers, and keep those damned Starblades from providing air support. Two, circle to their right, and we'll go left. Keep them engaged and don't let any of them break back to the landers."

I'd let a few Air Force fighter jocks have a turn in the seat of a Vanguard while we'd been training, and they'd all said that it was cheating. The flight-assist computer wasn't sentient like Lenny, but it was what they'd called *predictive AI*, turning our intent into reality without requiring the same sort of precision needed to fly an F-22. Which was the only reason I could fly one of the birds.

When I shoved the steering yoke downward, the gimbals spun, and the fighter took me into the atmosphere, the gravity resist kicking in automatically, the shields protecting us from the friction like we were wayward children who needed their hands held. And I suppose we were.

No more sensor dots. This close, the Starblades solidified into the familiar dagger shapes of the most common short-range fighter in the galaxy, their silver wings gleaming in the daylight glow of the sun. They were almost beautiful, if they hadn't been the weapons being used to try to kill us. By contrast, the Vanguards flying in formation behind me were brawny, curved like the shoulders of a lion charging into a pack of hyenas.

They opened fire first despite the fact that they were still at the outside edge of the range of their pulse cannons, and I barely felt the shudder as the thermal energy was translated into kinetic. But if they were at the edge of *their* range, they were well within *ours*. A nudge against the control yoke brought the targeting reticle of the particle cannon down over the center of mass of the lead fighter. The squeeze of the trigger came naturally now, far too naturally, like I'd gotten used to this, and that troubled me a little.

Not enough to keep from doing it again. The Starblades sparked like the old cap guns I'd played with as a kid, or maybe more like when I'd hit the rolled-up strip of caps with a hammer on the rear stoop. One time, I'd soaked the roll in gasoline from Poppa Chuck's mower can, and it had gone up in flames and left a black scorch mark on the cement. The fighters tumbled away, wreathed in fire like those caps, and this time my grandmother wasn't around to yell at me and force me to clean off the stoop.

The Starblade pilots weren't stupid, and they knew their birds were no match for ours head-on. They scattered, leaving behind the wreckage of five of their birds, splitting up to wingman pairs in a blossom formation like a sunflower opening up in the morning. They had to know they couldn't get away, and if they were anything like most of the Krill or Anguilar pilots we'd encountered, they weren't about to surrender, which meant one thing.

"They're splitting to get to the landers," I warned. "Stick with them! One fighter per two Starblades!"

Which I didn't like at all, but there were too many of them to match pair for pair. Gritting my teeth at the idea of letting Dagon and Wance fly off without me to watch their backs, I jerked the wheel hard to the left and banked in the direction of a pair of Starblades I'd picked at random.

The Starblades had the advantage here in the soup, which was what pilots called the atmosphere, and the Anguilar were going to try to take us deeper to push that advantage to the max. I had to catch these guys before they had the chance.

"Chuck?" I asked, not finishing the thought because he should know what I meant.

"Trying," he said, features screwed up in concentration. "Can't depress the turret any farther…"

I pushed the nose down just a degree, and Chuck's wordless grunt of satisfaction told me it was enough before a stream of red pulses put the exclamation point to the statement. One of the Starblades flared with crimson energy and went into a spin, and the other pilot finally made a mistake and panicked, jerking away from his out-of-control wingman.

Right into the targeting reticle of the particle cannon.

A weapon powerful enough to pierce the shields of a cruiser obliterated the tiny fighter, leaving barely enough debris to rain down to the surface. Trackless green grew closer and closer with every second, and I pulled up on the yoke, climbing again, determined to get back and check on the rest of my squadron.

"Charlie, is that you?" I recognized the voice, though it was thinner, reedier than usual, and the signal strength was weak.

I let out a relieved sigh and brought the Vanguard back level a thousand feet over the boreal forest.

"Brandy? Yes, it's us. Where are you?"

"The canyon north of the city. Get here quick, Charlie."

I choked on the next question and had to try again.

"Is it bad?"

"It's worse."

5

THEY CALLED THE CITY SANCTUARY.

I'd always thought it had been lazy, unimaginative, but Dani had told me once that it could be a cultural difference. I think, in the end, it had just come down to the fact that there was only the one real city on the planet, and it didn't make any sense to come up with another name until they had a second city.

That wouldn't be necessary anymore. The city no longer existed.

"What the hell did this?" Chuck asked, his voice barely above a whisper.

I understood. Every single structure had been reduced to a blackened crater, not one brick or board connected to another. Warehouses, factories, apartments, everything was gone. No smoke. It had happened days ago.

"Orbital bombardment," I answered Chuck's question, unable to take my eyes off the wreckage.

North into the hills, still running nap-of-the-earth, I spared a glance for the IFF and threat display. Most of the Starblades had fallen off the radar, only a handful still being chased around the continent by my pilots.

"Vanguard Two, this is One," I called to Laranna. "Reconsolidate the squadrons and home in on my position. The survivors are in the canyons north of the city."

"I copy, One," she replied, doing her best to comply with the broadcast codes I'd established, unlike Gib. "The landers are on their way down. I'll redirect them there."

"Haven't seen any enemy ground troops yet," Chuck said, leaning forward and squinting at the readout. "There're some thermal readings up ahead…"

Crimson threads exploded out of the forest along the dirt road out of town, seeking us out, and I fought an urge to pull away, my head knowing the shields would take it but my gut not so sure.

"Incoming," I said softly in counterpoint to the glowing arc around the fighter's forward shields.

"Armored vehicles," Chuck announced, traversing the turret. "We got a column down there…"

"Save your ammo," I told him, angling the control arm forward and pushing both pedals to the floor. Flying the Vanguard in an atmosphere was a lot like piloting a helicopter, if you substituted gimbal-mounted drives for rotor blades.

The fighter angled downward, the emitter of the particle

cannon swinging into alignment with the column of Anguilar armored vehicles barely visible through the trees. Bursts of scalar pulses still sought us out in a desperate fusillade, as if the infantry down there knew what was coming next. I might have felt worse about it if I hadn't seen the city. I touched the trigger, and artificial lightning connected us to the ground, blowing trees into crackling stumps, turning the packed dirt of the road to blackened obsidian…and blasting a half a dozen Anguilar APCs into nonexistence.

Mushroom clouds roiled black and angry red into the early morning sky, pointing the way north, and I followed their guidance like the Israelites in the wilderness. Only we weren't raining manna down from heaven on the Anguilar troops below us, more interested in the very fires of hell. Infantry abandoned their vehicles, trying to escape the death road by heading into the trees, but Chuck sprayed either side of the road with pulse fire. I ignored his efforts and theirs, blasting the vehicles to vapors and burning metal. Not as many boots on the ground as I would have thought, but they'd been here a week, and I knew the Strada warriors we'd left to guard this place wouldn't have gone down without a fight.

Totally involved in picking my next target, I didn't realize other fighters had joined my slow traverse of the road until another particle cannon joined my barrage, turning the road into a solid line of fire and smoke, the woods beside it expanding the flames as if Chuck and the other gunners were coloring outside the lines. Individual Anguilar troopers might have made it off the road, but they wouldn't get far, not with our troops landing back at the city, ready to sweep north in our wake.

I didn't know how many Anguilar troops we'd killed. It was impossible to tell from hundreds of feet above the tree-shrouded road and would likely remain that way even when our own infantry moved in behind us. The only count I needed, the only measure of success, was *all of them*.

It wasn't until we reached the river bar that our own dead became visible. The Strada warriors and Copperell militias didn't have military APCs, but I recognized the up-armored cargo trucks that had once been parked back in the city. What was left of them. Not disintegrated like the armored vehicles I'd taken out with the particle cannon, but ripped apart, blown to shreds.

The bodies remained where they'd fallen, gathered behind the trucks, using them for cover in a fight that had raged days ago. There wasn't enough left of them to identify their species. Too small for Gan-Shi, humanoid, but that was as much as I could discern from the air.

"Those are ours," Chuck said, voice haunted by the sheer numbers. This had been a last stand, a rear guard, and they'd sold their lives dearly.

More APCs littered the road beside the river, run off the road, burned by small-arms fire or explosives. The Anguilar body armor identified the dead lying around them. Hundreds of theirs, as many of ours, though most looked as if they'd been killed in airstrikes. The fighters had undoubtedly come from here to meet us, and any residual guilt I'd felt for downing them faded to nothing.

The road out of town split at the river, one path heading farther into the mountains up switchbacks and through tunnels, the other following the river through hoodoos and into the canyons. More wreckage, more casualties littered the road up through the canyon, some of it pushed aside, some abandoned at the center of the dirt track. Each shattered cargo truck was a kick in the gut, every motionless form sprawled across the ground a finger pointed my way, silently screaming "this is *your* fault!"

We didn't encounter more enemy troops until the end of the road, and this time, they weren't firing up at our fighters, they were charging forward into the narrows of the canyon, the choke point where the resistance forces had set up their front lines. Pulse weapons lit up the air with raw energy, static electricity crackling off the armor of the Anguilar APCs, but the return fire from the defenders heartened me, showing that at least some of them still lived. The Anguilar strategy was transparent—they were desperately trying to make it behind the resistance lines to force us to come down and smoke them out individually on foot, make it impossible for us to strike them from the air. Our guys knew it, too, and were fighting back with just as much ferocity.

"Wipe these assholes out," I growled, abandoning radio procedure myself, sure that no one would care.

The Anguilar were piled up, four vehicles across at the front and ten rows deep, unwilling to get out and advance on foot, probably figuring it would be suicide with the concentrated fire coming out of the canyon. It was like playing Galaga back in the pizza place in college, except that I had a full squadron of starfighters backing me up, ripping into the Anguilar ranks with a blinding cascade of particle beams and pulse bursts, racking up a score so high, it would have still ranked in the top ten thirty-five years later.

This wasn't a video game, though, a lesson hammered into my soul too many times over the last couple years. When you died, you didn't respawn, and once the game ended, you couldn't just take your quarters and go home.

"Cease fire! Cease fire! Cease fire!" I called over the whine of the jets as the Vanguard hovered in formation with the rest of the squadron.

A few stragglers took down running Anguilar soldiers with their pulse turrets before the entire squadron obeyed and the guns fell silent. Smoke billowed out of burning APCs, the very air shimmering with the ambient heat from soil turned to volcanic glass. Flames crackled in the trees, and a very small part of my rational thoughts worried about forest fires, but the river on one side of the road and the bare cliff face on the other would probably contain it.

A larger question was, where the hell were we going to land? The canyon narrowed quickly past the end of the road, barely room on either side of the river for the defenders to take up positions. Even now, with the attackers dead or dying, they stayed behind rockfalls and waited because there was simply nowhere else to stand. There was certainly nowhere for our planes to touch down, and from what I remembered of the Narrows on hiking trips with Laranna, it didn't get any better for miles.

We could land amidst the carnage and the fires where the Anguilar forces had been a few minutes ago—the Vanguards were tough enough to endure the heat. But *I* wasn't, and there was no point landing if getting out would kill me.

"Vanguard One-Three," I radioed, calling Dagon, my Copperell wingman, "this is Vanguard One. Ground troops should be advancing up the road in a few minutes. Maintain patrol of the area. If you see any Anguilar troops attempting to escape back down the road, let the infantry take care of them, but if you see any trying to head for the Narrows, you are weapons free. Take them out."

"Yes, sir," Dagon replied immediately. "Umm…I mean, copy, Vanguard One. Wilco."

Oh well. At least he was trying.

"Where are we heading?" Chuck asked as I fed power to the drives and climbed out of the canyon. "Back to the landing field?"

"It'll take hours to get back here from the landing field," I told him, staring at the view from the belly cameras as the Vanguard crawled above the roof of the canyon.

A thick layer of trees and brush lined most of the canyon rim, except for one spot just a few hundred yards long, burned clear to the rock by a nasty forest fire a few years ago. Lightning strike, Brandy had told us. It might have spread farther if the rain hadn't doused it after just a couple days. What it had left was barely enough nearly flat surface for a single Vanguard to touch down.

"I don't know that we've ever discussed the matter, Chuck," I told my gunner, "but I hope you don't have any problems with heights."

I CERTAINLY *DID* HAVE a problem with heights, but phobias were a luxury I didn't have time for anymore. The climb down the canyon wall to the river wasn't that bad. Plenty of handholds including tree roots and only one really nasty, tricky spot that had required an uncontrolled slide on the seat of my pants for ten feet or so before I caught myself on a rock outcropping.

A Strada waited for us at the bottom. I'd called ahead and told Brandy that Chuck and I were coming down, and she'd told us she'd send a guide to take us to the caves.

"Skyros?" I asked, racking my memory for the man's name.

He was one of Nareena's top lieutenants, a tall, rangy Strada warrior not that much older than me. His clothes were torn and stained with mud and dirt, a bloody bandage wrapped around his left thigh, and if word had reached him that the Anguilar forces here had been routed, it didn't affect his watchful stance or how tightly he clutched at the pulse carbine slung across his chest.

"Brandy says you're to follow me," Skyros said, his tone flat, as if behind that stern expression, he was numb with shock.

Other Strada and Copperell stood off to the side, eyes and weapons aimed downriver. Not one lacked a bandaged wound nor a haunted expression. I nodded to Skyros, and he motioned wordlessly to the others. The squad fell into a tactical formation around us with the sort of precision that couldn't come strictly from training. They'd been in constant combat for a week, and I was pretty sure that meant that all the sloppier soldiers hadn't survived this long.

"When did they land?" I asked Skyros, walking beside him, wishing I'd brought a rifle along instead of just my sidearm. Not that I thought I'd need it, but I felt naked and vaguely ashamed next to the vigilant troopers.

Skyros didn't answer immediately, plodding forward beside the river. The rush of the narrow stream echoed off the canyon walls, a background roar, the only sound for several seconds. I thought it had drowned me out, that the Strada hadn't heard the question, but he finally replied.

"There were six cruisers. The Liberator and the Starblade squadrons held them off for twenty hours. That was when we lost contact." He shook his head, shuffling to a halt for just a moment, like he couldn't talk and walk at the same time. "We did see the Liberator once more, though…when what was left of it reentered the atmosphere."

"Goddammit."

The curse was reflexive, exploding out before I could contain it. It might have been wrong, might have been cynical or heartless, but hearing that was nearly as big of a kick in the gut as seeing the dead soldiers. The Liberator ships were the biggest weapon we had in our arsenal, and we'd started out with six of them. Now, there were four. It was maddening. We'd sacrificed so much to build up our space forces, and it seemed like every two steps up meant a step back.

"They made orbit about three or four hours later." Skyros walked again, apparently having dealt with the demons the words had conjured up. "We thought they'd land immediately, but that was wishful thinking. They bombarded the city, but we'd evacuated everyone by then. We had a plan."

I nodded. Everyone knew about the evacuation plans. They'd been a fact of life here.

"The caves," I said.

"Yeah. The caves. But the problem was, they saw us from orbit. They knew which way we were headed, and they sent their ground troops after us. Nareena…she ordered the Copperell militia to stay with the civilians, and we all spread out from the landing field to the Narrows to slow them down as best we could. Waiting for the call to get through. Waiting for you."

"We came as soon as we got the message." It sounded lame even to me, but it was all I could say. "Is Nareena back at the caves?"

"She's dead."

I shouldn't have been shocked. I'd resigned myself to the possibility that they were all gone, and Nareena was the field commander of the Strada warriors. But I'd known her since we'd liberated Strada, and if she wasn't as close of a friend as Gib or Val, she was still a friend. Or she had been.

"And how many others?" I didn't want to know, but it was part of my responsibility to ask. There'd been 10,000 Strada warriors originally, but we'd split off 1,000 for each of the Liberators and another few hundred in the cruisers we'd captured. That left half the number here, 5,000.

"There are two thousand of us remaining." And if I'd felt like the news had been a punch in the stomach, for Skyros, the words came in a groan, as if they'd been tortured out of him.

Sanctuary's End

Three thousand people gone. One battle, one week, three thousand people dead. More losses than we'd suffered in any fight since the whole war had begun. I missed a step, nearly tumbled off the path, but Chuck caught my arm.

"Steady," he said quietly. "They need you to be strong for them."

I nodded and kept following.

"Of the Copperell militia, we've only lost a few dozen." Skyros's voice was still hoarse, but he pressed on, as bound to duty and honor as any Strada warrior. "They were kept back at the caves at first, but as our own losses mounted, we had to pull more and more of them out in the defense. The civilians…" He sighed. "The ones who lived in the town itself are all fine. They made it to the caves long before the bombardment, and we even managed to stockpile enough food for everyone. But the outlying settlements…we've had no contact."

"What about the Gan-Shi? Did they make it to the caves?"

He shook his head dismissively, showing none of the concern or agony he had speaking of his own people or the civilians.

"The Gan-Shi had been having problems with the townsfolk. A few weeks ago, Brandy made the decision to pack them into cargo trucks and send them to a new settlement about fifty miles downriver. We tried to call them when the evacuation started, but they didn't respond."

I pulled out my comlink and dialed up the frequency for the Vanguards.

"Vanguard Two, this is One. I'm heading for the caves. I need you to check on the Gan-Shi settlement. They've had no contact since the invasion."

"Right, I'll check it out. Charlie…how are the Strada?"

I wondered if I should tell her. There were all sorts of security reasons, morale reasons, comm discipline reasons why I shouldn't have said anything on an open channel, but those were all reasons I'd learned back on Earth in the National Guard and ROTC, and I didn't think they applied to the comlinks because, as far as I knew, no one could intercept the signals.

On the other hand, maybe there were some things that shouldn't be said over the radio, news better broken face-to-face.

"It's bad," I told her. "I'll tell you the rest when we debrief."

As I'd spoken to her on the comlink, the path had diverged from the river, the canyon splitting off, and we'd followed a dry streambed into a side channel. That ancient stream had cut into the side of the hill, and where it had once run was now a system of caverns. Maxx had found it exploring with the other kids four years ago, and Brandy had recognized its potential immediately.

Her work was visible just past the entrance, wooden braces shoring up the tunnels for safety, battery-powered lights just far enough in that they wouldn't be seen from overhead at night.

"Stay here," Skyros told his squad. "Guard the entrance. We don't know if any of the Anguilar made it past our pickets."

I wanted to tell him he was being paranoid, but he had good reason to be. I said nothing, just followed him…and the lights. The tunnel had started out barely tall enough for a man to walk without ducking his head most of the way, but a few dozen workers with power tools had carved out something taller and wider in just a few months.

Not too far into the passage, we ran into the first of the civilians.

"Charlie?" the older Copperell woman said hesitantly, squinting at me in the low light, letting the burlap bag slip off her shoulder. "Is it really you?"

"We're here now, Kara," I assured her. "You'll all be fine."

It felt like a lie. I had no idea if anything would be fine ever again, but it was what she needed to hear.

"Charlie? It's Charlie! They're here to rescue us!"

A dozen voices, a dozen questions, a hundred exclamations, and people poured out of side passages, crowding around us. Copperell, mostly, but there were plenty of others, a dozen species from a dozen star systems, with fear and desperation the only common denominators. And hope. I was the focus of the hope, and they all swarmed around me, the call going up and down the tunnels.

I tried to comfort them, then I tried to politely push through, and finally, I tried shouting at them to get back as claustrophobia took over and the press made it hard to breathe. It would be a hell of a thing to survive everything I'd gone through and then die from being crushed by the people who wanted me to save them.

"Get out of the damn way."

She didn't shout, barely raised her voice, yet the press of civilians parted like the Red Sea before Moses when the petite, demur Copperell woman walked through their midst. I was used to seeing her in a long, matronly dress, but the one she wore now was longer and looser to deal with her baby bump. More than seeing her visibly pregnant, what shook me about Brandy's appearance was how dirty and ragged her clothes appeared. The woman was detail-oriented and fastidious about her appearance.

"Brandy," I said, pushing through the crowd to pull her into a hug. "Thank God you're okay."

She didn't resist the embrace but returned it stiffly, and a sudden rush of fear hit me.

"Maxx?" I asked her. "Is Maxx all right?"

"Yes," she told me, emotion finally penetrating the cold mask she wore. "Maxx came here with the first of the evacuees."

"And Val?" I was afraid to ask the question, but I had to know.

"Val..." The mask cracked again, and her voice broke with it in a paroxysm of pain. "Val tried to reach the nearest settlements. He was caught at the edge of the orbital bombardment, but Vallon managed to carry him back to us. Come with me."

No one got in our way this time. No one said a word, as if they understood this was a rite of passage we'd have to undergo. Through the main tunnel, then into a branching corridor, this one more obviously dug out recently, the walls polished a smooth, slate gray. Past stacked boxes and around a wall of them set up as a barrier to the rest of the chamber.

Cots had been laid out in the subdivided room, most of them unoccupied, though a few held Strada and Copperell with serious wounds, amputations, burns. Except the one in the far corner, at the edge of the lantern light. No Strada or Copperell lay in that bed. He was human…what was left of him.

It was Val, though I could barely see his features through the oxygen mask covering his mouth. A blanket covered the rest of him, though it couldn't hide the burns sticking out under the edge of field bandages. The blanket flattened abruptly just past his knees. Standing over him was a medieval monk complete with a cassock, his beard streaked with gray, his eyes a bright blue, though today they were dimmed with sadness. Brother Constantine, who *had* been a monk until Lenny had scooped him up. Once he'd been the robot's personal assistant or something, but now he was attached to the resistance.

"Oh, God," I murmured, lurching toward Valentine McKee.

"Don't," Constantine said, catching my arm. "He's not conscious."

"We're keeping him in a medically induced coma," Brandy told me. "Otherwise, the pain…."

The word ended in a choked sob, and I thought she might crack, but that hard-won control took over again.

"We need to get him up to the *Liberator*. He needs the medical bay there."

I nodded, already grabbing my comlink. No time to carry him out in a vehicle, even if we could fit one into the Narrows. I'd have to get a lander to hover over the roof of the canyon, get him into a stretcher, and tractor it up.

"And then," Brandy said, that master spy mask slipping back into place, "we need to talk."

6

I STARED at the coffee cup, at the pale brown lapping at the rim, the steam rising from it. I needed caffeine, but I couldn't summon the energy to take a sip. I hadn't slept well in over a week and hadn't slept at *all* in the last thirty-six hours. There'd been too much to do.

Up to the *Liberator*, back down to Sanctuary to organize relief efforts and get the civilians into temporary shelters, check on the settlements, make sure that the badly wounded or sick got taken to the ship for treatment. Then back into a Vanguard to fly a shift on patrol, make sure that the other pilots got downtime. And now, back again to the *Liberator*, where I theoretically should have been in my bunk, resting.

But I couldn't close my eyes. Every time I tried, the images of those desperate men and women in the tunnels returned, the tableaus of destruction where Sanctuary town had been...and Val. Valentine McKee might have been born in the Nineteenth Century, but he'd adapted as well to this new world as I had. He'd found Brandy and Maxx and had become part of their family, then he'd become part of ours when Giblet, Brazzo, Laranna, and I had joined the resistance. He'd gone to Copperell with me on what had seemed at the time like a suicide mission and never batted an eye.

"Charlie."

I looked up sharply and realized Laranna had been talking to me for at least a few seconds, and I'd blanked out the entire thing. The galley had been nearly empty when I'd come in, but now it was packed with crewmembers and Strada warriors brought up from the surface, the low buzz of conversation snapping into place like the backing track in a recording studio. I wondered how long I'd been sitting here.

"Sorry," I told her, finally taking a sip of the coffee, the warmth and flavor an injection of alertness directly into my veins. None of the non-humans drank the stuff, which meant I'd had to buy a supply of it back on Earth and bring it aboard. Well, honestly, George had bought it for me, along with a deluxe coffee maker since I lacked a regular paycheck. "I'm kind of...out of it."

"We have tents set up for the civilians," she repeated patiently, pushing food around her plate with a fork but making no attempt to eat it. "They're not much, but they're all we could salvage. Thank God it's summer and there's no heavy rain in the forecast."

"What about the Gan-Shi?" I wondered. She'd reported back

on them a few days ago, but I'd had a million other things to think about since then, and all I could recall was that they'd only suffered light casualties.

"They say they don't require any aid." Her expression twisted in a scowl, and I thought I read suspicion behind it. "The Anguilar didn't bother bombarding them, didn't even send any Starblades to strafe their encampment. According to Warrin and Shindo, the enemy sent out a single scouting party, and the only casualties were a few males who went out to investigate the APCs. The Anguilar never came back." She shrugged. "Maybe they didn't consider the Gan-Shi a real threat and figured they'd take care of them once they dug out Brandy and the others."

"Yeah. What…" I stopped, took another sip to hide the tremor going through me, the twitching of my cheek muscles. "What are we doing about the bodies?"

Laranna leaned against the table, a tear trickling down her cheek that she showed no signs of shame for.

"There isn't enough time for a funeral ceremony for each of the Strada warriors here. They're being interred in a mass ritual tomorrow night, then we'll…" She sucked in a deep breath, her lip quivering. "We'll hold private vigils for them back on Strada when all this is over."

When all this is over. How many times had we said that these last two years?

"Nareena will be missed," I told her. "She was a good leader and a brave warrior."

"She's with Jax now," Laranna declared, a drowning swimmer seizing onto the only lifeline available.

Losing Jax the first time, waking up thirty-five years later to know he'd moved on with his life, had been as painful for Laranna as his death during the retaking of Strada, but I think having Nareena around had been a comfort, a reminder that Jax had found happiness even after her disappearance.

"Have you been to the med bay?" I asked her. "I was gonna head by there in a little while to check on Val."

"Don't bother."

I turned in my seat, not jumping in surprise mostly because I was too tired for that. Brandy pulled a chair out and sat at the table beside us, setting down her tray with a negligent clatter.

"What?" I blurted, imagining the worst. "Why?"

"He won't know you're there," Brandy clarified, showing no indication that she'd noticed my alarm. "Lenny is keeping him comatose while he's in the vat."

I shuddered at the thought. The vat was what we called the tank of oxygenated biotic fluid they used for the most serious cases in the med bay. You could breathe in the stuff but they'd told me it felt an awful lot like drowning, so they kept patients sedated while they were inside.

"So, they're using the…nano…what is that stuff again?" I asked, shaking my head.

"Medical nanites," she supplied, methodically cutting up her steak. It wasn't pork, but it was close enough that I'd decided to call it that. "Engineered bacteria designed to go in and repair tissue."

"Is he going to be okay?" I grimaced at how dumb the question sounded, but I was too brain-dead to put it any more delicately. "Can they fix him?"

If Brandy was offended by it, she gave no indication, just took a bite of her lunch and chewed it with purpose and determination until she could speak again.

"He'll live," she finally told us. "But he was without any real medical attention for days. It's a miracle he survived at all. Lenny told me that he's unsure how much can be done for him."

"How's Maxx taking all this?" Laranna asked, her hand inching toward Brandy's as if she wanted to comfort the woman but was afraid to touch her for fear she'd shatter at the contact—mentally, if not physically.

"He's scared." Brandy chewed dutifully, as if she considered it an obligation to the baby growing inside her and wouldn't shirk it no matter the circumstances. "He lost his father a long time ago, and now he thinks he's going to lose the man who's been his father for the last four years. He won't leave our compartment." Her steak devoured, Brandy threw down her fork and speared me with a glare. "Are you our commander, Charlie?"

"What?" I asked, feeling complete whiplash now.

She sighed as if I were a wayward child she had to lead by the hand.

"Are you *our* commander? The commander of the resistance? Because you seem to have spent a lot more time dealing with your friends on Earth lately. I could count the number of visits you've made to Sanctuary in the last few months on one hand."

My instinctive reaction was anger, but I knew that Brandy had to be in serious pain, and snapping back at her wouldn't accomplish anything. Besides which, she was one of the smartest and most quick-witted people I'd ever met, which meant getting angry would just make me look like an idiot. *More* of an idiot.

"Earth...*America* has the trained military we need," I told her. "If we want to take back Copperell, we need their help."

"Maybe," Brandy said, stepping on the last word. "But how badly? Everything they have, we gave them. You gave them the two cruisers, the Starblades, the weapons, the fusion reactors, the armor. It's been months now, and they still haven't given *us* anything in return. Are they part of our resistance, or are we just another ally of theirs to be used to protect them, to forward their interests? Because I will sacrifice anything to win this war, Charles Travers. I will even sacrifice the man I love more than any other if it means freeing the Copperell and all the other peoples of the galaxy from the terror and tyranny of the Anguilar." The passion in her tone balanced against the chill gleam in her eyes that could have frozen molten metal. "But if we've sacrificed this much, if the Strada have lost thousands and I've lost half my soul, and we have nothing to show for it but empty promises, then I'm done with you and your world. We all are, every one of my people."

I opened my mouth, but nothing came out. How could I reply to that?

"Brandy," Laranna interjected, stern yet gentle, "you're not thinking clearly. If it weren't for Charlie, the Anguilar would have rolled over all of us. How could you not trust him after everything we've been through?"

"My husband trusted him," Brandy shot back. "And now he'll

never walk again. He'll never be able to hold his son." She rested a hand on her stomach. "How do I explain that to him?"

"What would you have said to him if we *didn't* have the alliance with Earth?" I asked her, fighting very hard to keep calm, to tamp down not just the instinctive anger but a very real fear that everything was about to come apart at the seams. I wanted badly to look around and see if the people at the other tables were listening, but that would have been a sign of weakness. "Oh, yeah, that's right…you wouldn't have ever decided to try to have a baby because there was *no hope*. No hope of winning this war, no hope of driving out the Anguilar, no hope of ever taking back Copperell. You think the United States government is using us to advance their own interests…well, hell, of *course* they are! Just like we're using them to advance ours. That's what governments do. They aren't going to risk their entire planet being destroyed in an *interstellar war* that they just found out about from some kind of cockeyed altruism!"

I threw my hands up, unable to hold the frustration in any longer.

"For God's sake, Brandy," I exploded, "*you* were right there when we had all those planning sessions trying desperately to figure out anyone who had the power and the will to help us. You know how many times the two of us and Gib and Val went on ops we had every reason to think we'd never come back from. You know that Brazzo and Dani *didn't* make it back." I dialed it back, seeing the stares coming from the other tables. "I know you're hurting, and I'm sorry. I'll do everything I can, give everything I have, up to and including my life, to drive the Anguilar off

Copperell. But this"—I motioned around us—"had nothing to do with whether or not President Louis is dragging his feet. This is on *us*, and we'd better find a way to deal with it or we won't have to worry about whether the American government wants to help the resistance, because there'll be no damned resistance to help."

She stared at me with a gaze so fixed it might have been the laser designator for a missile launcher, but eventually, she nodded.

"Come with me. We have to talk to Lenny. You're the commander," she acknowledged, but then tilted her head to the side. "And you have some decisions to make."

I THOUGHT we'd head to the bridge, but it only took a couple minutes before I realized Brandy was taking us to the medical bay. Which made sense because Lenny would be there, taking care of Val. The robot didn't actually have to be *on* the bridge to monitor what was happening there because he basically *was* the ship, or I should say that the ship was an extension of him. In some sense, all the Zoo ships were, and all the robot bodies controlling them.

But taking care of Val might require Lenny to actually be present because as well-trained as the Copperell technicians were, none of them had the qualifications to operate the medical equipment in the hospital. Hell, even if he'd abducted an ER surgeon from the current-day US, I doubt they would have been able to learn to use the tech in the medical bay.

I came to a stop just inside the doorway, grabbing the door frame for support. The tanks were lined up in the center of the chamber, four of them, reminding me too much of the stasis pods. I remembered waking up in one of the pods like it was yesterday instead of almost two years ago, and it wasn't a pleasant memory, but it had nothing on this. Val floated naked in the tank, and if there was anything good to be drawn from the indelible image, it was that the fierce, weeping burns were gone, healed by those nanite things in the two days he'd spent on the ship.

His legs were still gone below the knees, one arm amputated at the bicep, the other at the elbow, and if the stumps were sealed with fresh, pink skin, that only made them seem more permanent.

"Jesus," I murmured.

"Great Spirits preserve him," Laranna whispered almost at the same time, and maybe we were both saying the same thing.

"He is stable," Lenny told us as if he hadn't noticed our shocked reaction.

Lenny was…well, there was a reason I still hadn't brought him down to meet the folks. The first time I'd seen him in the lander, just before he'd stunned me and stuck me in a stasis pod, I'd been scared shitless. It had taken me a while to figure out how to describe him, but the closest comparison I'd settled on was the robot in the old movie Logan's Run, the one in the ice cave, except Lenny had multiple arms…if need be. They retracted inside his gleaming, silver body when not in use, and each of them could be fitted with whatever tool he required at the moment. Right now, he had four of them extended, and the accessories attached to them defied description.

Unlike his face. That I could easily describe, but no one would have believed me back home so I'd never bothered. Lenny's face looked like a modern art sculpture of a young Michael Keaton. Like Mr. Mom-era Michael Keaton. Or maybe his Batman movies, although I hadn't seen those until I'd returned to Earth and gotten access to Dani's collection of movies. I never would have thought Keaton could pull off Batman, but there you go.

"He should be kept in the tank for another twelve hours," Lenny went on, "and then, of course, we have a decision to make."

"You mean you can't grow back his arms and legs?" I asked, looking between Lenny and the tank. "I've seen what you can do with that nano-bacterial whatchamacallit stuff."

"If he'd been brought to me immediately after the injury, it might have been possible. Now, that's no longer the case. We'll have no choice but to implant prosthetics."

"Then what's the decision?" Brandy snapped. "You just said we'd have no choice."

"There are two different types of prosthetic replacement available," Lenny explained with seemingly infinite patience. "I can attach limbs that will operate much like his biological arms and legs, and coat them with artificial skin that will be difficult to differentiate from his natural flesh. He'll even be able to feel to some extent, depending on how much nerve damage there is at the stumps."

"That doesn't sound bad," I ventured cautiously. "Why does it sound like there's a *but* coming somewhere?"

"But," Lenny confirmed, "there is another option. It would require extensive surgery, implants that would strengthen Val's spine and hips, a battery pack in his abdomen, and a few other modifications, but it would be possible for him to be equipped with bionic limbs that would greatly increase his strength and durability. He might consider this a plus if he intends to continue to fight the Anguilar."

"He's done enough fighting," Brandy told him, the flat declaration leaving no room for debate. "How long will it take for him to be ready for the prosthetics?"

"I can begin prepping him for the procedure in another day or two." The metal eyes drifted from one of us to the other, which I knew was an affectation, as was his entire face. His actual sensors were somewhere else, down in his chest, giving 360-degree coverage. "You didn't come here simply to check on Sgt. McKee."

I looked around the medical bay, checking for techs or other patients, but it was empty. The other wounded had been treated and released.

"How could the Anguilar have found this place, Lenny?" Brandy asked the robot. "We had a conversation not that long ago about how unlikely it was that they'd stumble across this system by accident."

"They did not find it by accident, Brandine." He said it with not a trace of uncertainty or doubt, and I suppose there wouldn't be. Lenny didn't guess. "I checked our hyperspace communications relay after the battle. The programming had been altered. Subtly," he admitted, cocking his head to the side as if in admiration. "I was barely able to detect it, and whatever routines it had executed had been erased immediately afterward, but the maintenance systems for the maneuvering thrusters showed they'd been fired within the last two weeks."

"Someone sent a signal," Laranna hissed, disbelief in her voice and her expression that likely matched my own.

"It had to have been the Gan-Shi," Brandy said, pacing across the floor in front of the tanks. "One of them must have sent a signal to the relay just after they arrived…"

"There is no evidence of this," Lenny cautioned, looming over her, rolling into her way as if to stop her pacing and her train of reasoning. "The hack might have been accomplished at any time since the relay was put in place. Perhaps whoever installed it was simply waiting for the system to be unguarded. We have taken in hundreds of refugees in the last two years before the Gan-Shi came. It could be any one of them."

"We need to vet every single refugee and find out if they had the opportunity," Laranna said.

"I'm afraid there's no time for that now," Lenny told her. His gaze turned my way. "You know why."

I nodded.

"The Anguilar cruisers got away, and they know we're here," I explained. "They'll be coming back with reinforcements. I already sent the call back to Strada and Thalassia. The cruisers and the other Liberators are on their way."

"We're making a stand here?" Laranna asked, her shoulders

squaring as if she were readying herself for a fight. I opened my mouth to reply, but Brandy beat me to it.

"No," she said, shaking her head. "If we stay here, they have the advantage. They have more ships, more troops, and they can just keep throwing them at us until we're overwhelmed. We don't have any other choice." Brandy nodded to the image of Sanctuary, the world that had been her home for years now. "We have to evacuate."

7

"We were extremely fortunate," Warrin told me, head tilted back slightly as he spoke, like he was intent on enjoying the midday sun despite the circumstances. I recalled how bright the Gan-Shi had kept the lights in their underground city back on Wraith Anchorage and figured this sort of weather must be heaven for them. "Once the Anguilar scouts saw we were no threat to them, that we had no weapons, they disengaged and left us here without further attacks."

Shindo didn't seem quite as sanguine about the whole thing, his expression dour—although that was a fine distinction from the normal Gan-Shi look.

"We still lost three males killed by the scouting party. And two of our young males were injured badly." He sighed, which sounded more like a horse whinnying. "My people have been unsettled for months now, first moving from Wraith Anchorage to this world and then from our encampment outside Sanctuary town to this one."

This encampment was rougher than the one I'd seen outside the town, many of the tents still broken down, the wooden huts nothing but bare slabs and two-by-fours, waiting for someone to get around to rebuilding them. Even more incomplete were the expressions on the faces of the women and children, a sense of loss not of their pitiful tents and shacks but of the stability they'd known for generations. And if that stability had been at the cost of misery, poverty, and the exploitation of their young males, well, better the devil you know.

The one good thing about the place was that it hadn't been around as long, so the smell hadn't had time to settle in. The stench still reminded me of a stockyard, but at least I didn't feel the overwhelming desire to cover my nose and mouth.

"Perhaps," Shindo said with the slightest note of hope in his voice, "since the Anguilar were not interested in our people, we could just stay here. Once they see you've left, they might not bother with us."

"That's a fantasy, Shindo," Chuck sighed. He'd come with me since he'd dealt with the Gan-Shi before, and because Gib and Laranna were on patrol in their Vanguards. "If they don't find us, they'll take out their frustrations on you."

"Chuck is right," Warrin said, surprising me.

Of all the Gan-Shi gathered around us, he was the last one I'd expected to support our position. The Elder female stood silent behind him and Shindo, her arms crossed, her gaze hard. I got the impression that she and her sisters thought we humans weren't worth her time, but perhaps I was being unfair and the females just figured it was their business to handle the relations within the tribe and the duty of the males to deal with outsiders.

"We can't stay here without the aid of the resistance," Warrin went on, motioning broadly to take in the others. "We could feed ourselves, this is true, but we have no trained technicians to maintain power plants, water treatment, sewage…disease would ravage our people. Perhaps in time, we might be able to take care of ourselves, but even back at Wraith Anchorage, we required the infrastructure of the station to survive. For now, we must accompany the resistance to a more secure location."

"I will have the herd prepare for the move," the Elder said, speaking up for the first time. She speared me with a glare. "And your resistance will provide food and shelter during the trip?"

"Of course," I assured her. I wiped sweat off my forehead with the back of my hand and staggered slightly. No sleep last night, either…or not much. The mass ritual for the Strada warriors had lasted well into the early morning. I really just wanted to get back in the lander where it was cool and let Chuck fly us back while I grabbed a nap. "There's enough of you that it's going to take at least two trips to take everyone to the new settlement. Maybe three. We'll get resupplied with food, medicine, and bedding when we drop off the first load."

"And where will you be taking us?" Warrin asked. "This is a goodly world, with open plains and sunshine. I would not have our herd stranded in a wasteland where crops would not grow nor the sun shine."

Chuck offered me a curious glance of his own, as if he wouldn't mind hearing that himself. This was something I hadn't talked to him or Brandy about, had barely had time to discuss with Laranna in the brief interludes we had between one or both of us running off to perform frantic and desperate duties in the limited time we had left before the other ships arrived.

"Earth?" he suggested, shrugging. "I mean, it's close. We can reach Earth in a week. And I think they'd be okay with it. Not sure where, but probably somewhere in the US or Canada?"

"That would be a last resort," I told him, shaking my head. "Too much politics involved."

"Strada then?" He was just guessing now, because he'd never been to Laranna's homeworld, but I couldn't suppress a snort of laughter.

"I wouldn't send my worst enemy to live outdoors on Strada. There's some nasty predators there at night...I know, I had to run through the jungle with the bastards on my heels once. No, we're going to Thalassia."

"Where?" Shindo grunted, cocking his head toward me. "I have not heard of this place."

"A former Anguilar outpost," I explained. "We liberated it from them a few months ago." All I remembered of the world was the area right around the one large city, but I racked my brain for the landscape further afield. "It's a little drier than this place, at least the part I saw, but there's plenty of good land to grow crops. And the winters there are milder than here."

Warrin nodded, apparently satisfied with the description, though I thought Shindo still wanted to debate the issue.

"The population there is light on the ground," I added. "They won't be pressured by your people settling in. They'll be grateful for the company." That might have been overselling the whole thing, but it was true that the Thalassians only inhabited a small portion of one continent.

"Our males are supposed to be learning to be soldiers with your people to fight the Anguilar," Warrin pointed out. "Will this still be possible? You wanted us to aid you in the liberation of Copperell."

"That may have to wait." I shook my head. "This move is going to push things back enough as it is. Thalassia is a good three weeks in hyperspace. There may not be time to adequately train your people." I sighed. "Hell, I'm not even sure we'll be able to go through with the attack. Just moving everyone to Thalassia is going to take months." I turned back to Chuck with a bleak expression. "And I don't know if Louis or Gavin are gonna wait long enough for that. This might derail the entire thing."

"You can't allow that to happen," Warrin said with a lot more conviction than I would have expected from the older Gan-Shi. I frowned at him.

"Thanks for the encouragement, but why is it so important to you?"

"Because they can't be allowed to get away with this!" His volume rose along with his ire. "This is the second home they've forced us out of! They destroyed the world we'd built for ourselves, the one we'd just managed to take back for the herd.

And now, they've come here and chased us off this land. They'll do the same again, to us and others like us who only wish to be left alone. In the end, there will be no peace until they've been defeated."

I nodded slowly.

"All right, then. We'll figure something out." I had no idea what, but since when had that stopped me before? I closed my eyes and recalled the population numbers we'd come up with when we'd transported the Gan-Shi here. "You have six thousand adult males, eight thousand juveniles of both sexes, and seven thousand adult females, right?"

Warrin and Shindo looked at each other as if each expected the other to answer the question, but finally, the Elder stepped forward, awarding them both with an exasperated glower.

"Approximately," she confirmed.

"Then I need twenty-five hundred children and five hundred adult females prepped for immediate transport up to the *Liberator* by this time tomorrow. Try to keep families together, but if you have to foster some of the kids to make it work, then you have to. We're starting the evacuation with the *Liberator* immediately. We'll leave the Vanguard fighters as a rear guard until the rest of the starships arrive to take the next load."

"I don't like splitting up the herd," Shindo said, his chin tucked against his chest, his face sullen and stubborn. More sullen and stubborn than usual for a Gan-Shi. "It feels wrong."

"You'd rather we stayed here and waited for them to kill us?" Warrin asked him. He was obscenely talkative for one of the bulls, I'd noted. Shindo didn't reply, true to form, but the Elder did.

"We'll be ready," she promised. "You keep your end of the bargain."

I nodded, clapped Chuck on the shoulder, and led him back to the lander.

"The landers will be the weak link," I told him, ducking inside the hatch and heaving a relieved breath at the shade and the remnants of the cold air from our flight in. "Even round the clock, it's going to take nearly a full day to load up a Liberator."

"There's another weak link to all this," Chuck pointed out, taking a quick look behind us to make sure the Gan-Shi weren't still listening.

There was no danger of that, since Shindo and Warrin seemed to be arguing with each other and the Elder was yelling at her sisters, the senior cows of the herd, chivvying them into action. Chuck slapped the control to close the hatch behind us. His brow furrowed and his jaw worked like he was chewing the words before he spat them out.

"What's the problem, Chuck?" I asked him, powering up the engines, smiling as cold air rushed out of the vents.

"You know what the damn problem is," he accused. "We're pulling all our ships out of Strada and Thalassia, leaving Earth with only the two cruisers. We're gonna be leaving everything wide open for an attack, and I think that's exactly what the Anguilar want."

"You might be right," I told him, feeding thrust to the belly jets. Clouds of dust obscured the tents of the Gan-Shi camp for a moment until we cleared it.

Everything made more sense from the air, a pattern emerging from the apparent chaos of the encampment. The Gan-Shi were an orderly bunch in their own way, or at least the females were. I had some doubts about the males being organized or cooperative enough to submit to training, but if I could have convinced the females to forego the whole pacifist, weapons-hating thing, I would have recruited them for the infantry instead.

"But I don't know what else to do," I continued once I had the lander angled for orbit, the rear engines burning bright. "We leave anybody here, they're dead. And yeah, it's crossed my mind that's exactly what Zan-Tar is thinking, and maybe if someone smarter than me was in charge, they could figure out a better way to handle this." The lander's navigation system locked onto the beacon from the *Liberator*, and I glanced over at Chuck. "What about you? You're George's son. Some of his big brains must have made it into your DNA. You have any brilliant ideas? That don't involve leaving a bunch of civilians to die?"

His brow furled in thought, but finally, he tilted back his head and hissed out a breath.

"No. I have a gut feeling we're doing exactly what that bastard Zan-Tar wants, but he's got us backed into a corner. How the hell did he find this place?"

Chewing on my lip, I debated whether I should tell him. So far, Brandy, Lenny, Laranna, and I had kept it close to the vest, but if I couldn't trust Chuck…

"Someone used our hyperspace comm relay to send a message."

Chuck's head snapped up, eyes going wide.

"And we don't know who," he surmised, "or else we'd be doing something about it."

"Yeah." I winced. "Brandy thinks it's the Gan-Shi, since they're the latest refugees to arrive."

"And you don't?"

"I think I'd need to know why one of them would betray us to the Anguilar," I explained. "And how they'd have had the chance to make the connection to make the deal to begin with. It's not like the Anguilar knew the Gan-Shi would be coming here."

"I get that. But if it's not them…"

"Then it could be anyone," I agreed. "Brandy takes in any Copperell who asks for asylum, and I've already met Copperell turncoats. It could be someone who's been here for years."

"Well, this all just sucks," he commented, slumping in his seat, arms crossed over his chest. "It's like watching a train wreck, except I'm on the damned train." Chuck eyed me sidelong. "You've been dealing with all this a lot longer than I have, Charlie. What're you gonna do?"

"One thing at a time. Evac everyone someplace defensible, then get back on the horse and see how the Anguilar react. There's a couple possibilities here. One, if Brandy's right and it's a Gan-Shi, then this might have all been a last-minute thing and they could have just sent whatever forces they had available to probe the signal they got. If that's the case, then we can still move forward with our plan to invade Copperell."

"And if it's not?" Chuck pressed. "If this was someone planted a long time ago?"

"Then this could just be the beginning." I tapped the side of the control yoke rhythmically. "We could be dancing to the enemy's tune."

"Whatever happens, I know one thing for sure." He laughed softly. "I'm glad I'm not the one in charge."

8

This was taking too long.

"Vanguard Two, this is Vanguard One..." I shut my mouth, tired of playing fighter pilot, tired of the space suit, tired of being strapped into this seat, even tired of the view despite the blue and green beauty of Sanctuary. And just plain tired. I made sure I was on a private channel and threw in the towel. "Laranna, you copy?"

There was the chance she wouldn't. The wing stretched out in a patrol array near the orbit of Sanctuary's moon, close to minimum safe jump distance, but the thing about orbits was, there could be a whole planet between us. But according to the IFF signal on my sensor screen, her squadron was just around the curve of Sanctuary, well within relay range of the *Liberator*. The massive ship drifted slowly by below us, waiting patiently in low orbit for the Gan-Shi to finish the first phase of the evacuation.

"I'm here, Charlie," she replied, not bothering to lecture me about abandoning my own comms protocols. I had a feeling everyone's commitment to them was only skin deep.

"You have eyes on that last group of landers?" I asked. "They were supposed to be in the air an hour ago."

At least the clock in my Vanguard's main display said it had been an hour. Trapped in the tiny cockpit since the very beginning of the load-out, I'd lost all sense of time, and I would have been willing to believe that days had passed. The worst part was going to the bathroom, an arrangement awkward enough that I refused to talk about it to anyone who hadn't had to go through it themselves.

"I see them," Laranna told me. "They'll be passing the terminator in a few seconds."

The terminator was the technical term for where the light side of the planet met the dark side, and almost before Laranna finished speaking, the cluster of bright blue sensor icons representing the landers popped into existence there. Transitioning from light to dark, which wasn't a disturbing image at all and definitely wouldn't make this whole process even more stressful.

"Okay, I got them now," I transmitted to Laranna. Them and the Vanguards, all three squadrons of them, the *Liberator*, the cargo shuttles, and shitloads of empty space that could light up with hyperspace jumps any second.

The worst thing about commanding a whole wing of the starfighters wasn't the suit, wasn't the smell, wasn't even the bathroom facilities. It wasn't even the knowledge that they'd all put their lives in my hand. It was the constant vigilance. Not the same sort of vigilance I'd learned trying to become an infantry soldier. That was easy, natural. Listening for footsteps, voices, watching for movement. This was like playing a flight simulator video game for hours on end except I had to watch two dozen *other* people play the same video game and make sure they didn't screw up.

"Getting edgy?" Chuck wondered, and I would have thought he was teasing except for the fact that he sounded utterly miserable.

"The longer this takes," I reminded him, "the bigger a target the ship becomes. I want her out of here."

"Once she's gone, it's just us, just the Vanguards, alone here for over a month. It'd be a perfect opportunity to finish off the rest of the resistance."

"Thanks for trying to make me feel more confident about my decision," I said, offering him a dry smile. "It's our only play. We lay low, camouflage the fighters in the forest, and if they come back, we try to catch them flat-footed."

"Camping out for six weeks," Chuck grumbled. "In the middle of summer. Can't say I'm really looking forward to it."

"You're a Ranger!" I laughed sharply. "Isn't this like, your thing?"

"It *was*. But I've kind of gotten used to the whole pogue life. Air conditioning, nice, soft beds, warm food. You guys have spoiled me."

"I'm not especially looking forward to it myself," I agreed. "Particularly since we're going to be running patrols the whole time. At least Laranna'll be there." I looked sidelong at Chuck. "You got anyone back home yet, or have we kept you too busy?"

"Oh yeah, I just have all sorts of chances to meet women," Chuck scoffed. "As long as I don't mind if they have horns or feathers or something."

"Don't knock it till you try it."

"Hell, if I could find a Strada girl like Laranna, I'd go for it," he agreed. "I mean, the green thing doesn't bother me at all, and I kind of dig a woman who can kick my ass, but the Strada just hang out with each other. All they talk about is hunting and swords and knives and the best ways to disembowel a man."

I grunted acknowledgement.

"Yeah, I suppose Laranna and I met under unique circumstances." I nodded at the sensor screen. "Looks like they're about to dock."

"Maybe we could squeeze a few more shuttle loads into the old girl?" Chuck suggested. "I mean, I know it'd be cramped and uncomfortable, but if it would wind up saving lives…"

"It's not just that it'd be cramped. The ship is pretty advanced, but there's a limit to how much CO_2 the atmospheric plant can scrub. We're pushing it now with four thousand extra people aboard. I wish we had some stasis pods. Then we could jam people in like cordwood."

Chuck visibly shuddered.

"You'd never get me into one of those damn things. Too much like being dead."

I was about to agree with him that I'd never get into a stasis pod again, but a warning buzzer drowned me out. It was unwelcome but not unexpected, like a saying I'd read once about death—I knew it was coming, but I was hoping not so soon.

"Vanguard Wing, this is Vanguard One," I transmitted, surprised by how calm my voice was. "Hyperspace jumps detected. Enemy in system. All squadrons, form on me."

Chuck had fallen silent, too stunned for even a curse.

"Cheer up," I told him. "We don't have to wait around wondering if they're going to come back." He offered me a grim smile.

"Joy."

SPACE WAS BIG.

I hadn't had a real sense of how big it was until I'd started commuting through it, but now I understood. Even with technology that was almost magic compared to the space shuttles and Sputniks from my day, it still took hours to get anywhere unless we took a shortcut with micro-jumps through hyperspace. Yet even with the arc of Sanctuary spread out beneath us, the moon a golf ball in the distance, and a tableau of stars glittering in the firmament thousands or even millions of light-years away, even with tens of thousands of miles between us, the enemy force still seemed to fill the space around us.

Ten Anguilar cruisers bulled their way through holes in space, and squadrons of Starblades exploded from their launch bays before the wormholes had even completely closed behind them. I'd heard it said that the old MLRS Multiple Launch Rocket System could, in two volleys, put a piece of shrapnel in every square meter of an entire grid square a kilometer on a side. This was the space equivalent of that, every square mile of space between us and minimum safe jump distance seemingly filled with angry, gleaming metal.

No one fired yet because no one was in range, but drives flared as both sides charged headlong into each other, knights on some medieval battlefield. Or, in our case, maybe the Light Brigade charging straight into the Turkish guns.

"Lenny, get that damned ship going! I want you out of here with those civilians in ten minutes."

"You won't survive without us," Lenny said, and I rolled my eyes, though he couldn't see me.

"And none of us will, including those civilians, if you stay. There's too many of them, and there's no time to argue." I reached into my memory for the name of the Copperell who was on duty as chief of the bridge crew. "Rosan, take a few shots on your way out if they present themselves, but for God's sake, get into hyperspace and send word to the other ships to turn back."

If it wasn't already too late. We'd put out the call for the other Liberators and cruisers over a week ago, and the fact was, they were overdue. I didn't wait around for Lenny's response, hoping the bridge crew would follow my orders even if he hesitated. Rosan controlled the ship in combat, anyway, since Lenny's programming forbade him from using weapons.

"Vanguard Wing," I broadcast to the rest of the fighters, "split up by wing-mate pairs and head straight for the cruisers. Ignore the fighters. They can't do significant damage to the *Liberator* before she jumps."

"But they can blow the shit out of us," Gib pointed out, "if they gang up on the Vanguards while we're otherwise occupied."

I risked a frantic look away from the sensors and targeting screen to check the comm readout and relaxed when I saw that Gib had, at least, switched to our private channel instead of broadcasting that to the entire wing.

"They can," I replied, "but that's our job."

"That's *your* job, human. You're the commander. I'm just the best pilot you've ever met."

"Does that mean you're not going to do it?" It wasn't a serious question. I knew Gib better than that.

"Oh, for God's sake, of course I am. What else have I got to do?"

I laughed softly.

"Good luck, buddy," I told him.

"You, too. See you on the other side."

"Dagon," I said, switching frequencies to my wingman. "You're with me. Hang tight, and don't let anyone shoot me down."

"Copy that, Vanguard One," he replied with a gentle, chiding tone. Oh yeah. Comm discipline. I'd forgotten.

"Hang on, Chuck. Gonna be a bumpy ride."

I'd read an article sometime back around the time one of the Star Wars movies came out that had criticized them for their fighters acting like airplanes in an atmosphere, and I'd felt very superior for making that point in an argument about science with George one night after too many beers. As an aside, I've often thought that it was the fact I'd had too many discussions like that which had kept me from having more girlfriends in college.

But I'd been short-sighted and so had whoever the science reporter for Time or Newsweek or whatever it had been, because flying the Vanguard in space was as close to operating an F-16 as it was possible to get. The gimbal engines spun us away from our course, the inertial dampeners turning what would have been unbearable angular momentum into the feeling of a gentle bank in an aircraft. Gentle enough that I could even move my head without tweaking my neck muscles like last time, checking the rest of the wing.

They'd broken expertly, just like we'd drilled a thousand times, the way Tamura had trained us back when we'd awoken the Kamerian pilots from stasis. There was a saying in martial arts that I'd learned way back when and had reinforced for me by Laranna when she taught me the Strada way: soft targets, hard weapons, hard targets, soft weapons. When you hit someone in the jaw, the smart thing to do was to use your elbow because using your fist was likely to get you a few broken knuckles.

The same thing applied to fighting high odds in the Vanguards. Soft targets—say, two or three cruisers—could be handled by hitting them hard, mass attacks by full squadrons, firing in collimated volleys. But when there were just too many ships to pull that off, when the target was too hard, the weapon had to be soft, slippery, difficult to grab onto. They were big, we were small, and their particle cannons couldn't be aimed independent of the orientation of the cruisers. Their pulse turrets were meant to hold off fighter attacks, but those were normal fighters, which lacked defense shields.

And that was about the last rational thought I had before instinct and training took over. Looking back, I could see every second of the fight, every turn and roll and shot, but that was hindsight. In the moment, I didn't see, I didn't hear, I merely sensed.

Particle cannons blasted between fighters, a futile attempt to throw off our attack because even though Anguilar starship captains might be amoral pricks, they weren't stupid, and they knew they couldn't hit small, fast-moving targets with a fixed weapon. It was almost beautiful in a way, the coruscating fireworks show put on by the Anguilar as a sign of our defeat, a celebration of finally discovering our bolt hole and rooting us out.

They wouldn't get all of us, but enough. Enough that Lenny would have to go back to the drawing board with his Excalibur algorithms and find just the right people to lead his resistance, wait years more for it to all come together, and in the meantime, Thalassia and Strada and Earth would be on their own, and if they were lucky and smart, they'd make an alliance and try to hold the Empire off. Emphasis on *try*.

The cruisers had fired at extreme range, but we knew better, waiting because we were only going to get one clear shot before we passed by them and had to reverse thrust. We had to wait, not just to be in the effective range of our cannons but to be close enough to make sure they would penetrate the cruisers' shields.

"It's like playing chicken with an oil tanker," Chuck murmured. "In a rowboat."

He wasn't wrong, but he'd left out all the other little chickens. They'd run ahead of their motherships, pinpricks of silver backed with the glow of their drives, and they weren't shy at all about blasting us with everything they had. Crimson threads of scalar energy sought us out, Dagon and me, a web of destruction for anything lacking shields.

"Shit!" Chuck blurted as the Vanguard shook like a car with bad shocks on a rutted road.

A halo of white surrounded us, blanking out the optical cameras, but we still had the sensors…and Chuck still had his own pulse turret. I'd always thought it would be more dramatic if the gunner's seat rotated with the turret, but I suppose the fighter had been designed for efficiency instead of cinematic appearance, and the controls were more like an arcade game. One of the old-style games I'd played as a kid, not the home systems Chuck had showed me. Those were cool, but there was something simpler, sleeker about the old joystick-and-button setup, and Chuck could have been one of the old geeks who used to leave their date at the table at the pizza place in order to waste some quarters in Galaga or Gyrus or Defender.

He would have been good at it. Chuck's first burst speared directly through the cockpit of a Starblade, and a thermal bloom flared white on the sensors. He moved to the next target, and another fighter blossomed with a brief explosion of flame from Wance in One-Three, covering our six. And then I couldn't pay attention to those small battles anymore because I had my own target, and it was a hell of a lot bigger.

The cruisers were all alike, which seemed unimaginative, but the Anguilar had never been accused of having any sort of artistic style. They did share an ominous, sharklike quality, predators of the deep black, and it was easy to appreciate that with one of them bearing down on us. Pulse turrets sought us out, red lashes scourging the night and our shields lit up again, absorbing the energy, the fighter shaking like a bone in a dog's teeth as the shields turned radiation into kinetic energy.

The cruiser was so close, our entire forward view was a gleaming wall of silver, and I had a fraction of a second to pull the trigger. I don't remember touching the firing control, and the particle cannon discharge took me by surprise…though I imagine it surprised the Anguilar crew even more. This close, barely a hundred miles away, pierced the cruiser's defenses as if they weren't there, the shields lighting up in futile protest like the barn door closing after the horse had escaped.

The blast struck the cruiser just aft of amidships, as close as I could get to the engineering section, a magnificent eruption of heat and vaporized metal exploding from the impact, but it was Dagon who took her out with his follow-up. I was too busy pulling away from the looming hulk to witness the hit, but I couldn't miss the aftermath. The supernova detonation of the ship's reactor probably lit up the skies on the dark side of Sanctuary if anyone was outside to watch, and it blotted out everything on the rear-facing cameras, turning the screens a harsh white.

It shrank in the rear screens with alarming rapidity as our

mutual acceleration sent us sailing past each other, and the real fun began. I didn't bother warning Chuck this time, figuring he'd get the hint when his acceleration couch swiveled along with the drive pods. My own seat barely locked into place before the engines roared their defiance of Newton's laws of motion, but Sir Isaac wasn't going to go down easy, and he smacked me right across the face.

The braking burn punished us with the ruthlessness of a nun at a Catholic school, and my vision blurred for a moment, in synch with the fuzz across my thoughts. Desperation cried out for my attention, a distant scream on a dark night, but it didn't register with my conscious mind until my brain fought its way out of the fog.

What I expected to see once my vision cleared was the rest of the wing doing the same thing we were, braking for another run at the cruisers. I also expected to see the Anguilar starships and their short-range fighters performing a similar maneuver to meet our attack, unless they played it smart and cut one loose to go after targets on the planet while the others kept us busy. The *Liberator* should have been long gone, safe in hyperspace, on her way to Thalassia.

What I got instead was a good news-bad news joke. The good news was that our first attack run had been successful. Three of the ten cruisers were out of the fight, two of them vanished into burning nebulae of hot gasses while the third tumbled past Sanctuary, her drive dark, blooms of heat escaping from the gaping hole in her aft spine.

The bad news was, the *Liberator* had turned away from her escape run to make a beeline straight at the cruisers…and they were ignoring the Vanguards to burn straight for her.

"What the hell?" Chuck exclaimed.

I couldn't have put it better myself.

9

"Rosan!" I fairly bellowed into my helmet mic. "What the hell are you doing? I told you to get out of here!"

"Sorry, sir," the Copperell woman said, not sounding apologetic at all. "We're not leaving you here to die…and we're definitely not abandoning all the civilians on the surface. If we're going down, we're going down together."

"Goddammit, get me Lenny on this line right now!" I wanted to smack Rosan in the head and only the facts that one, she was a female and I'd been taught never to hit a woman, and two, she was tens of thousands of miles away at the moment made me refrain.

"I can't interfere, Charlie," Lenny said immediately, as if the two of them had rehearsed the lines. "We're in combat, and my programming forbids me from taking part in armed hostilities against sentient biologicals."

"Jesus, is he a politician robot?" Chuck wondered, sounding more bemused than upset by the whole thing.

Which was easy for him to say. He had the luxury of being able to sit back and watch me make decisions.

"Brandy, this is Charlie," I broadcast urgently. "Tell me you can hear me."

Seconds crawled by as our Vanguard and the others spread out around us killed our momentum, waiting with the impatience of a hungry lion for the drives to take us back the other direction. And a few minutes ago, I would have been just as impatient to get back into the fight, but now all I wanted was to get between the enemy and our ship.

"Charlie," Brandy replied, her voice so much calmer than mine, "who do you think ordered Rosan to turn back? Those people down there are my friends. They looked to me for leadership and protection, and I'm not giving up on them without putting up a fight."

"What about Maxx?" I demanded, wondering if everyone but me had suddenly gone insane. "What about all the children on the *Liberator*?"

"What about all the children on Sanctuary?"

The navigation board informed me we'd reversed course, and the automated systems confirmed it by swinging the hull of the Vanguard around to match our direction of travel, the seats staying in place with a carnival ride effect that tormented my inner ear. I used the interruption to think. There was an old saying that Sgt. Redd had shared me with me, a future officer. Never give an order you know won't be obeyed. It just increases the chances that the troops will disobey your orders in the future and makes you look weak.

Brandy wasn't thinking straight, and Rosan, a Copperell, was more loyal to Brandy than she was to me. They were going to join battle with the Anguilar, and there was nothing I could do to stop them. The good news was, there were only seven cruisers left, though there were still a shitload of Starblades, but the bad news was that they weren't going to be surprised again, and if they went by the MO they'd shown the last two battles, they were going to concentrate on targeting the *Liberator*.

Which meant my strategy had to change. I'd been thinking we could attrit the cruisers until they retreated to a safe distance and let their fighters whittle us down, which wasn't an ideal plan, but it was all I had. Now, the plan would have to be for us to support the *Liberator*.

"Vanguard Wing," I said, my gaze locked on the weapons rangefinder, waiting for the red line to intersect the nearest cruiser, "reform in squadrons. One-Three, you take first squadron, and I'm at the point of the spear. We're forming an escort for the *Liberator*, triangular clusters. Everyone copy?"

"Vanguard One-Three, I copy," Dagon replied.

"Vanguard Two, I copy," Laranna told me.

"Yeah, I hear ya," Gib drawled, passive-aggressive to the last.

"Rosan, do you understand the plan?" I growled, still not happy with her.

"*Liberator* copies." And all of a sudden she was big on properly following proper protocols.

Oh well, I could fire her later. Or maybe transfer since it

wasn't as if we had a whole list of trained candidates for technical work. The IFF transponders and the threat identification board came together on the main tactical display, making sense of the flares and reflections and blurred motion of the optical viewscreen. Sides reformed like metal shavings drawn together by a magnetic pen on one of those old Wooly Willy toys, except their collection was a good deal larger than ours, which was what made the whole thing a stupid idea.

"It's probably just as well," Chuck said dolorously, "that I don't have a girl back home." He tilted his head toward me. "You know we're all going to die, right?"

"We were all going to die a few minutes ago," I reminded him, maneuvering into a position just above and forward of the *Liberator*'s angular bow. "The only thing that's changed now is that the ship is going down with us."

"Gonna suck that Dad won't know what happened to me." He shrugged. "Gonna *really* suck if the Anguilar hit Earth and we're not there to help them."

"Yes, I think we can all agree that the whole situation sucks. Get ready. Thirty seconds until we're back in particle cannon range."

And this time, there was no hope of swinging wide out of the cruisers' firing arcs and hitting from the side because they were intent on ignoring our threat to take out the ship. We'd have to exchange broadsides like this was an 18th-century naval battle, and if they missed us, it would only be blind luck…or because they were aiming at the *Liberator*.

I'd kicked around several strategies and picked one at random, because it was just as likely to succeed as any other.

"Vanguard Wing and *Liberator* fire control," I said, speaking clearly but rapidly since we only had ten seconds, "target the bridge area of the cruiser I designate Alpha." I tapped a fingertip against the closest of the Anguilar ships in the sensor display, and it glowed red, a stylized letter *A* popping into existence beside the avatar.

Just a touch against the steering yoke and the reticle drifted upward, but I didn't pull the trigger yet. Five more seconds, and I had to make sure everyone else would fire at the same time. Tension crackled in the space between us, the unnatural suspense of wondering which of my friends would die in the next few seconds…because somebody would. Maybe me, maybe Laranna, maybe Gib…but when the cannons fired, someone would die.

So completely focused was I on the target, the buzzing of the threat warnings, the flashing lights telling me we were in firing range that I didn't notice the wormholes opening from hyperspace until the three massive ships emerged from them, coming out nearly on top of the Anguilar formation. Lightning crackled before the nose of the ships had completely emerged from that eldritch dimension, atomic particles flashing across hundreds of miles, almost point blank out here.

And an enemy starship died, split amidships by the particle blasts from a Liberator and one of our own captured Anguilar cruisers, the newly christened *Marauder*. I wanted to marvel at how providential their arrival was, but they'd given us an opening, and if this was indeed God at work, it would be pretty ungrateful not to take advantage of His providence.

"Fire!" I yelled, jamming down the trigger. "Fire now!"

Two dozen particle cannons discharged as one, lighting up trans-lunar space like a midsummer thunderstorm...or like one of those photographs of the Empire State Building being struck by lightning. No lightning rod on cruiser Alpha though, and nothing could have stopped the barrage of atomic fury unleashed from every Vanguard and the *Liberator*. The cruiser didn't just come apart, didn't just explode, she disintegrated, nothing left of her but a ball of fusing atoms, expanding so quickly that she consumed a dozen Starblade fighters...and nearly took us with her as well.

"Pull up," I warned, chanting it more than shouting it because none of my pilots were suicidal. "Dammit, pull up..."

The controls of the Vanguard were pretty intuitive, which came in handy in situations like this with waves of nuclear fury coming straight at us. All I had to do was pull backward on the steering yoke, and the drive pods rotated downward, adding upward thrust to our forward momentum, taking us in an arc away from the roiling clouds of plasma. The rest of the wing had the good sense to follow, but the *Liberator* was too massive and had built up too much momentum to change course so abruptly, and she barreled ahead through the maelstrom of energy.

Her shields glowed so bright they drowned out her outline, turning her bulky oblong into a huge sphere of white, like an angel from the Old Testament...and like one of those angels guarding Daniel, the shields guided her through the fiery furnace unscathed. I let out a relieved breath, turning my attention to the rest of the Anguilar strike force, hoping to wipe them out while they were still in disarray.

But just like that, in the space of less than a minute, there were only five enemy cruisers left against three Liberator ships, a cruiser and twenty-two Vanguards. Apparently, those were longer odds than the Anguilar were ready to face because just like the last time, they turned and ran. Polychromatic rings shimmered in space, and the cruisers seemed to elongate as the gravity well distorted the light waves between us and them just before they zipped out of our dimension and into another.

Leaving behind all those poor fighter pilots. Like a swarm of light bugs when the back porch lamp abruptly turned off, the fighter squadrons milled around in a disorganized mass for a moment before most of them turned en masse, aiming for the planet.

"Giblet," I said, surrendering to his lax radio procedures and paying him back for it simultaneously, "take your squadron down there and clean those bastards up."

"Yeah, right. Always me."

Most of the fighters had turned, but not all. A half a dozen had decided a suicide charge was the best way to go out and burned straight for the *Liberator*, firing their pulse turrets in enraged futility. The ship's point-defense guns barked back at them and the fighters winked into glowing clouds of vapor one at a time. Except the last one. Zoomed in on my tactical display, it was easy to spot when the burst of scalar pulses grazed its engine compartment, taking out the drive in a shower of sparks and sending the little fighter careening out of control. The pilot was doomed to drift into the outer system and die either from lack of oxygen or hypothermia. Unless...

"Rosan," I called, "if you can follow orders long enough to manage it, send a lander out to capture that pilot. Brandy could use some intelligence. In more ways than one."

"I can't believe you guys showed up when you did," Chuck fairly gushed, looking like he wanted to grab Captain Calabro and pull her into a hug. "That was like some miracle shit."

The Peboktan female stared at him in bemusement, her fists planted on her hips. Peboktan were, for the most part, engineers and technicians, but a few carried that technical know-how into a penchant for commanding the ships they worked on, and Calabro had been recommended to us by Mallarna, our Peboktan chief of engineering for the entire fleet. She'd assured us that Calabro was just as good at captaining a ship or flying one as Brazzo had been, and as far as I was concerned, that was the highest reference anyone could have.

"It was hardly a miracle," she said, her buglike features scrunched up in consternation. "We would have been here twenty hours ago if we hadn't listened to Lenny and waited for the other Liberators to arrive."

"I felt it would be more efficient," the Lenny robot added.

Oddly, he gave me the creeps because it wasn't *our* Lenny... and yet it was. We'd decided to meet on *Liberator 2*, since the main ship had taken some damage sailing through the plasma cloud and a repair crew had been dispatched to patch her up. Calabro, this version of Lenny, Laranna, Chuck, Rosan, and Brandy had all gathered, and I wanted to tell the last two that it took some serious balls for them to show their faces in front of me, but that could wait until I spoke to both of them in private.

"You said we needed to evacuate the planet," Lenny went on. "That is going to take more than one shipment, and I felt that it would be a better use of our resources to load as many ships at once as possible. The last Liberator will still be another ten days getting here, of course, but that would make the gap between our coverage of the planet shorter."

"Well, that worked out so well," I murmured. "Why don't you leave the strategizing to us next time?"

He didn't respond, and I wondered if it was because he was offended. The other Lenny wouldn't be, but he'd told me once that although they were the same AI programming, any time they spent apart and out of communication was an opportunity to grow independently of each other. Lenny had seemed to think that was a good thing, but it worried me. It was hard enough to figure our version out, much less try to account for variables in different incarnations of the robot.

"I don't care," Chuck insisted. "You guys showing up when you did saved our asses, and I can deal with that."

"It's most unfortunate that we lost a Liberator," Lenny commented. "I feel as though I've lost a part of myself, just as with the last ship. Not to mention it severely attenuates our combat capabilities."

I raised an eyebrow at the robot.

"Have you been talking to Chuck?" I wondered. "Getting all the latest US military jargon down pat?"

"I have absorbed all the data from your internet," Lenny reminded me, "via the network between the Liberators. That includes the terminology your people use for military operations."

I grunted, not at all comforted by the idea that the Lenny robots knew more about my world than I did.

"Brandy," I said, fixing her with a glare, "did you get anything out of the prisoner?"

If she felt any shame for the incident, she didn't show it, her expression defiant, and she shrugged in response.

"He's a Krin," she told me, "which means he's a violent, stubborn son of a bitch and told me to go screw myself in so many words. I put him in a bare metal cell naked and set the temperature to just above freezing. Give it another four or five hours, and he'll be more talkative."

"That sounds pretty close to torture," Chuck said, frowning.

"What's your point?" Brandy snapped.

"That's against the UCMJ," he replied, as if that explained everything. Then he seemed to realize that she probably wouldn't know what that meant, and he elaborated. "It's against United States military regulations."

"And I should care about that why? I don't work for your government. None of us do."

"Yeah, but I can't be a part of…"

"Then leave," Brandy growled at him.

"Enough," I interrupted, raising my hands, palms up.

"Brandy, let's keep your techniques to yourself in front of Chuck. Just give us the results when you have them. Lenny, get with"—I shrugged—"the other...Lennys, and get every single one of these ships packed to the gills with civilians. Ignore the protocols for CO_2 scrubbing, just jam everyone that'll fit."

"It won't do them any good if they arrive at Thalassia as corpses," Lenny objected. "There's no way to keep that many biologicals alive in this ship for more than two hundred hours."

"We're not going to Thalassia," I corrected him. "There's no way we can leave the civilians here that long, not with the Anguilar coming back to probe us every couple weeks. Whoever we leave behind is as good as dead."

"Where the hell else is there?" Chuck wondered.

"Laranna," I said, grabbing her hand, "could you stay here with the rest of Third Squadron and wait for the last Liberator? I'm afraid Chuck and I are going to have to go with the caravan."

"Of course," she said immediately. "But where are we taking them?"

"The only place left," I said. I nodded to Chuck. "The place you suggested. Which is why I have to go along. We're taking them to Earth."

10

"Why do we have to accompany you?" Shindo asked, staring out the airlock field of the *Liberator*'s hangar at the outlines of the Western Hemisphere. "Neither of us is a diplomat."

"We're here to represent our people," Warrin said, chin in the air as if he were posing for a Gan-Shi recruiting poster. "We should be proud."

I exchanged a look with Chuck, and he rolled his eyes.

"You should be grateful to get the hell off this ship before anyone else," I told them, slapping the security pad on the side of the lander. "I know I sure as hell will be."

"You said it." Chuck shuddered, his nose wrinkling. "I mean, it was bad enough I had to share my compartment with you"—he nodded toward me—"*and* that damned Copperell who wouldn't stop snoring. But the reduced rations were the worst. I'm starving, and I will injure you bodily if we don't stop at a drive-through on the way to the White House. Not to mention how badly this damn ship smells with thousands of people jammed into it."

Some of them were here on the hangar bay, cots and pallets and sleeping mats lined up along the far bulkhead, Copperell and Strada gathered atop them, staring at us. No Gan-Shi, though. I don't think they liked being this close to the outside, and really, neither did I, but I'd gotten used to it.

"I just hope they don't force us to take a shower before we meet the President," I said, heading up the ramp. I'd rather be flying my fighter, but it only held two, and those two weren't the size of a Gan-Shi.

"I still don't understand the concept of your government," Shindo admitted, the ramp swaying under his weight as he boarded. "You said it has a president, two full bodies of elders, as well as a court that can overrule them all?" He snorted, and the entire spacecraft shuddered as he fell into one of the chairs behind the cockpit. "It seems most awkward. How do you ever get anything done?"

"We don't, mostly," Chuck admitted, waiting for the other Gan-Shi to board before he closed the hatch behind us. "That's a feature, not a bug. Most of the important stuff that happens is done by private enterprise."

Warrin and Shindo stared at Chuck, uncomprehending and he leaned his head back against the copilot's seat with a weary exhalation, clearly not looking forward to having to explain the western economy to the two aliens. I rescued him by getting on the radio with traffic control.

"Attention Space Command," I called, "this is Resistance Lander Zero-One requesting clearance for orbital insertion."

Once upon a time, the whole procedure would have been a formality, since no one on Earth had anything that could have taken down a lander, much less threatened the *Liberator*, but the two American cruisers, the *Victory* and the *Endeavor*, patrolled out in trans-Lunar space, and squadrons of Starblades could scramble out of Andrews and Edwards at a few minutes' notice. Had to make sure to ask nicely now before coming down from orbit.

"Lander Zero-One, this is Space Command. You are cleared for deorbit and landing at Joint Base Andrews. Please follow the beacon."

The woman tried to sound blasé and professional, but she couldn't quite keep the excitement and wonder out of her voice. And who could blame her? She'd gone in just a few months from the Space Force being a bunch of desk-bound geeks who supervised satellite launches to being in charge of the most powerful weapons in the history of humanity, from writing reports about signal intercept to dealing with aliens. If I hadn't been desensitized to the whole business over the last couple years, I'd still be as giddy as a schoolgirl every time I got behind the controls of a fighter.

Oh, who am I kidding? I *was* as giddy as a schoolgirl whenever I climbed into a cockpit. Who wouldn't be? Not that the lander was as fun to fly as a Vanguard or even a Starblade. The things were pretty much automated, and I only had to sync the navigational computer to the beacon and let it take us down.

That was okay in some ways, though, because it let me enjoy the ride. I'd landed on dozens of planets since Lenny had abducted me, but there was something different about Earth. I was probably biased, but she was more beautiful than any of those other worlds. Too many people for my taste, though that was more of a function of two decades-long wars depopulating too many of the planets rather than anything special about Earth.

"You ever think about coming back for good?" Chuck asked me, as if he'd somehow been listening in on my thoughts. "I mean, once all this is over." He grimaced. "Assuming we live through it. Have you ever thought about settling down on Earth again?" Chuck motioned down at the expanse of North America spread out before us, bathed in daylight. Every detail stood out clearly, at least where the clouds didn't cover. The ridged splendor of the Rockies, the glittering thread of the Mississippi River…

"No, I don't think so," I said without any hesitation. "There's really no place on Earth that I'd consider home anymore. Poppa Chuck's farm got sold at auction after he died, Mom and Dad are gone…and forget Florida. It's like one giant subdivision now."

"There's no law that says you have to live the places you lived before," he reminded me. "It's a big world."

"It's an even bigger universe. There are a lot of cool places out there where nobody lives at all, and I won't have to pay through the nose for a house." I grunted. "I saw what the real estate prices were in northern Virginia the last time we visited your dad. I couldn't afford a house there even if I'd retired as a general."

"Thank God for family money," he agreed. "But you've also

got some pull. The government, as much as they were annoyed with you for what happened at Wraith Anchorage, owes you a lot. They could declare a bounty for the ships you provided them, and you'd be filthy rich."

"I hadn't really thought of that," I admitted.

"If I were you, I'd consider asking for a nice little ranch in eastern Idaho, maybe southern Montana. I hear Bozeman's nice. I mean, it's a real city, but it's a lot less people than out east."

I laughed softly.

"Yeah, and I'm sure the neighbors won't be freaked out at all by the green lady moving in next door."

"You get a big enough ranch," Chuck pointed out, "you won't have any neighbors. As for Bozeman, well…it's a college town. Green skin is probably the *least* weird thing around campus."

"I'll talk to Laranna about it," I promised. "But right now"—I glanced back at the two Gan-Shi in the rear seats—"I think we're gonna have enough convincing to do for one day."

"You want us to take in *how* many aliens?" Parker Donovan exploded, coming up from his seat with irate disbelief written across his face. I exchanged a look with Chuck and sighed.

"Parker, please sit down," President Louis said, fingers pressed to his temple like he'd developed a headache. "We have guests."

The Gan-Shi of course, but the massive aliens weren't the only guests. Uniformed Secret Service had escorted them into the Situation Room because there was no way they were going to leave the President of the United States alone with two raging bulls who could kill him with their bare hands while absorbing a dozen bullets each. The agents even carried the new pulse rifles for insurance, ready to mow down the Gan-Shi males at the slightest provocation.

Besides the security arrayed around the perimeter of the circular room, at the table were Louis, Donovan, and General Gavin, and there were also some people I'd met but barely talked to, and a couple new faces that I had only seen before and never met. A tall woman with salt-and-pepper hair and a very fashionable pants suit eyed the Gan-Shi with poorly concealed alarm and distaste, wringing her hands in her lap like she expected the bulls to go on a rampage at any second. She was Hatty Blakefield, the Secretary of Housing and Urban Development, and I really had no idea why she'd been invited to the meeting other than maybe 30,000 aliens would need a lot of housing.

Madison Barrett, the Secretary of State, I'd met before, but she'd had little input during the more straightforward military confrontations with the Anguilar. She was short and elfin, yet still she gave me the impression that people could underestimate her at their peril, and I wouldn't have wanted to face her down in a dark alley. She didn't seem intimidated by the Gan-Shi at all, nor did she pretend to be outraged at the request for asylum. Instead, she watched with shrewd eyes and said nothing.

Then there was the slender, almost skeletal man with thick glasses and the fashion sense of a mortician, or perhaps one of the Earp brothers. A black suit, black bow tie and a very plain white dress shirt that went well with his cadaverous looks and hollow eyes. He hadn't offered his name, but I'd seen him on a news report by chance. Something like Lisbon, I thought, and he was the Attorney General, though I was just as much in the dark why he was here as I was the HUD director.

The last of the unusual suspects I had never met, never even seen before. He was a doughy, soft man a couple inches shorter than me and fifty pounds overweight, and he looked like a bear squeezed into a child's raincoat in his gray suit, the fabric pulling and bunching in all the wrong places, as if it had never been meant for someone of his size.

"Thirty thousand for the moment," I answered Donovan's question, keeping calm, hoping that President Louis would prevail in this argument. "But this is just temporary. We're going to move everyone out as soon as possible, but we need to hold off until after the attack on Copperell. I don't know how the Anguilar found out about Sanctuary, but I do know that at least part of why they attacked now was to keep us on the defensive, keep us reacting. We need to consolidate somewhere secure, somewhere we don't have to worry about our civilians being attacked, and then we can get back to the plan."

"And temporary," the chubby man put in, speaking for the first time, "means how long?"

"This is Secretary of the Interior Wayne Rigsby," President Louis said by way of introduction.

"Well, Secretary Rigsby," I replied, nodding to him politely, "that's uncertain at the moment. We hope the operation will be short because the longer it goes on, the less likely it is we win, but it could still wind up being months. And that's months *after* we actually launch the attack. So if you want a wild-ass guess, let's call it a year."

"My people," Warrin put in, leaning forward, his chair groaning in protest, "will be most grateful for your hospitality. We are a simple folk and can make do with simple accommodations, as long as we have the space and ability to grow our own food under the open sky."

"The Great Plains," I put in, motioning expansively to Rigsby. "That'd be my first instinct. Or maybe somewhere in Colorado like where we were training the Rangers."

"That could work," Rigsby said, nodding. "It's all federal land. Military base, of course, but it's bordered by BLM and national forest."

"Now hold on a second," Donovan objected, though this time he stayed in his seat. "We're forgetting a few things here. First of all, is this even legal? I mean, we have immigration laws, and while they're not meant to handle a situation like this, they still apply and this isn't some matter of two or three refugees on a boat. We're talking thirty *thousand* non-humans. That's basically an army, and we have no way of vetting them. "

"We're not asking for them to be given townhouses in New York City," I reminded Donovan. "If you're worried about security, putting them on the grounds of a military base should let you keep a close enough eye on them."

"As for the legality," Lisbon cut in, adjusting his thick glasses, "I believe we can get away with it, at least for a while. Particularly if we couch this as admitting asylum seekers on a temporary basis with the assurance they'll move on eventually."

Louis nodded, tapping his chin with a fingertip.

"All right. What are your other concerns, Parker?"

Donovan's features screwed up as if he was unhappy that his first—and likely most pressing and convincing—issue had been addressed so easily. His lips pursed, and I figured he was gathering his thoughts for another assault, when the HUD secretary spoke up.

"Another issue is public perception," she noted. "We're going to be providing housing for thirty-thousand non-citizens in the midst of one of the worst housing crises in history. That's going to cause some heartburn among the opposition."

"We have the first of the fusion reactors nearly complete," General Gavin objected, sounding aggrieved. "Once we get the fabricators working, we'll have virtually free prefabricated housing we can put up anywhere within power transmission distance. Hell, we can even distill fresh water from seawater at very low cost with that kind of power. We could build a city in the middle of the desert that would house tens of millions of people and provide them food and housing at no cost. You really think they're going to give us a hard time about this?"

"It's politics," President Louis told him, casting a jaundiced eye his way. "Of course they will. They're already making noises about impeachment again, and that's before they even find out that our biggest allies just lost their base of operations to the enemy. How do you think *that* will play out?"

"That was going to be my next point," Donovan agreed. "This is going to make you"—he jabbed a finger at me—"look weak. And if *you're* weak, then *we're* fools for allying with you, aren't we?"

"Then we don't pitch it that way," Gavin said, elbows on the large, circular table. He nodded toward Shindo and Warrin. "We tell them that you gentlemen and your people are simply refugees from the war with the Anguilar, and we've agreed as part of our alliance with the resistance to take you in. No offense meant, but your appearance is going to be notable to our media and the general public, so you'll draw the attention away from the others."

"There are still nearly ten thousand of those *others*," Donovan pointed out. "How the hell can we hide that?"

"Call them advisors," Chuck suggested, his eyes popping open like a light bulb had snapped into existence above his head. "Spread them out among the fusion reactor construction site, the fabricator crews, the ship works in New Mexico building the shuttles. We can say they're dependents of the workers."

"That's not a bad idea at all," Louis admitted, nodding slowly. "You're going to be a general like your father someday, Major Barnaby." His gaze flickered around the room. "All right. I'm not making a commitment yet, but let's look into making this happen. Wayne, see to the land we're going to need. I'll leave it up to you to decide where, but make it someplace suitable for our friends in the Gan-Shi." He smiled genially at Warrin and Shindo, but they didn't respond. I wasn't sure they *could* smile. "And make sure it's someplace we can maintain security." Warrin frowned and made a sound like a bull about to charge. "For your protection," Louis added. "We don't want curiosity-seekers or reporters coming in there and interfering with your people. I'll get the Secretary of Agriculture to provide you with seeds and farming equipment, Housing will get you temporary shelters set up, and you won't be disturbed as long as you stay on the land you've been granted."

Warrin didn't respond, but his grimace might have lightened a shade.

"I'll need to get with the Secretary of Energy for the additions to the production details for the ships and reactors, but no one'll question that too much." Louis's brows knitted. "But there's only one way this will work, and that's if the actual story, the actual reason for the refugees being here doesn't leave this room. If it does, I'll know one of you leaked it, and I'll make sure whoever did it never works in government again."

"Sir," Donovan interrupted, not sounding very cowed by the threat, "aren't we forgetting one thing?" He half-rose in his seat, palms on the table, and glowered at me. "You said it yourself, Travers, you had a leak somewhere. The Anguilar found out where your home base was, and someone had to have sold you out. Someone on your world, Sanctuary. If we bring those people here, we're possibly bringing a traitor into our midst."

And there was no arguing against that. It was undeniable, and it had eaten at me the entire way here. We had a mole, a needle in a stack of thirty thousand needles, and no way to find them.

"You're right," I admitted. "It's a possibility. But that's why we're here. Sanctuary was vulnerable because it was too isolated to defend if it wasn't a secret. Lenny made it the home base of the resistance when we didn't have the means to defend ourselves. We would have had to move it eventually to stay in line with our new strategic reality." Yeah, yeah, I know, I sounded like a Pentagon briefing, but that was the kind of talk Donovan was used to hearing. "If the spy is here, there's nothing more they can do to hurt us."

President Louis's smile was canny, knowing.

"If this whole supreme galactic military commander thing doesn't work out," he said, "you might want to consider running for office. Because you've definitely got the talent for bullshit." I started to protest, but he waved it away. "Fine. Barring any major unforeseen problems, I'll allow this to move forward. But on one condition." He wagged a finger at me. "Quid pro quo, Charlie. You need a favor from us, I need one from you."

"Of course, sir."

Because what else was I going to say? But that damned smile really made me wish I'd had any other choice.

11

"Please kill me," I murmured aside to Chuck, but then forced the grimace away for a polite smile and a half-bow as the Chinese ambassador stepped into the office.

It was, at least, a very *nice* office, with an incredible view and the sort of furniture that was just the combination of classic and comfortable that only a VIP could demand. I suppose that was what I should have expected from the Secretary of State's private office, particularly when it was someone like Madison Barret.

"Mr. Ambassador," the woman said smoothly, pushing the door shut behind the older Chinese man, "please allow me to introduce you to Major Barnaby of the US Army, and of course, Charles Travers, the commander of the resistance forces."

"A pleasure to meet you, sir," I told the ambassador, hoping to hell I could get away with not saying his name because I'd forgotten it about two seconds after Barret had announced him.

I usually had a pretty good memory for that sort of thing, but we'd started off with representatives from Britain and worked our way east, and I'd lost track of things right around Poland. I'd also lost count of how many hours this dog and pony show had been going on.

I should have been out there with the rest of my troops overseeing the unloading of the ships. The process had been going on for nearly three days straight, and I'd yet to inspect the living quarters for the refugees. I also should have been wearing combat fatigues or, better yet, just a T-shirt and jeans instead of the monkey suit they'd forced me into. Not even a dress uniform, because of course, I wasn't in the US military anymore, and if I had been, that wouldn't have played well with the concerned ambassadors of all these countries who weren't comfortable with us dumping a huge load of military power into America's lap.

It wasn't even just a normal suit, which I could have lived with at least for a few days despite my loathing for ties. No, they'd commissioned some fashion hack to make me their idea of what space-age formal wear should look like, sort of a cross between a Nehru jacket and a circa-1979 prom tux. I felt like a huge idiot wearing the getup, but the various diplomats had been…well, *diplomatic* enough not to mention it.

"Please, have a seat, Mr. Ambassador," Barret invited, guiding the distinguished, straight-backed diplomat to a chair beside mine. Chuck sat in the back of the office, not as a slight to him, Barret had explained hours ago, but to deemphasize the military involvement with the resistance. "I trust traffic wasn't too bad?"

The Chinese ambassador laughed harshly in a voice like a

cobblestone street, a man who'd spent his youth smoking way too many cigarettes.

"You Americans complain of your traffic as if it were a badge of honor, but I would like to see one of you brave enough to attempt driving in Beijing at rush hour."

"Even I'm not brave enough to drive in the traffic you guys have nowadays," I confessed, the polite smile easier to fake after practicing it all day. "I didn't even own a car before I…left Earth. I feel safer in a spaceship."

"Yes, I have heard your story, Mr. Travers," the ambassador —I really badly wanted to ask him his name—said, disbelief written across his face in a thin smile. "You say you were born in the 1960s and abducted by aliens in 1987. And you expect us to believe this?"

It wasn't the first time I'd heard the accusation, but it was the rudest, and I was about to tell him I didn't care what he believed, but Barret stepped in and played peacemaker, which I suppose was her job.

"Mr. Wei," she said, finally repeating his name after I'd lost interest in being polite to him, "we have very detailed records of Mr. Travers from when he was in college ROTC and the Florida National Guard, including photographs and fingerprints. We also have DNA samples given to the authorities by his parents after his disappearance. There is no doubt that the man sitting beside you is exactly who he claims to be."

"Yes, you would say that, wouldn't you?" Wei shook his head. "Pardon me, Madame Secretary, I know you must abide with the wishes of your president, but I didn't come here today to be part of this grand deception you've performed on the world stage. I am here only to reiterate that if this insane alien war you've dragged our world into should affect the People's Republic of China, we *will* hold you responsible. You think your new weapons will keep us in fear, but these sorts of technological toys never stay secret for long. Sooner or later, we will share in the weapons you now have, and you will regret taking this action without our consent."

For all that this guy looked like a shopkeeper dressed up for his daughter's wedding, there was a threatening ferocity in his tone and the set of his intense, dark eyes, and under normal circumstances, I might have found that combination and the unusual setting intimidating enough to watch my mouth. But the circumstances weren't normal, and I'd already been pissed off before he walked in.

"No, you won't," I told him, flatly, as emotionless as I could manage. Barret glared at me, but before she could interrupt, Wei asked the question I'd anticipated.

"We won't *what*, Mr. Traver?"

"You won't build your own starships," I clarified. "You won't even build anything equivalent to the Starblade fighters. Building them requires technology humans wouldn't have developed on their own for centuries, if we *ever* did. Because no one in this galaxy did. It came here from another galaxy, and it was discovered so long ago, not even the sentient AIs that are the oldest intelligence we know of remember how it happened. If I hadn't convinced the resistance that they needed Earth's help against the Anguilar, no nation on Earth would have star travel or gravity-resist technology, and there is absolutely zero chance you could copy it even if I sent you a cruiser in pieces with a technical manual. You don't know how to build the machines to build the machines. You can't even make the stuff that makes it possible because it requires an artificial black hole just to produce it." Barret half-rose from her chair like she wanted to put a hand over my mouth and prevent me from revealing state secrets, but I'd just exhausted everything I knew about the science of producing a starship. "So please, if you just came here to threaten us, don't bother. It's empty. It's stupid. You're alienating the only people who can give your country things you *can* produce, like fusion reactors, automated fabricators, room-temperature superconductors. I'm not a scientist, but I do know that stuff is what'll transform Earth from a bunch of squabbling nitwits grasping for the last scraps in the bowl into a world at peace because what's going on in Europe or the Middle East isn't nearly as important as all the energy and resources that are coming in from the rest of the Solar System."

"Yes, and all of it conveniently controlled by the United States," Wei sneered. "We will all be dependent on them, the entire planet under their thumb."

"Not if we win this war," I corrected him, smacking my palm down on the Barret's desk hard enough to make both him and the Secretary of State blink in surprise. "If the Anguilar win, the best-case scenario is that you'll be stuck in this Solar System, trapped here because they don't want to expend the troops and resources to try to take a planet as heavily populated as Earth. You'll be cursed with the knowledge that there's a bigger universe out there that you'll never be a part of." I shrugged. "But if we win…the whole galaxy is open. There are dozens of systems out there, and no one government is going to be able to run all of them—it's just too big. Which means if China doesn't want to depend on the US for interstellar transport, well, you can just make a deal with one of the other governments or independent shippers who'll be doing business with the highest bidder once the Anguilar aren't around anymore."

A thoughtful frown creased Wei's features, counterbalanced by the worried version crossing Barret's face. She had, I imagined, just registered that as a possibility and didn't care for it at all. I could understand why, but since I wasn't working for the US government anymore, it wasn't my job to secure a generational hegemony for them. My job was to beat the Anguilar.

"And anyone who has a significant role in defeating the Empire," I added, "is likely to be remembered more fondly by the people who own those ships. They might even be interested in a long-term partnership."

Wei rubbed at his chin, staring at me like a starving dog at a squirrel.

"We might need proof of this. My government would very much like to have a representative on one of your ships."

"I'm sure that can be arranged," I told him, eyeing Barret meaningfully. She nodded with obvious enthusiasm, seizing what was clear even to a neophyte diplomat like me was a wonderful opportunity to bring the Chinese government into this fight on our side. "You can contact me through the White House, and we'll set up a short patrol through the next few closest systems."

That part I had down pat because he'd been the fourth ambassador who'd requested a ride-along. I figured we'd take them all at once and let them set down on the first habitable we came to so they could tell all their friends they walked on another planet. Good publicity for the cause, and if the Chinese threw their economic and military weight behind the war, definitely worth it.

"Very well," Wei said, and by this time, I knew his tone. It meant he'd reached the limit of what he'd been authorized to say and everything else was going to be his own words. "Tell me something, Mr. Travers, just a curiosity raised by the reports I've read from your accounts."

"Yes, Mr. Wei?" Some juvenile part of my brain that had never grown up wanted to counterpoint the man's name with *no way*! But I managed to control myself.

"If your description of events is accurate, then you are a daring and resourceful military leader, and I have to believe you have some sense of military history."

"It was a hobby of mine during college," I confirmed. "Although I'm mostly familiar with American military history."

"Then I hope you can understand something peculiar about your war," Wei said. "Although you're dealing with unimaginable distances and amazing, miraculous technology, the numbers of actual people involved, both combatants and noncombatants, are staggeringly miniscule."

I nodded. It was something I *had* thought about.

"It's a little like the Seven Years War," I agreed. "A world war in a lot of ways but with small populations in the colonies, relatively small numbers of ships, and armies numbering in the thousands. Plus a lot of use of local militias. That's why getting troops and equipment from…Earth is so important." I'd almost said *America*, but that would have been impolitic.

"It has been very interesting meeting you," Wei said, standing abruptly and offering a hand. I jumped up, unprepared for the sudden goodbye, and grasped his hand. His grip was firm and dry and stronger than I would have thought. "I hope we are able to speak again."

When the door closed behind the Chinese ambassador, the air went out of me, and I leaned heavily against the desk until Barret glared at me and I stood straight again, taking my weight off of her desk.

"*That* was a lot closer to being a complete disaster than I'd like," she growled at me, then offered Chuck a baleful glare. "I thought you were supposed to keep Mr. Travers in line, Major Barnaby."

"Ma'am, I'm just a military liaison," he protested, spreading his hands. "I've never had any training in being a diplomat. I thought I was here to make sure Charlie didn't punch any of those self-important assholes." Chuck patted me on the shoulder. "And may I say, you showed an admirable amount of self-control."

"I hope that's it," I said, rubbing a hand over the back of my head. I needed a haircut. "Because if I don't get some lunch, I'm going to gut, skin, and cook the next ambassador who comes through that door. Who's next, anyway? Australia? New Zealand?"

"No more ambassadors," Barret assured me, a cat-ate-the-canary smile on her face. "The Australians are satisfied with the technology we're passing onto them, and the Kiwis probably aren't even aware that there's an interstellar war going on."

"Oh, thank God," I sighed. "So, where's the nearest Mickey-D's?"

"We'll bring you some food," she told me, nodding at the door. "There's a gentleman waiting for you outside. He'll take you to an office where lunch is waiting for you. And then, one last conversation you'll need to have."

Pain lanced through my temples, and I rubbed at them.

"I thought you said no more ambassadors?"

"Oh, trust me, Mr. Travers," Barret said, "this man is many things, but he's no ambassador."

12

I leaned back in the chair and polished off the last of the club sandwich, not quite satisfied but with at least the edge taken off my hunger.

"You want another water?" Chuck asked, offering one of the plastic bottles we'd found in the office's mini-fridge, but I shook my head.

"I want a beer," I replied with a hint of a whine. "Jeez, Chuck, you'd think I asked them to settle the Gan-Shi in Manhattan condos instead of giving them a few hundred acres in the middle of nowhere North Dakota."

"I'll tell you a secret my old man told me, Charlie," he said, wiping his hands off with a napkin that had come with the bagged lunch. "Politicians collect favors, but they hate owing them. You came here and gave us all this technology, gave us two starships, and yeah, we're supposed to help you fight your war, but we haven't done it yet. The President owes you a favor, and he didn't like it, so when you asked him to take in the Gan-Shi and the Copperell, he was happy to have the chance to have *you* owe *him*."

"And not hesitant at all about calling in that marker." I motioned around at the room. It was tiny, unadorned and poorly-lit, with not a hint of personalization, like it was shared by several people who didn't leave anything of themselves behind. "Whose office is this, anyway? It's a dump compared to Barret's."

"She's the Secretary of State," Chuck reminded me. "Whoever this is…" He made a face. "Maybe the janitor? Although that wasn't a janitor who brought us here."

No, he hadn't been. Dark suit, bland expression, hadn't said a word. I'd thought Secret Service, but I'd been around plenty of them the last few months and this guy didn't seem like one. A fed of some kind, but I didn't know which.

"Not FBI," I mused. "He would have been wearing ID and a badge."

"A spook," Chuck declared, gesticulating with a finger. "Don't know the flavor. CIA, NSA, DIA, something."

The door opened, and I jumped up automatically, hand going for a pistol I wasn't wearing before I realized where I was. It wasn't the guy in the suit, though…it was *another* guy in a suit. A slightly more expensive suit, a slightly older guy, but just as spooky, with that used-car salesman vibe I'd gotten from the other CIA types I'd encountered dealing with the US government. Slicked-back dark hair with a touch of gray, just enough over fighting weight to tell me that he did most of his work in an office and didn't get out early enough to visit the gym regularly.

Behind him was…a different kettle of fish altogether. Not as old as Suit Number Two, older than Suit Number One, he still had a trace of silver in his well-kempt beard, but that was the bigger point. He *had* a beard, and I hadn't seen a single other person in the White House who did. There was something about his eyes as well, and the set of his mouth that were…*different*. It's hard to describe, but I'd found out dealing with aliens the last couple years that the language a person speaks shapes their face, and this man hadn't grown up speaking English. The clothes were the second tell. Everyone else I'd seen in the White House fell into one of two categories—tailor-made high-fashion suits that cost more than I would have made in a year as an Army officer or off-the-rack business wear that a junior functionary could afford.

Not this guy. He wore a leather jacket in a place and a season not suited for it, over a black shirt and black jeans that even from my limited exposure to the modern day I was sure weren't in fashion in the United States. He also wore a visitor badge on his jacket's breast pocket, which meant he didn't work here.

"Charles Travers," Suit Number Two said, not a question or a greeting but more of an accusation. "Major Barnaby. I'm Taylor Richford." He pushed the door shut behind them. "And this is Mr. Kononov. He has something he needs to speak to you about."

Neither of them offered to shake hands, so I didn't either.

"You have some experience with my country, I think,"

Kononov said, his Russian accent confirming all of my suspicions.

"Not very pleasant experience," I confirmed. "They've tried to kill me twice."

"Yes." He smiled. "I would apologize, but neither of those actions were my decision, and after I finish speaking to you, you'll understand why I feel no responsibility for them."

"Sit down," Richford invited, moving over to the other side of the desk.

I'd sat in the office chair while Chuck and I had eaten, and Richford didn't show any trace of proprietary resentment so I figured this wasn't his office. Instead, he took one of the uncomfortable, straight-backed chairs meant for the presumably rare guests in this place. I shrugged and took the swivel chair while Chuck and Kononov stood. I wondered if the Russian standing was meant to make me feel uncomfortable, but I wasn't going to give him the satisfaction.

"You're KGB, right?" I guessed, eyeing Kononov.

"FSB," he answered without hesitation, then grunted a humorless laugh. "Though that is, as you Americans say, just rebranding. I understand why you'd call it that. You left this place when we were still the USSR. I wish I could say much has changed." He tossed his head in the sort of shrug no American would have made. "I was a young boy when the Soviet Union fell, but old enough to understand my parents' elation at the idea things would be better. That elation lasted long enough for me to finish university, and then everything was back to the bad old days. Except this time, the country was being run by the openly criminal rather than the secretly criminal."

Chuck's eyebrows shot up.

"That's very…self-aware of you. Not what I've come to expect from the Russian government."

"If I were to speak this way in front of my superiors, I'd be thrown in a secret prison and never heard from again." Kononov sat on the edge of the desk, the fingers of his right hand twitching in a way I recognized from a couple of the sergeants in my ROTC cadre after they'd banned smoking in the building. "If anyone even knew I was here, I'd be subject to…intense questioning. But I've come to the conclusion that there's a difference between loyalty to the Motherland and loyalty to the man running it."

"That's fascinating," I put in, holding up a hand, "and I'm sure there's some really important James Bond, cloak-and-dagger style shit going on here, but I have to ask…what does it have to do with me? I'm not with the CIA." I eyed Richford significantly. "And I'm not in the US military anymore. So why am I being included in this top-secret conversation?"

Kononov and Richford exchanged a look, and the man I presumed to be a CIA agent nodded to the Russian spy.

"Tell him," Richford urged. "We've talked about it. There's nothing else we can do."

Kononov nodded but took a moment to curse softly and pull a pack of cigarettes. He shook one loose and let it hang from his mouth, unlit, his fingers shaking.

"There's no smoke detector in here," Richford told him, and

the Russian nodded gratefully, fishing a lighter from his jacket pocket and inhaling a lungful of cancer.

I didn't especially care for the smell of cigarettes, but I was used to it. Chuck, though…from his reaction, Kononov might as well have pulled down his jeans and taken a dump on the floor.

"You must understand," the Russian went on after steeling his nerves with the nicotine, "what I am about to tell you can't leave this room. I know you have no obligation to the government, but…"

"Oh, they pretty much have me where they want me," I reassured him, scowling at Chuck for being right.

"You remember the Anguilar attack on your capitol?" Kononov said.

"I'm not likely to forget it."

"During the attack," the Russian agent continued, ignoring my sarcasm, "the enemy managed to land a shuttle unnoticed by you or the American government. They touched down at a secret base in Siberia, reachable only by the air."

"And how the hell did they know about the base if it was so damned secret?" Chuck demanded, the edge to his voice showing that he had a fair idea exactly how they'd known.

"They'd been in contact with the FSB," Kononov confirmed. "And through us, directly to President Sverdlov."

And there it was, the other shoe. The reason we were here. I didn't know much about the international situation while I'd been gone, but I'd heard about Sverdlov. Former KGB, a real throat-cutter.

"They've been there ever since," Kononov explained.

"Feeding our researchers and engineers enough technological crumbs to ensure our cooperation."

"The Russians are making a deal with the Anguilar," I said, shaking my head. I suppose I shouldn't have been surprised, yet I was. Not that the Russians would want to make the deal but that the Anguilar would be subtle enough to think of it. That had to be Zan-Tar.

"No." Kononov punctuated the denial with a palm smacking down hard on the desk. "Not Russia…President Sverdlov. He has done this as he's done everything since he came to power: unilaterally, without thought for the future of our country."

"I can tell you what your future is," Chuck said grimly. "If the Anguilar attack again and we and our allies know you betrayed us to them, the very last thing we do will be to nuke the hell out of you."

"And the Anguilar won't give a shit," I added. "To them, you'll be tools to be used and discarded."

"You see my dilemma then," the Russian agreed, taking another deep drag before blowing the smoke into the far corner of the room. "I can't take this to the FSB because they're part of it. If I try to go to the military, I'm likely to be considered a traitor. Sverdlov purged most of the generals independent enough to consider defying him years ago."

I looked over at Richford, an ugly suspicion forming in my mind.

"Wait a second. If you and the President know about this, why am I here?"

"We need to excise this problem ASAP," Richford said, his

expression as flat as if he were speaking of getting his BMW serviced. "If we allow the Anguilar a bolt-hole on Earth, allow these negotiations to go on, it's going to come back to bite us in the ass."

I waited for him to expound, but he and Kononov just stared at me as if that had explained everything.

"You have Delta Force and SEAL Team Six and whatever to take care of things like this," I told them, coming out of my chair, steam pressure building up behind my eyes. "And if you need to get past Russian air defenses, you have the Starblades we gave you."

"The US government," Richford said, not moving from his seat, hands still clasped in his lap, "can't afford to take any such action directly."

"Well, why the hell not?" The steam finally exploded, and this time, I made no attempt to bottle it up. "You could land a whole squadron of Starblades in Red Square, and there's not a damn thing they could do to stop you! Surely, you could land a special ops team in the middle of freaking Siberia!" I motioned above us. "With the cruisers and the fighters, you could shoot down an ICBM attack…even a sub-launched missile attack. You know that, and so do they."

Kononov had smoked the cigarette down to a nub and looked around furiously for somewhere to stub it out.

"*Suka*," he muttered and crushed it against the desktop. I recognized it from one of my Military History instructors as a Russian curse word. "Nuclear warheads are not dangerous only when they're at the end of a missile, Mr. Travers. Only more detectable."

"What Mr. Kononov is saying," Richford put in, "is that the Russians have between hundreds and thousands of nuclear warheads they could dismount from their ballistic missiles and donate to terrorist groups. As things stand right now, the Middle East will be totally irrelevant within a matter of years due to the fusion reactors and high-temperature superconductors you've shown us how to manufacture. That's not good news for terrorist groups based in the area since it means absolutely no one will be paying attention to their causes…unless they can attract notice by, oh, I don't know, setting off a nuclear warhead in a seaport at Long Beach. The Russians can claim plausible deniability, and there's no way we could respond in kind without turning the entire world against us."

"That's if Sverdlov even cares about retaliation," Kononov sneered. "If not, he could simply smuggle warheads in on cargo ships flagged under other nations and strike the entire western world. What would it matter to him if you invade then? He might prefer it. General Winter has destroyed many armies, and even starships might not be enough to defeat him."

"And if we do it?" I asked, looking between the two of them. "How does that make it any better?"

"You're not in the US military," the Russian agent reasoned. "If you attack in your Vanguards and use only alien troops…"

"…*and* if you can show the world the Anguilar operatives you've captured," Richford interjected, "then not only would world opinion be on our side, but Sverdlov would also look weak."

"And if he looks weak," Kononov continued for him, sounding enthused for the first time since he'd entered the office, "then he *will* be removed. This is the one opportunity we'll have to do it peacefully before he can take down the rest of the country with him."

"But only if me and my troops do it," I finished. "Where the hell is Donovan? Or at least the CIA director? Shouldn't they be in here?"

"Plausible deniability, Mr. Travers," Richford reminded me, grinning like a man who knew he'd won his argument. "Everything said in any of the meetings you've had with the President or any member of his cabinet has been recorded and can be played back for a Congressional hearing, a Senate subcommittee, or a meeting of the UN Security Council."

"But not in an office without even a working smoke detector," Chuck surmised. He shook his head and offered me a bleak expression. "You have to make the decision. And I won't be able to go with you."

"Oh, yeah," I sneered. "Because I really have any other choice." A thought struck me, and I pointed a finger at Richford's chest. "You're probably some off-the-books type. I bet Richford isn't even your real name and you think you can drop this on me then disappear. But I'm gonna share a little secret with both of you." I added Kononov to the conversation with a harsh stare. "If you're conning me, if there aren't Anguilar spies at this base, I can scan this entire continent from orbit and find you just by the

DNA profile my comlink has already recorded." I patted the breast pocket of my suit jacket. "And I'll take both of you off this planet where there is no Hague or Geneva Convention, where no law can touch me and turn you over to the coldest hardest intelligence chief you've ever met."

Richford said nothing. A real cool cat. But Kononov blanched, beads of sweat breaking out on his forehead.

"My intelligence is solid," he insisted. "I have the location along with photographs of the aliens." He motioned at Richford. "Or, rather, he has it."

"I've already transferred it to your comlink," the CIA officer said quickly.

"And I suppose you want me to give you dates and times?" I asked him, but he just as quickly shook his head.

"No. Tell me nothing. Major Barnaby, you weren't present for this conversation, and you know nothing about it. Are we clear?"

"What conversation?" Chuck asked, spreading his hands innocently.

"Good." Richford stood and offered us both a nod. "Then we'll leave you here. Give us five minutes before you open the door." He smiled thinly. "And I look forward to never seeing you again."

Kononov bowed his head slightly, then took a moment to brush the ash off the desk into his hand and slip it into his jacket pocket, along with the cigarette butt. The two men left, and once the door was closed, there was no indication they'd ever been here. I sat down on the desk and rubbed a finger across where the Russian had stubbed out his smoke.

"You can really do that?" Chuck asked me after a beat, his eyes wide as if in horror. "Take someone's DNA remotely from your comlink and find them anywhere on the planet?"

I laughed softly and tossed my water bottle into the trash can.

"Of course not. I don't even know how to make the thing do much beyond talk to people. Come on, let's go." I waved at him. "We have an assault to plan."

Chuck put a hand on my arm before I got to the door, a grin on his face.

"If you're really going to do this, I have something you're going to want to take with you."

13

IF I HADN'T KNOWN BETTER, I could have sworn the hard-driving guitar-heavy music blaring out of the cockpit speakers of the Vanguard was some Led Zeppelin song I'd missed during my long absence from Earth. But instead, it was a group Chuck had introduced me to called Greta Van Fleet, and the song was Highway Tune. I tapped a foot against the deck beside one of the control pedals and hummed along, letting the beat take me away from the night-shrouded forest beneath us.

"Is this atonal caterwauling necessary?"

My first instinct was to tell Shindo that I'd heard what his people considered music and he had no business criticizing anyone else, but then I glanced back and barely contained a guffaw. The Gan-Shi looked ridiculous, his knees jammed up to his chest, arms crossed over his knees and still barely fitting into the back of the cockpit.

"What?" I asked him, trying to keep my face neutral. "You don't like my taste in music?"

Beside me in the gunner's seat, Skyros smirked. He'd mentioned at least a dozen times that he'd rather have me put a kettle over his head and beat it with a metal rod than listen to another classic rock song. He'd done a good job taking over for Nareena, though he'd needed a little help from Laranna to settle in.

"I know not if it's your personal taste," Shindo admitted, "or perhaps your entire species', since I've yet to hear anything from the workers at the encampment that I can tolerate." His brow furled, the horns shifting. "Of course, I can't say which I find more objectionable, the music or being jammed into an aircraft built for two tiny humanoids."

"I did give you and your people the choice," I told him, eyes drifting back to the red dot hovering ahead of us, tantalizing and foreboding at once. "We could have just squeezed two more Strada into the same space."

"Not that they would have been any happier," Skyros added. "But the cockpit might have smelled better."

Shindo snorted and tried to lean forward threateningly…and came up short against both the safety harness and his own legs.

"You Strada and humans smell just as bad to us," he said, huffing like a steam engine. "And taking part in this raid will be proof that whoever the traitor was, it isn't one of us."

I didn't think it would prove anything, in point of fact, but I didn't want to say anything to discourage him. Things were complicated enough already.

"I don't like this," Brandy had said when she'd heard the plan.

I'd called everyone up to the *Liberator* because I wasn't sure how secure any possible meeting place downstairs would be, even the White House or the Pentagon. We were talking about Russian spies, and if I'd learned anything reading up on the history I'd missed, it was that the federal government leaked like a sieve. Mr. Richford, or whatever his real name was, had at least gotten that much right.

"There's a lot not to like," I'd agreed, watching Russia pass below us on the bridge viewscreen. They had to know we were up here, could see our ships on optical even if their radar wouldn't work on the hull. "But if it's true, I don't see that we have any other choice."

"What I don't see," Giblet had countered, taking a sip from the bottle of beer he'd brought along with him from the galley, "is how the hell we're going to pull it off. I mean, sure, we can get down there, and there's not a lot they can do to stop us in the Vanguards, but a lander doesn't have shielding, and if they have heavy weapons around this place, they could take it down." He'd shrugged. "Particularly if they have Anguilar advising them. One of the first things those bastards would give them is software that'd pick up on the drive signature from our spacecraft."

He wasn't wrong about that.

"You didn't bring a beer for me, did you?" I'd asked, still looking at the screen.

"You kidding? Of course I did." Gib had produced another bottle from behind his back, grinning.

"You brought it for yourself," I'd accused, twisting off the cap.

"Well, yeah. But I'm not a monster."

"I meant to ask you, Brandy," I'd said after taking a sip, "did you ever get anything out of that Krin?"

And the reason I hadn't asked was that I hadn't been able to get away from Chuck long enough to make sure he didn't hear anything he was uncomfortable with. Not that I was sure *I* was comfortable with it, either. True, every Krin I'd ever run across had been a raging asshole, but that didn't make it okay to torture them, and keeping someone naked and cold for days at a time was pretty damn close to torture. If she planned to go any further than that, I needed to rein that in right now.

"He got more talkative once he got hungry," she'd told me, smiling with a hint of cruelty I'd never noticed before. "And sluggish. The cold does that to Krin after a while. According to him, the initial attack on Sanctuary was a last-minute operation. The Anguilar had a small strike force waiting for a signal, and when they got it, they sent the attack with no preparation." The smile had faded away, transformed into murderous rage barely contained. "If they'd come at any other time, come when the Vanguards were there, or the cruiser, or the *Liberator*, it would never have been so…successful. That had to be part of the transmission the mole sent, that there was only the one Liberator ship." Brandy had shaken herself like a dog waking up from a nap, and the rage dissipated behind her eyes, settling back down to the cold cruelty. "Once you showed up and chased them off, they went back to the nearest Anguilar colony and got reinforcements. They have orders not to waste their cruisers, but his fellow pilots heard rumors that the fighters and ground troops were expendable." Brandy had smirked. "He wasn't too happy about that, but when the alternative to being in the Anguilar military is working in the mines for them, there's not much of a choice."

"But he didn't know anything about who the mole was?" I'd asked, but she'd just shaken her head.

"He's a low man on the totem pole. It's not something his commander would have shared with him…if even he knew."

"And I guess he wouldn't know a damned thing about the situation down here," I'd mused. The beer wasn't great, and I couldn't fathom why Gib preferred Corona to Heineken. "What did you do to him after he spilled his guts?"

I'd been hoping and praying she wouldn't say she'd killed him. I didn't have any problems killing enemy troops in battle, but summary executions would blur the line between us and the bad guys way too much for my taste.

"Put him back in his cell." She'd shrugged as if the matter was unimportant. "You never know when we might need more intelligence from him, and we could make some sort of deal to strand him on an isolated settlement."

I'd tried not to appear too obviously relieved, though I was.

"This is a secret base, right?" Skyros had asked, and I'd looked over at him in surprise, having forgotten he was present. I was used to Nareena representing the Strada forces. She'd been a calming, steadying influence on all of us, the voice of experience with most of her life spent fighting the Anguilar. "I mean, these Russians of yours, they don't wish the other nations to be aware of its existence, correct?"

"That's the general idea," I'd agreed.

"They may not have that many troops guarding the place then. If we took all of the Vanguards, that would be thirty of us, which might be enough."

"No," Gib had said, shaking his head. "We'll want at least some of the fighters in the air providing fire support."

And that was when it had hit me.

"The flight from orbit is short." I'd pointed with the spout of the bottle at the Russian subcontinent as it traveled past us, wishing it was a physical window instead of a holographic projection so I could have tapped against it. "Maybe short enough that we could squeeze a third passenger into the Vanguards."

"Ooh," Giblet had hissed, grimacing. "That's gonna suck for whoever has to ride it down. But yeah, I suppose. Two infantry per bird, that's thirty, and we can still keep the fighters aloft after we drop them off."

"We won't need all of them for air support," I'd amended. "Say, we keep half of them in the air and the other half on the ground, then we can put our total effective ground force almost at thirty. If we're in combat armor and bring along a couple plasma guns, that should be enough."

"We have plasma guns in our arsenal," Lenny had said, speaking up for the first time in the little planning session, "but I have observed that they are awkward and unwieldy for use by dismounts without armored transport."

A smile had slowly spread across Gib's face.

"Awkward and unwieldy for us normal-sized humanoids, but not for the Gan-Shi."

"Surely you're not serious," Brandy had fairly exploded, staring at him wide-eyed.

"Yes, I *am* serious," he'd countered, "and don't call me Shirley."

"Oh, Jesus," I'd moaned. "I never should have let you watch that movie."

"One of those damned cows is a traitor!" Brandy had insisted, throwing up her hands in obvious frustration. "What's it going to take for all of you to realize that? Do one of you need to wind up with your arms and legs burned off, laying in the med bay next to my husband before you see what's happening?"

She'd gotten shrill and loud enough that quite a few heads had turned on the bridge, and I slipped an arm around her shoulder. She'd tried to jerk away from me, but I spoke quickly and quietly, hoping she'd take the hint.

"Brandy, everyone here knows what you and Val have sacrificed, and you might be right about the traitor being among the Gan-Shi. But we can't treat twenty-thousand of them like every single one is a mole. If we take twenty-two of them on this mission and one of them betrays us, we'll manage to ferret out the traitor on an operation that's not do-or-die for the resistance."

"And if we lose more people in the process?" she'd demanded. "Can you live with that?"

"I guess I'll have to," was all I'd been able to come up with as a reply. "Gib, go get us a couple landers ready. I'll let Space Command know we're on our way."

I WISH we'd had time to wait for Laranna and the last Liberator ship, but they weren't due for at least another week. No Laranna, no Chuck, no Nareena, no Val. And Gib would be staying in the air for cover, which meant I'd be leading the raid on the base myself, backed up by Skyros, a Strada I'd never gone into combat with before, and Shindo, a Gan-Shi I didn't know if I could trust.

"We'll be in visual range in about ten seconds," Skyros told me.

And we'd be the first since I was at the front of the formation. Only two squadrons because Laranna had kept hers back at Sanctuary, which was at once too many birds and not enough. Too many because the more fighters we had in the air, the better chance we'd be spotted from the ground. And not enough because I would have felt so much more comfortable with another twenty or thirty ground troops.

If there was a bright side, it was just how remote this place was. I'd never been to Siberia, never come any closer to it than orbit, and I hadn't had a clear idea of just how unbelievably big the area was until I'd flown across it nap-of-the-earth all the way from the Alaskan coast. We'd flown at night, even though the shelter of darkness was more psychological than real. If the

Russian satellites or ground radar could pick us up during the day, they'd have even less trouble at night.

I *could* tell the difference from the view out the cockpit, though just barely. The enhanced optics built into the screens illuminated every detail of the tundra that had replaced the forest a few hundred miles back, though it was all much of a sameness after a few seconds of looking at it, but there was a blue tint to the unbroken clumps of brush and the trackless mud.

Well, not exactly trackless. There *was* one set of tracks, the railroad kind, winding their lonely way through the wasteland. It was beautiful in a way—the sort of way that one of the astronauts had described the Moon, a magnificent desolation. I could imagine taking a days-long luxury train ride through the area just to say I'd done it, but not setting one foot off into the muddy slog. And never doing it again. It was a good place to hide a secret base.

The installation had once been an oil drilling platform, or so I'd been told by Lenny, who had researched it via his downloaded image of the internet once I'd given him the coordinates. It had been shut down years ago and never reopened because the Russians couldn't tempt any western workers to come repair it and didn't have enough skilled engineers of their own. Yet it *wasn't* completely shut down, evidenced by the thermal readings glowing red and yellow on the sensor screen. No movement, no trains on the ancient tracks, just rust-covered buildings suspended on stilts driven deep into the mud, down to the permafrost. If not for the faint readings on thermal, I could have believed Kononov had been lying to us and the place was abandoned.

Until one of those rusted, metal roofs split apart like the petals of a flower and a surface-to-air missile battery spun on its gimbals, the pincushion wall of slender projectiles aimed right between my eyes.

"Oh, damn," I murmured. "Skyros…"

He nodded silently, adjusting the aim of the pulse turret but an instant too late. Smoke and fire billowed from the sides and back of the launcher as every single one of the SAMs spat out with the urgency of a base commander who knew the game was up.

I shouldn't have been worried. The Vanguards had the most advanced electronic countermeasures of any spacecraft except the Liberator ships, which should have sent the weapons spinning off out of control, but this close, only a few miles away, it wasn't impossible that they could be guided in visually. And I *still* shouldn't have been worried because there was no conventional warhead the Russians had that could penetrate the shields of our Vanguards.

And yet, I *was* worried and I acted instinctively, yanking the trigger of the proton cannon. It wasn't aimed anywhere specific except in the general direction of the incoming flight of missiles, yet this deep into the atmosphere, it didn't have to be. Like an artillery shell, it could be addressed *to whom it may concern*. Air heated to plasma and fled from the beam of atomic destruction that had doomed it, sending waves of static electricity and burning oxygen ahead of it. Consuming the missiles in spectacular orange and white detonations of their rocket propellant.

All but one. It didn't impact a Vanguard, perhaps set off via a proximity fuse or perhaps detonating sympathetically with the rest of the warheads. I wasn't an expert on SAMs or their chosen warheads, but I figured this one would be like any other missile warhead, with a load of high explosives at the core of some kind of fragmentary material. I figured wrong.

The light of a sun ripped apart the night and threw my Vanguard out of control.

14

A NUKE. They launched a nuke at us!

It was my first thought, and I didn't have time for a second, totally involved in not plowing my fighter into the mud at supersonic speed. The explosion, whatever it was, had sent the Vanguard tumbling away, only the automatic stabilizers keeping the starfighter from spinning end for end like a football at the kickoff. We went into a flat spin, which wasn't *that* much better, but at least the Vanguard was equipped to pull out of it. I tilted the left grip of the steering yoke one way, the right another and did the same with the control pedals, unable to make out a damned thing through the kaleidoscope view of the main screen, royally screwed if we were attacked again but not knowing what else to do.

The left drive pod spun one way on its gimbals while the right stayed pointed the other and I ran headlong into a brick wall. At least that was what it felt like to me, and if the labored grunt from Shindo was any indication, it wasn't any better for the others. But the Vanguard stopped its spin, hovering only a couple hundred feet above the charred and blasted ground, the view growing steady just in time for me to see Gib coming in just behind me, blasting the SAM turret with his proton cannon.

The launcher and the building beneath it disappeared in a ball of white fire, laying waste to more of the tundra, as if anyone could tell the difference.

"That was a plasma warhead," Gib told me as if I should know what that meant. "The Anguilar have been sharing some of their more obsolete toys with your Russian friends."

A dull ache had settled into my head, neck, and back from the pounding the explosion had dished out, and I had to blink my eyes to clear them from involuntary tears. Only then could I check the external sensor readings, hoping they wouldn't show the ground below radioactive. That would be the end of this mission, and it would probably mean a hell of a lot of trouble for President Louis, since the Russians would blame *us* for a nuclear attack on their sovereign territory.

No radioactivity, just a temperature spike to somewhere around 120 degrees Fahrenheit. Uncomfortable but not close to fatal.

"Watch our backs, Gib," I told him, spinning the drive pods downward and gradually cutting power. Sort of gradually...I wanted down and wanted it quickly. "Landing force, follow me."

The Vanguard was a brute, built to take a beating, and I put her to the test, landing hard, the impact not quite as punishing as the plasma warhead against our shields but still bruising, throwing me forward against my safety harness.

"Out!" I tried to yell the command, but it emerged as a hoarse croak since I hadn't had the chance to pull in a full breath to replace the one the landing had driven out of me.

Deciding to lead by example instead, I yanked the quick-release for my harness and grabbed my pulse rifle from its niche in the cockpit bulkhead beside me. The next step would have been the hatch control, but Shindo beat me to it, probably more eager to be out of the fighter than I was.

The Gan-Shi didn't so much step out of the cockpit as he did fall out of it headfirst, and when he hit the ground, it was on all fours like the bull bison he resembled, his hands and feet sinking inches into the thick mud. Rising from the crouch, lit up by the interior illumination of the cockpit, Shindo looked savage and atavistic, as if he were about to charge into a pack of wolves to save his herd from predation.

Flipping down the visor of my combat helmet, I jumped down beside him, stance wide, knowing before I hit that my boots would be stuck up to the ankles in the mud. Fighters landed behind us, the glare from their jets throwing long shadows onto the metal buildings, the blackened and scoured spots where the explosion had reached them shining brilliantly. Bits of mud splattered against my armor and onto Shindo's bare back—he and the other Gan-Shi had refused my offer to have custom armor fabricated for them, saying that they had no experience fighting in it and wouldn't be comfortable.

"Get the plasma gun," I told him, motioning to the small

cargo hatch in the side of the fighter. It couldn't carry much, and we hadn't used them for anything yet, but as it turned out, they were a perfect fit for the plasma weapons.

I'd only used the things once before, back when we liberated Strada, and even then, we'd had to mount them on their equivalent of a horse because they were so damned heavy. Shindo pulled the six-foot-long weapon out of the niche one-handed and swung it around like it was a carbine.

"This way!" I told him, waving toward the largest of the buildings.

Maybe I should have waited for the others, but the longer we gave them to get prepared, the more casualties we were going to take…and as much as I'd been brought here by Lenny to be a commander, a leader, the only way I knew how to lead was from the front. The main entrance was up a short flight of skeletal metal stairs, mud clogging up the grating the only hint that the place had seen any use lately.

The double doors showed the same signs of disuse…from a distance. But as I got closer, the details came into focus, lit up to daylight by my helmet visor's enhanced optics. The rust on the door and the walls wasn't real, just painted on, camouflage—or *maskirovka*, as the Russians called it. Ironic that I'd wound up here, invading Russian territory after four years of training to push back a Russian invasion of our territory during the Cold War. I pointed at the center line where the twin barriers met, no visible mechanism to open them.

"Shoot it here," I told Shindo. "And make sure you close your eyes just before you pull the trigger."

The Gan-Shi was at least smart enough to back up twenty yards or so before hefting the gun, though I was concerned that still wouldn't be enough. I stepped just in front of him, letting him aim the gun over my shoulder, and waited.

"What are you doing?" he demanded, and even though I faced the wrong way to see his expression of disdain, I felt it.

"Protecting you from splashback," I said impatiently. "Since you were too stubborn to wear armor. Pull the trigger before I do it myself."

I hoped he closed his eyes because even through the polarized visor, my own vision whited out at the sun-bright splash of plasma. A wash of heat dried all the sweat I'd built up beneath my armor with the feeling of a day spent on the beach at Daytona in the middle of Spring Break concentrated into a half a second. Before either my eyes or the visor could adjust to the blinding flare, the concussion hit, and I stumbled back a step into Shindo's chest, pinpricks of pressure my only clue that red-hot shrapnel had blown back at us.

Smoke and afterimages cleared in a moment, and where the thick, sturdy, well-camouflaged double-doors had been was a glowing, steaming hole through the metal…and a stairway leading down. That was a shock, given the permafrost. I'd read up on the geology of the area in a file Lenny had put together for me before the mission and thus had some idea of how difficult it would be to construct an underground base here, much less keep it secret. But I guess if you want a secret base, putting it somewhere most people would think impossible was a good start.

The plasma had melted through the doors and splashed

across the roof as it sloped down into the descending staircase, charring the metal there black and stripping away a broad swathe of it to reveal the insulation beneath. But the biggest effect the blast had besides opening the door lay burned and smoking on the floor, the remains of three men in Russian camouflage fatigues. Not enough was left to tell for sure if they'd been Wagner Group mercenaries or Spetsnaz commandos, but the charred and melted wreckage of a pair of heavy machine guns told the story of their intent. They'd seen us coming at the last second and run up here to try to set up an ambush, the poor bastards. It was hard to blame them for the situation—they were just following orders, although that defense hadn't worked out too well for the Germans in World War Two. Lucky for these guys, they wouldn't have to worry about a trial.

"I should go first," Shindo said when I moved ahead of him.

"Yeah, you'll be so useful trying to take corners with that giant cannon," I told him, wishing he could see me rolling my eyes.

I was lucky he could even hear me. It had taken a ten-minute-long debate with him, Warrin, and the other males who'd come along to convince them to carry a comlink on their belts and wear earplugs so we could talk to them during the assault.

"Just be ready if I need you to blow out any more locked doors," I told him.

Going down stairs while wearing a helmet wasn't a fun experience, since the only way to see my own feet was to lean forward and physically look down, taking my eyes off potential threats. I was very tempted to push up my visor and take my chances since the stairwell lighting was mostly intact, but being a leader meant setting an example. As much as I hated wearing an enclosed helmet, as much as it felt like trying to fight inside a barrel and added a layer of insulation from reality, the smart and responsible thing to do was to keep the protection and the night-vision capabilities.

"Sir," Skyros called over the helmet radio from somewhere behind me, "we're on the ground and coming in behind you. Giblet and the cover squadron are back in the air."

"Put the Gan-Shi in the rear and have them watch our egress," I ordered, speaking softly out of instinct even though no one could have heard me through the closed helmet.

"Yes, sir," Skyros confirmed, though he couldn't conceal the doubt in his voice at the thought of letting the big bulls have a free shot at our backs. He and the other Strada trusted Brandy, and she had been pretty vocal about her belief that the traitor was one of the Gan-Shi. My own thought was that it was better to find out who we could depend on now, even if we had to do it the hard way.

If Shindo had picked up the subtext, he didn't mention it, and I tried to shut out the nagging worry of having the Gan-Shi standing behind me with a weapon that would leave very little behind if he shot me point-blank with it. The stairwell didn't help, since it seemed to go on forever, twisting around one landing after another, and at each one, I had to cut the corner and check around the other side of it.

I'd gone down three stories and encountered no further enemy, and I didn't like the implications of that at all. It meant that after the machine gun crew had rushed up to meet us, whoever was in charge down below had told everyone else to stay downstairs, probably in a nice defensive position. That meant that they'd be harder to dig out, but it also meant they were expecting help. A few minutes ago, that wouldn't have worried me, since I'd been sure the most advanced Russian missiles or jet fighters were no match for the Vanguards.

Then I'd had the chance to experience this new plasma warhead thing firsthand.

Stop borrowing trouble, a still, small voice whispered inside my head. *Do the job that's in front of you.*

I tried to remember who'd told me that, and I thought it might have been Poppa Chuck or maybe Sgt. Redd. Either one would have been right, though I figured they would have been talking about different things entirely.

Four floors down and not so much as a single door yet. Whatever was down here, the Russians badly wanted it hidden. Laranna had taught me a method of checking corners, and when I'd showed it to Chuck, he'd said it was called slicing the pie. I sliced the pie around the corner of the next landing and the pie almost had me for dessert.

I don't know what tipped me off, what made me jerk back in time. I could say instinct, but the truth is, there was likely some cue I'd missed on a conscious level, a change in the echo of my steps, a thickness in the air, or just a miniscule increase in the ambient temperature or the light filtering up from the next level. Whatever it was, it saved my life, because I pulled my helmet back from the corner just a fraction of a second ahead of a burst of gunfire that punched fist-sized holes in the sheet metal siding that lined the walls.

Even with the helmet shielding my ears, the roar of the heavy machine guns pounded a drumbeat directly into my sinuses, banishing thought or any hope of calling to alert the others. I had one notion, one piece of training that had stuck with me from my Army days even though it wasn't something the resistance or the Anguilar used much. Something the others hadn't bothered to carry because none of them had trained with them, but I'd procured through Chuck.

Grenades. The reason neither the Empire nor the resistance used them was because of the armor I wore, the same sort of armor both sides came equipped with in the war. It was too good. Any grenade that could penetrate the armor would be powerful enough to possibly injure the person who'd thrown it. I'd asked Laranna why no one built a grenade launcher and had it patiently explained to me that the weight one would take up could better be put to use firing a more powerful pulse blast that could do more damage anyway.

But the Rangers Chuck was training in North Dakota had an advantage over the Imperial troops—over ours, too, if it came down to that. The powered armor wasn't something anyone had tried in recent memory, and it allowed them to wear thicker protection…and to throw a grenade farther. Since they were Rangers, whose main job was to shoot people and blow shit up, that meant they really wanted more powerful grenades.

Powerful enough that I wouldn't want to throw one of these things out in the open, but around the corner and down the stairs seemed pretty safe. For me. No pin on this one, just flip up the safety and press a big, red button. I whipped the cylindrical grenade hard enough to bounce it off the far wall, aiming high so it wouldn't get nailed by the streams of slugs still spraying out of the stairwell.

A flash of light and rolling thunder echoed up from around the corner of the landing, concussion rattling the siding over the walls and sending me stumbling backward a step. I caught myself against the far wall, but before I could push back around the corner, Shindo swung the barrel of his plasma gun on target and fired down the stairs. If the light and heat had been overwhelming outside on the tundra, here in the enclosed space of the landing, it was like I'd set off that grenade inside my helmet.

Gritting my teeth, I rushed up beside the Gan-Shi and brought my rifle up to my shoulder. There was nothing left to shoot at. The bottom of the next landing was a crater, the metal of the steps and what I assumed used to be a pair of heavy machine guns on tripod mounts melted and twisted into Daliesque shapes, small fires crackling where nothing should have been able to burn. I tried not to look at what was left of the soldiers who'd been manning the guns. Given a few hours and a crime scene unit, we might have been able to piece together how many of the Russians there'd been, but all I knew at the moment was that they weren't going to be shooting at us anymore.

Suddenly very grateful for the helmet and its air filters, I descended slowly, the muzzle of my pulse rifle following my eyes. A haze of white smoke clouded the landing below, but it wasn't stationary. It billowed through a door blocked open by a body.

This one was more or less intact, blood stains adding new patterns to his camouflage, and it looked as if he'd been trying to get clear when the grenade fragments had caught him. A Kalashnikov rifle lay beside him, just beyond the reach of his fingers.

"Sir, you okay?"

Skyros appeared beside me out of the smoke, his face just visible through the visor of his helmet, eyes flickering between Shindo, the carnage, and me. Shindo watched with a neutral expression, a few minor burns on his arms and chest from the plasma discharge. The barrel of the weapon glowed red in the dim light filtering through the doorway, the overhead lamps of the landing shattered by the two explosions.

"Yeah. Spread out behind me in a tight wedge and follow at one-second intervals. Shindo, you're with me."

I didn't especially want him up with me, particularly given that he'd already gotten parboiled from the plasma gun, but I wasn't sure if we'd need heavy artillery up front. He didn't question the command, though, and if the red patches and missing body hair bothered him, his expression was as stolid as ever.

The door opened into a hallway narrow enough I wasn't sure if Shindo would be able to fit through it with the gun, a perfect chokepoint if the Russians had another ambush set up. Doors lined the hall on either side, unlabeled, and I paused at each one, then pushed it open and shoved the barrel of my rifle inside first. Nothing. They were someone's living quarters, simple and unadorned, and unoccupied. Small, barely twelve by twelve, each of them had a pair of bunk beds and little else. The last one was a large, communal bathroom with rows of showers.

Ducking down, I checked under the bathroom stalls and saw nothing. Someone might be hiding there still, standing on the toilet seat like in the movies, but not enough to pull off an ambush. I left kicking in the stall doors to the others and kept moving.

The hallway opened up into an intersection, the left dead-ending in a large, darkened room stacked high with shipping crates, the right corridor heading down to a larger suite of rooms, brightly lit, the silver of some kind of lab equipment gleaming the reflection of the overhead lights. There was nowhere else to go. The Anguilar had to be inside that chamber if they were anywhere in this facility, and that meant whoever was guarding them had to be there as well.

How many would that be? There'd only been enough bunk beds for twelve people…maybe twenty or so if they slept in shifts, and we'd already killed at least seven or eight. The last of them wouldn't be thinking about an ambush, not back there. They'd try to hold out. Maybe I could talk them out of it. I tilted up the visor of my helmet.

"Hey, you, in there!" I called. "I know you're in the lab. Give up the Anguilar and we'll leave. They're all we want. You can keep whatever technology they already gave you, I don't give a shit. But we're not going to let you make a deal with the Anguilar. They'd stab you in the back anyway. Turn them over to me, and you can walk away."

No reply at first, and when it came, it was in heavily accented English.

"You risk open warfare, American. Even if you left now, our nation will strike back at you."

"I'm an American," I corrected him, "but I'm not with the American government. I'm Charlie Travers, the leader of the resistance against the Anguilar, and whatever help you think you have coming, it's not going to be enough. We have enough firepower to bury you under this place if we wanted to. We could destroy a city if we wanted to, and there wouldn't be a damned thing you could do about it. But all we want is the Anguilar."

"The only way you will have them," the Russian said, "is if you come through us."

I sighed and glanced back at Skyros, motioning for him and the others to move up.

"I guess we have to do this the hard way."

15

"On three," I told Skyros, priming the grenade.

I didn't *want* to use it. Throwing it into the lab meant chancing that I'd take out the Anguilar, too, and it was important that we take them alive. But I also wasn't going to run into a hail of heavy machine gun bullets, despite the armor. Skyros motioned back to the rest of the Strada.

"We're ready."

"Three." I counted down on my fingers, my rifle tucked under my arm. "Two. One."

I tossed it, harder this time, farther, then pushed Shindo back away from the door, not wanting to take the chance he'd do something stupid again. I didn't know what was in these new grenades, but I'd had the chance to toss a couple live M67s during training, and the detonation from one of the old models was a dull crump, a slight flash, a black billow of dust. This was ten times the power of one of the old grenades, more like a land mine, and even from this far away and with thick, metal walls in the way, the detonation still felt like a punch in the chest.

The echoes from the blast hadn't died when I rushed in, the details of my surroundings washing over me like a wave breaking at the shore, only bits of it registering in the bare seconds I had to think about them. Bare metal, not so shiny as before, pitted and burned now. Instruments I didn't recognize, most of them damaged and smoking, and I could only imagine they had something to do with the technology the Anguilar had offered the Russians in exchange for their alliance.

Chairs toppled by the blast, some of them regular office models, torn and shredded but cheap-looking before that, I judged. Others were tall stools meant for use at the tables with the instruments, tossed around like jacks on a playground, a couple of them twisted and broken. But the chairs were the only thing twisted and broken on the floor. No bodies, no blood. At the other end of the lab, though, were rows of silver cabinets, freezers or refrigerators maybe, each of them six feet tall, their surfaces scored by shrapnel.

I'd taken a step toward them when I noticed the wire. It ran from one of the refrigerators to a large, plastic desk crammed into the corner of the room, and I could only plead inexperience that I didn't recognize it immediately for what it was. Instead, I wasted nearly a full second, assuming the dull, green wire was an electrical cord before the thought struck me, training I hadn't had in years and only briefly then.

Mine.

"Get back!" I yelled, turning, pushing Skyros away before throwing myself at Shindo, blocking him with my body.

Something kicked me square in the back with the force of a pro football punter, and like the luckless pigskin, I went flying toward the dome ceiling of a stadium, the lights glaring into my eyes. Sort of.

The lights were flashes of stars inside my head, and the punter was probably something simple, like the old MON-50, the Soviet-era equivalent of a Claymore mine. Stuffed inside that desk, the wire running to the troops hiding inside the refrigerator. The thought floated inside my head like a stray birthday balloon, lost and never to be seen again unless it was snagged by a tree or a power line. I felt like that balloon myself, heading for the sky until I came up short against a mighty oak tree—well, it was actually a Gan-Shi, but Shindo was certainly as solid as an oak.

I knocked him over. I couldn't have done it on my own in a fight, not without all that C-4 propelling me, but I got no satisfaction from the accomplishment since it hurt me a lot more than it hurt him. I'd been kicked square in the back by the explosion, then slammed straight into Shindo, stopping my flight abruptly, my nose squashing up against the front of my visor hard enough to break it.

My back rested on the floor. I didn't remember hitting the ground, just a blur of motion and the unmistakable sight of Shindo falling over from the impact, then a brief blackness, and I was on the floor. It was all I knew for a moment, my position, the fact that I was down and Shindo was down and God alone knew what had happened to everyone else. I couldn't see through the wash of light dancing in front of my eyes, couldn't think, could barely feel beyond the vague knowledge that I was in serious pain.

I figured the lights were just a symptom of the concussion I surely had, but then I realized in a flash of insight that what had actually happened was that my visor had been damaged in the blast. I needed to push it out of the way, needed to see. I couldn't hear anything, either, which probably meant the helmet radio had been damaged by the blast as well, but that seemed trivial compared to the inability to see possible threats.

The only problem was, when I tried to move to push the visor up, my body didn't want to cooperate, like my arms and legs were trapped in quicksand. The pain lurked in the background, ever present, but it wasn't the pain stopping me, it was the fog across my thoughts, as if the signals weren't getting from my brain to my hands. Nothing could penetrate the fog, not fear, not desperation, not reason. I tried anger.

I'd survived being abducted by an alien, survived pirates, survived more battles with the Anguilar than I could count, survived mutant monsters, traveled from one side of this galaxy to the other, and I was *not* going to die here in a hole in the ground in the middle of Siberia. Screw the Russians, screw the Anguilar and screw *this*.

My hands moved as if of their own accord, though I sensed that it was more a case of them following orders from my brain just a few seconds late. The visor was stuck, and rather than struggle with it, I yanked the gasket seals of the helmet loose and pushed it off. The room was darker than it had been, either because I suddenly lacked the light-intensifying optics of the visor or maybe because the overhead fixtures had been destroyed in the blast and all the illumination came from outside in the corridor.

A glance behind me showed Shindo still flat on his back, his arms and legs thrashing, and a squad of Strada in the process of scrambling to their feet, and if there was any good news to be had it was that no one was dead. The bad news was all up front.

The doors to the refrigerators swung open soundlessly, or rather whatever sound they made was drowned out by the ringing in my ears, and half a dozen soldiers in Russian camouflage burst from their hiding place, AK-12 rifles swinging up from where they'd held them down at their sides while crammed into the storage cabinets. From behind them, four Anguilar in dress officer's uniforms scrambled out, the pulse handguns they carried more dangerous than the 5.45 mm slugs of the AKs.

But to get to them, I'd have to go through the Russians.

Somehow, I was up on one knee. I didn't remember doing that, felt like I was missing seconds of time, little breaks in the reel of my memory. Reaching for the service pistol holstered at my hip, I found my rifle instead, still slung around my shoulder. I'd figured it had been lost in the explosion, but somehow the harness attaching it to my armored vest had survived the concussion and the hail of ball bearings, and who was I to look that gift horse in the mouth? I pulled the trigger the second my hand found the grip, not trying to use the sights, just walking the crimson flashes across the target.

Concussed, battered, bruised, my hands numb, I felt an odd

separation from the actions, as if someone else fired the rifle, as if the Strada behind me were the ones cutting down the Russian special forces. They should have surrendered. Anyone else would have surrendered. *I* might even have surrendered…to the Russians, anyway, if not the Anguilar. These guys didn't. In retrospect, I respected it. They had their duty and their orders were likely to not give up the Anguilar to us no matter what. In the moment, I hated their guts, not for fighting us but for making me do this.

The Russian Spetsnaz soldiers went down, disappearing from sight behind the cover of a worktable as if the pulse rifle had disintegrated them…and so did two of the Anguilar. There'd been no way to avoid it, since they'd jumped out of the cabinets just behind the Spetsnaz commandos, but I cursed myself anyway, still unable to hear my own voice, and tossed the rifle down.

I did something stupid. It wasn't the first time, but at least I had the excuse of being concussed. The last two Anguilar were both armed, their handguns drawn and firing, and I charged straight into them anyway. My shoulder slammed into the gut of the one closest to me, and I carried him into the other Anguilar officer, taking them both back into the door of one of the refrigerators. It had swung shut behind them, and the three of us hit it hard enough to wobble the heavy cabinet on its moorings…and to send the pulse pistol of the poor son of a gun in the back flying away from him.

A flash of heat seared the left side of my face, the snap-crack of a pulse gun discharging penetrating the ringing in my ears, and I was dimly aware that the first Anguilar I'd tackled had fired his pistol just past my head. Grabbing his wrist, I forced the weapon upward and brought a knee up between his legs.

One of life's little gratifications was that all humanoid males in the galaxy seemed to share the same weakness. The Anguilar's breath gushed out, stinking of whatever carrion the aliens considered a delicacy, and I stripped the pistol out of his hand, then slammed an elbow back into his jaw. He went limp and I made a grab for the other survivor, but Shindo had beat me to it. The big Gan-Shi had seen better days, was bleeding from a dozen shrapnel wounds in his arms and legs and had added a few more burns to the total from firing the plasma gun unarmored, but it didn't appear to bother him. He wrapped his fingers around the Anguilar officer's neck and lifted him off the ground one-handed. The Anguilar kicked and writhed, pounding his fists against the Gan-Shi's forearm in utter futility before his eyes rolled up in his head and he went limp.

"We want him alive," I reminded Shindo, smacking him on the shoulder.

The Gan-Shi scowled down at me but negligently tossed the alien aside. My hearing had improved enough that I winced at the heavy thump the Anguilar made when he hit the floor.

"Any casualties?" I rasped, then realized most of them wouldn't hear me since I didn't have my helmet radio anymore.

Skyros had my back, though, and pushed up his visor to report to me.

"No serious injuries," he told me, then shrugged. "Not counting you, of course."

I looked down at myself and spotted the blood. I'd taken shrapnel all over the place, obviously, since a damn land mine had gone off basically in my face, but the armor had done its job and absorbed most of it. Even alien armor had its weak spots, though, usually at the joints, and a shard of shining, heated metal protruded about three inches from my left shoulder.

"Aw, shit," I murmured, sagging to the side and barely catching myself before I fell over. "I hate it when that happens."

"Steady," he said, putting a hand on my right arm. "Let's get you back to the fighter and get the hell out of here."

"Bring the prisoners," I reminded him, but he was already nodding.

"It's taken care of."

I don't know how I was the one to notice it first. I had no right being observant and every excuse not to be, but something about the desk caught my eye. The lab had two desks…well, it had before one of them had exploded and taken all the equipment within ten feet with it. One on each side of the room. The only one remaining was on my right now that I'd turned around to head back out of the lab, and I just happened to be looking that way when someone's foot slipped out from beneath it.

I didn't shout, just pulled away from Skyros and made a shushing gesture, then pointed at the desk. Skyros's eyes went wide, and he pushed down his visor, I guessed to give orders to the others without being overheard. I didn't wait for him to organize things, just slung my rifle over my shoulder—the one without a shard of metal sticking out of it—and pulled my handgun.

Slow or fast? I gave the question a heartbeat's reflection and decided on fast, mostly because I'd always been an impatient son of a gun and partially because I wasn't sure how much longer I could stay conscious. I walked up to the desk and kicked the side, aiming the handgun at the open end.

"We know you're in there. Get out now, or I'm about to find out how well cheap plastic protects you from scalar energy pulses. I've got a feeling it's not going to be very effective."

I was taking a risk that whoever it was spoke English. With the Spetsnaz, it had been a good bet, but this guy wasn't any kind of special forces or he wouldn't be cowering under a desk.

"I…coming out."

The voice was male, high-pitched, and ragged with stress. A Russian accent, of course. The movement had been a shoe, black but not a dress type, more what waiters and other service types who spent a lot of time on their feet wore. The man wearing it was young-ish, about my age, with shaggy, dark hair and a gaunt build, his cheeks hollowed out like a jack-o-lantern left outside until mid-December. I'd expected a suit or maybe a lab coat, though that might have been a product of me watching too many movies, but instead, he wore a set of dull, gray coveralls.

"Keep your hands up," I warned him as he scuttled out from under the furniture.

"Da, I will," he promised. He looked awkward and slightly ridiculous crawling out with his hands raised, but I was past caring about that. "Do not shoot me!"

"Who are you?" I demanded, keeping my pistol on him.

"Nikolai," he told me. "Nikolai Luzhkov. I am a…" His face screwed up as if he were hunting through his memory for the word. "Technician? I operate…machines." He motioned at the wrecked equipment. Then his eyes fell on the dead Spetsnaz commandos, and he went pale. Pal*er*. This guy hadn't seen the Sun for quite a while as it was. "There are…" he stammered. "There are two others, plus an engineer and two physicists, but they were called to Moscow two days ago to make report. Just me and the Major and his people." He nodded toward the two Anguilar being restrained by the Strada. "And the aliens. Can you…can I go with you? You must take me from here soon."

"Why?" I wanted to know, irritated. It was going to be hard enough cramming the two Anguilar into the Vanguards. "They're sure to send someone to check the place out in a few hours, if they haven't already. You'll be fine."

But he was already shaking his head violently.

"No, you not understand…the Major." Luzhkov motioned at one of the Spetsnaz bodies. "He knew you were coming. He set…bomb." His brow furled. "Nuclear bomb. It will go off soon. We have to leave, now!"

Shit.

"Skyros!" I yelled at the Strada, waving to get his attention. The Strada flipped up his visor, looking confused. "Get everyone out and off the ground now! This place is about to blow!"

I wished I had handcuffs. Grenades, I had, but no handcuffs. I tapped Luzhkov in the shoulder with the barrel of my pistol and motioned at the door.

"If you want to live," I told him, "then start moving."

THOSE DAMNED STAIRS.

They reminded me of the ones we'd taken down to the cache on Haven where we'd found the Vanguards, exasperating on the way down and exhausting on the way up, though this time, we also had a ticking clock to worry about. A clock we couldn't see, nor did we know how much time was left on it.

"Come on!" I yelled at the Strada ahead of me. "For God's sake, if I can make it up the stairs with a piece of metal sticking out of my arm, you guys should be freaking running!"

Luzhkov certainly had no issues running up the stairs, and I hadn't once needed to prod him with my pistol to keep him moving. The man practically danced with impatience, as if he had energy enough to climb the stairs three times while we did it once.

"We must hurry!" he insisted. "The Major said it would not be long!"

"Sorry, sir," Skyros grunted, the legs of one of the Anguilar officers sticking out from under his arm where he and the Strada in front of him carried the alien up the stairs. "But the prisoners won't sit still, and I'm afraid we're going to drop them."

Shindo grunted and pushed between Luzhkov and me, then tapped Skyros on the shoulder.

"Give him to me."

I was about to tell the Gan-Shi to leave his plasma gun

behind, but Shindo just shifted it to his left hand, grabbed the Anguilar by the arm, and tossed the prisoner over his right shoulder. The big guy had been burned, peppered with shrapnel, and knocked over by a flying Charlie Travers, but he charged up the steps toting the massive plasma gun and the squirming, cursing Anguilar as if it was nothing. The Strada carrying the other prisoner chased after him as if his performance had shamed them into trying harder, and it was only another two minutes before we emerged into the light of a new dawn.

I blinked, wondering how the hell we'd been down there long enough for the Sun to come up until I realized where we were. Northern Siberia was pretty damn close to the Arctic Circle, and this was mid-summer. There wasn't a hell of a lot of night to be had at this latitude. The Vanguards waited for us, their landing gear half-buried in the mud, obscenely exposed here in the light of day, and now that Gib had landed his squadron to pick up the infantry, we had no air cover. What we did have was a half a dozen Gan-Shi scanning for threats with their plasma guns. I searched the sky with every other step through the morass, expecting a flight of MIG-35s any second, probably armed with the same sort of plasma warheads that had nearly blown me out of the air before.

Nothing but pale blue skies stared back at me. Maybe that made sense if there really was a nuke under the installation…and maybe that made sense, too. This base was their version of Area 51, sort of, as top secret as top secret got.

"Get the prisoners on board," I yelled to no one in particular and knew it the second the words were out of my mouth. None of the Strada could hear me, and they were doing their job anyway without me giving orders.

Shindo high-stepped to one of Gib's fighters and dumped the Anguilar officer into Gib's cockpit before heading back for my ship. I grabbed Luzhkov by the arm and guided him into the cockpit.

"It's gonna be a tight squeeze so you might want to breathe shallow for a while. But it's the best we can do."

He didn't complain, scrambling into the far corner of the cockpit and hugging his knees to his chest, eyes darting around as if he expected the world to end any second. When Shindo jammed himself into the fighter beside him, though, his eyes went wider, and he groaned softly as the bulk of the Gan-Shi pressed him harder into the bulkhead. I knew how he felt. The rush of adrenaline had deserted me, and the wound in my shoulder throbbed, a warm trickle of blood dripping under my armor, taking another shred of my consciousness with every drop. My vision blurred slightly, and I considered whether I should try to pull it out and apply a dressing now.

Except there was that whole ticking clock thing.

"Skyros," I told the Strada as he settled into the gunner's seat. "I'm gonna get us off the ground, but if I pass out, you're going to have to be ready to take over."

I probably should have let him pilot us away from here, but I wasn't quite far gone enough yet to let anyone else drive. Besides, it wasn't as if I had to worry about red lights up here.

The fighter didn't seem to care if I was a little woozy, the jets screaming to life as I fed them juice from the power cell. Yet even over their racket, I still heard Luzhkov's sigh of relief when the landing struts pulled free of the mud and we blasted away from the installation. The pods swiveled with the ship, and the nose angled upward into the morning sky.

"We have to get to safe distance," he told me, voice breaking with fear. "I don't know how powerful the bomb is…"

Pretty damned powerful, as it turned out. We were ten thousand feet up when the flash of light washed out the rear cameras and seemed to surround us even at an altitude of almost two miles. Light moved faster than sound and the concussion wave moved at the speed of sound, so I had a fraction of a second to clench my teeth and tense up, holding tightly to the controls and hoping the shields would be enough to protect us.

And praying.

Ten thousand feet, as it turned out, wasn't *quite* far enough. Turbulence hit the fighter like a physical blow, about as violent as the point-blank detonation of the plasma warhead, except this time I was ready for it. The controls fought with me, as if the Vanguard was a living thing and had gotten pissed off at me for abusing it so frequently, but I held it steady, tilting the drive pods at a more shallow angle, giving us some extra stability.

Stable enough that I had the presence of mind to check the sensor screen and make sure that none of the fighters in our two squadrons had been caught by the blast. Enough that I could spare a moment to check the rear camera view. Where the Russian installation had been was now a huge sinkhole, gouts of steam blowing up streams of meltwater from the permafrost. No mushroom cloud, but the blast would definitely be detectable from orbit.

"I think this is gonna be a problem," I murmured.

But hey, at least my shoulder didn't hurt so bad anymore, so I had that going for me.

I passed out.

16

"Ow."

Pain. That was the first thing I experienced, a pounding, throbbing pain in my head. The cottonmouth came close on its heels, the sort of intense, desert dryness that made it hard to breathe. Then more pain from the blinding light when I tried to open my eyes. I pressed my hands into the sides of my head and sat up, still not knowing where I was or how long I'd been out.

"Water," I croaked, hoping someone would hear me.

"Here, Charlie."

A warm grip pulled my hand away from my head and pressed a cup into it. I drank carefully but greedily, gulping down the cold water until my tongue didn't stick to the roof of my mouth. Shielding my eyes with one hand, I opened them a slit until they adjusted to the light.

Laranna stood above me, concern written across her face, and I blinked hard, sure I was hallucinating.

"Hey," I said once I'd figured out that she was actually here, and that *here* was the ship's medical bay. I lay on one of the treatment beds, disconnected from any of the hookups, tubes, and gadgets I'd seen used for whatever witch-doctor crap the high-tech machines did to heal us up.

I took her hand in mine and squeezed it so the next question I asked wouldn't be taken the wrong way.

"How are you here already?" I wanted to know. Then I looked around. "And how long have I been out?"

"The answer to the second question would answer both."

It wasn't Laranna's voice, and I worried again I might be delusional until the towering, robed figure of Constanine stepped into my peripheral vision. He hadn't changed his fashion sense since leaving the ancient cache at Haven to join the resistance, but he had, at least, taken up regular bathing and washing his clothes. Probably at the insistence of the people who had to work around him.

"You were kept sedated for four days," Constantine told me.

Yelping, I jumped out of the bed, then grabbed at the sheet and pulled it around me when I discovered I was naked. And the floor was *cold*.

"What the hell?" I demanded, looking between the two of them. "I had a little shoulder wound! Why would you keep me out for four days?"

"You also had a small brain bleed," Brother Constantine said, tapping the side of his head demonstrably. "From what Skyros told me, you were mere feet away from an antipersonnel mine detonating. The armor was sufficient to keep most of the shrapnel from penetrating, but it can't stop physics. The shock wave still battered your brain inside your skull, and if Skyros hadn't rushed you straight into the med bay after docking with the *Liberator*, you would have died in minutes. Once the bleed was stopped, we had to leave you in the tank for the better part of two days to repair the damage to the surrounding tissue."

"Oh." I sat back down and felt at the side of my head. They hadn't even needed to shave me, for which I suppose I was grateful. I'd shaved my head once for the ROTC Ranger Challenge competition, and it hadn't been pretty. I'd thought Jill was gonna break up with me.

"You were extremely lucky," Laranna added in a chiding tone. She had my clothes tucked under her arm and passed them over to me with a sigh. "I know I couldn't convince you to sit out these sorts of operations, but you do *not* need to be the first one through the door."

"Oh, like you wouldn't have done the same thing," I scoffed, turning away from Constantine to pull on shorts and jeans. Fortunately, my bed had the wall on one side so I wouldn't have to flash the other patients in the clinic.

"Of course I would have," Laranna agreed. "But I'm not the commander."

I couldn't argue with that, even though I had no intention of giving up being point man whether or not it would have been the smart thing to do, so instead, I pulled on my shirt, slipped into my Nikes, and turned to kiss her. She pushed me away for a second, still glowering, but then sighed and pulled me into an embrace. The kiss was sweeter still for the fact that I was lucky to be alive to experience it. At some point, how close I'd come to death was going to hit me, but not yet.

"I'm sorry," I told her. "I'll be more careful. How are the rest of the civilians? Are they getting settled into their new homes?"

"Your government had the trailers ready," she confirmed, gears shifting at the sudden change in conversation tracks. "The engineers and technicians we already had working on the reactors and fabricators have pitched in to make sure there's plenty of food, bedding, and clothes for them." Laranna shrugged. "No one is very happy about the situation, but they're making the best of it, as long as it's temporary."

I took a whiff of myself, decided that they'd bathed me while I was under, and debated whether I should be grateful or disturbed by that.

"Thanks for taking care of me, Constantine," I told the former monk. I took a quick look around and saw a couple of the Strada who'd been on the mission with me getting minor treatment from the other medical technicians. "Where's Val? I thought you were keeping him here until the implant surgery."

"He wanted some privacy," Constantine said, bowing his head slightly as if in respect for Val's sacrifice. "Brandy took him back to their quarters."

"Have they decided which way he's going with the…" I shrugged. "The cybernetics?"

"I have not been informed." Constantine's head tilted to the side. "I would think they'd have asked my opinion, considering."

Oh, yeah. I'd forgotten about that. Unlike Val, Gib, Laranna, and me, Constantine hadn't made his way into the future in a stasis pod. He'd lived every year of a millennium, second by second, and he'd done it because of the mechanical implants Lenny had given him. I'd never seen any visible evidence of them, but then, he never showed up in public wearing anything more revealing than a cassock, and I'd often wondered if he was a smaller version of Lenny underneath that robe.

"Which choice did you go with?" I asked, feeling daring since he'd brought it up.

"Charlie Travers," he told me, laughing softly, "I was not given a choice."

And with that, he walked off, apparently uninterested in satisfying my curiosity.

"Damn," I murmured. Shaking it off, I turned back to Laranna, who eyed me with her arms crossed.

"I hope you don't think our discussion is over."

I groaned and massaged my temples, pretending my head still hurt. Well, not exactly *pretending*—it did still hurt, but not enough to prevent the scolding Laranna was set to deliver.

"Can we do it later?" I begged. "I need to find out the status of the prisoners we took."

Four days…so much could have happened. I needed to find out what those Anguilar knew, and I also needed to make sure that Russian technician was being taken care of. Maybe Brandy could get away with keeping a Krin in a cold cell, but the Russian was a different story. We were going to have to give him back, eventually, and he'd better be ready to tell everyone we treated him in accordance with international law.

"You have more to worry about than the prisoners," Laranna warned me, following me out of the medical bay.

"Sir." A Strada warrior nodded to me as we passed each other in the doorway of the medical bay. "Glad you're back on your feet."

"Thanks, Morro," I told him, the fact I was able to recall his name a comfort since it meant my brain was still working. "You going in to get patched up?"

"No, I told my life-mate Olave that I'd meet her here after she had her leg checked by the medical techs. A shell fragment cracked her tibia when the bomb went off down inside that bunker." Morro chuckled, eyeing me up and down with an expression of disbelief. "Honestly, sir, I can't believe you survived that. I mean, you were *right there* when the explosion happened. Then you just jumped up like it was nothing and shot down the human soldiers and captured the Anguilar all by yourself. And you even managed to fly your fighter back up to the ship before you passed out."

"Almost," I corrected him. "Skyros had to dock with the *Liberator*. I was unconscious at the time."

"And almost dead," Laranna reminded me, digging her elbow into my ribs. "Don't forget that part."

"You're okay now, though, right, sir?" Morro asked, his expression suddenly concerned.

"I'm fine," I assured him. "Go take care of your wife. She's waiting for you."

He offered a final nod and a wave to Laranna before heading on inside. I let out a breath and stared at the floor for a second.

"You understand now?" Laranna asked me quietly, guiding me down the corridor.

"Yeah." I glanced aside at her. "I mean, I've always thought that if I was irreplaceable, I wasn't doing my job right. I can't be the only one who can lead the resistance in battle."

"They don't just need you to lead them in battle, Charlie," she said. "I've told you that before. We have Strada, Copperell, Gan-Shi, and a half a dozen other different races fighting under the same banner, and they need someone who can bring them all together. Besides which..." Laranna frowned, brow wrinkling in thought. "Well, the Anguilar Empire has a lot more troops, a lot more spaceships, and there's no rational reason to believe we can beat them. Except you. They believe in you because you keep beating the Anguilar, and if we lose you, God alone knows what they'll have to believe in. I think the whole thing might just fall apart."

"*You* could lead them." We'd talked about that before, too. "Everyone respects you."

"If you're not here," she said firmly, "I will be in no condition to lead anyone. In fact, I pray to the spirits each night that if you die, I die with you. I believe that is the main reason you lived through this insane stunt you pulled, the spirits listening to me."

And *that* was definitely an idea I'd rather not consider.

"What were you saying about the prisoners not being my only problem?" I asked, so desperate to change the subject that I'd rather hear bad news. She cocked an eyebrow at me as if I were a wayward child.

"Really? You invaded Russia and set off an atomic warhead on one of their bases!"

"*I* didn't set it off," I objected. "The Russians set it off."

"And you think they're going to admit that? It's all over your news broadcasts, that President Sverdlov you told me about last time claiming that Russia has suffered a nuclear attack from America. He says that we're helping your country conquer the world, and the only chance anyone has is to band together and, ironically enough, resist."

"Oh, this sucks," I moaned. Now my head really did hurt again.

So distracted was I by the news that I almost didn't notice where we were heading. It wasn't the bridge and it wasn't the operations center. In fact, I didn't recognize this section of the ship at all, which had to mean they'd remodeled it recently. That happened sometimes, the ship's hallways and compartments being rebuilt by Lenny's construction bots, which made every trip into the bowels of the *Liberator* a new journey through the labyrinth of the minotaur.

Or maybe it was just the concussion.

"Where the hell are we going?" I wondered.

"The brig," she told me.

"I didn't know the ship *had* a brig."

"It didn't until we suddenly had prisoners to worry about." She made a turn into an intersection I didn't remember, nearly running into a pair of Copperell guards in combat armor, rifles slung over their shoulders.

"Sir, ma'am," one of them said, nodding to us. "Brandy is waiting for you in the interrogation room."

"We have an interrogation room, too?" I demanded in a soft hiss after we'd passed by the guards.

Laranna shrugged away the question, and we found ourselves in a narrow corridor lined with thick, metal doors, each with a small window into the compartments. I paused by the first of them and peered inside. The Krin sprawled over a bare, plastic cot, and I wasn't sure how cold the room was, but at least he had clothes on. A plastic tray on the floor and strands of gristle from some kind of meat still left on it were evidence he'd been fed, as well, so at least Brandy had listened to me about that.

In the next cell was Nikolai Luzhkov. His accommodations were spartan, but compared to the Krin's, they were a five-star hotel. The bed had sheets, blankets, and a pillow, and the room came equipped with its own sink and toilet. The Russian sat cross-legged on the floor, his expression somewhere between glum and bored.

"We need to get him somewhere nicer," I told Laranna. "A regular room, not a cell, and he needs to be allowed to eat in the galley, under guard. It's important."

"I can go tell the guards…" Laranna offered, and I nodded.

"Now, please. After what you told me, the sooner, the better."

"All right." She turned to head back to the intersection but paused. "But after you talk to Brandy, you need to call Chuck. The President has been trying to get in touch with you ever since you got back, but I told him you were badly injured and unconscious."

"Shouldn't I talk to the President first, then?" I asked.

"Chuck said to have you call him first," she insisted.

"Okay," I assented. "Just get the Russian to a private room. Guarded but not locked. Actually," I added, a thought striking me, "give him a tour of the ship. And kind of be…flirty."

"What?" Laranna snapped, eyes narrowing. "You want me to *flirt* with him?"

"Not exactly," I said, holding my hands palms out. "Just be friendly and…keep him distracted enough that he won't ask to call home until we get the chance to make sure he's willing to tell the truth about the demolition charge they set."

She still looked skeptical, but she nodded.

"All right, I can do that. What are *you* going to do?"

"Nikolai is for damage control," I explained. "Reacting to what already happened. I'm hoping Brandy has something for me that gets us in front of whatever comes next."

Laranna kissed me before she left.

"Good luck."

The next cell was dark and empty, the one after it occupied by an Anguilar officer. He looked the worse for wear, his uniform torn and stained with mud, a cut over his eye angry and red and untreated. No bunk at all in this room, not so much as a scrap of bedding, and the only accessory was a bucket left in the corner, uncovered. I felt bad for whoever had to go into that room to clean up after him, though I honestly didn't feel bad for him. I'd yet to meet the Anguilar soldier who deserved sympathy.

He certainly felt bad for *himself*, that much was clear from his posture, curled up in a corner as far away from the bucket as he could get, knees drawn up, head ducked down. Maybe trying to sleep despite the harsh lighting, maybe just sulking.

The last cell was as brightly lit as the one before but empty, the door left hanging open, letting out some of the ripe stench of four days' worth of unwashed Anguilar, and I hurried past it. No more cells, though I suppose they could build more if we needed them, and the corridor dead-ended in a heavy, armored hatch, windowless but guarded by yet another Copperell.

Copperell rather than Strada. I wondered if that was because Brandy understood we needed the Strada for ground troops or perhaps that she'd picked soldiers who'd be loyal to her personally rather than me.

"Is Brandy inside?" I asked the guard. He said nothing, just stepped aside and tapped a code into the security lock set in the wall next to the massive door.

A magnetic lock snapped aside, and the door opened a couple inches with a pneumatic hiss. The Copperell grabbed the external handle and pulled it open just far enough for me to squeeze through, then closed it after me with an ominous thump. A chill crawled up my spine, and I thought at first it was a reaction to the stygian darkness inside the chamber until I realized Brandy was keeping it just a hair above freezing in the room. I wished I'd brought my jacket with me...or that Laranna had brought it to the medical bay.

The only light in the room was a circle near the center, harsh and glaring but utterly focused on the surgical table tilted up at an angle with the Anguilar officer strapped down to it. Brandy stood over him, a silhouette against the hard glow of the overhanging light, a monster from an old horror movie.

At least I'm sure that's how the Anguilar saw her. Thick, plastic straps held him down at the forehead, chest, wrists, thighs, and ankles, and his uniform had been cut away over his chest. The faint down of vestigial feathers shifted with each heaving breath he took, and terror was writ across his aquiline features, sweat pouring off his face, streaming down the silvery metal of the table.

"Hello, Charlie," Brandy said quietly, ice dripping off of each word. "You're just in time. I was explaining to Captain Jai-Latan here exactly what he had to look forward to in the last few days of his miserable life."

She pulled a small cart out into the circle of light, the blades, torches and other nefarious-looking instruments I couldn't identify stacked there rattling with the rumble of the wheels on the grating of the floor. Brandy hesitated for a moment before grabbing a small torch, its flame hissing to dull blue life with a flick of her thumb on the control.

"This, for example, will come in very handy after I begin stripping the skin off of Jai-Latan's body. I'll need it to cauterize as I go, so we don't lose him before he has the chance to share with us every bit of information he has that might be useful."

I should have said something, but I was frozen in place, speechless, as if Laranna had casually announced she was leaving me or Poppa Chuck had admitted to being a Democrat.

"I don't know anything," the Anguilar pleaded, trying to

shake his head but coming up short against the restraints. "I can't tell you anything…I'm just a pilot!"

"Oh, I don't believe that, Captain," Brandy said, bringing the flame a few inches closer to his face. "Particularly since you had nothing to fly at that base. And with only four of you hidden there, there's no way they wouldn't have assigned each of you more than one duty. But you can keep saying that as long as you like."

Her smile was a rictus grin as she leaned over him.

"I have all day."

17

I suppose I thought she was bluffing or else I would have moved more quickly, but I was still encased in a fugue of disbelief right up until she touched the outer edge of the Anguilar's ear with the flame. His scream broke me out of my trance, then I grabbed her wrist and pulled the torch away from him. The Anguilar's breathy sobs heaved loudly in the background, but my attention was on Brandy's eyes, hard and unyielding as metal.

"This isn't how we do things," I told her, prying the torch loose of her grip and switching it off. Brandy jerked her hand away from my grasp, scorn replacing the cold hatred in her expression.

"Then you don't *really* want to win this war," she hissed, close enough that spittle hit my cheek on the plosives. "You don't have the stomach for what needs to be done, and you're going to get us all killed trying to be a saint among sinners."

"If you don't want me in charge," I told her, determined not to lose my cool, particularly not in front of the prisoner, "then you can get together with the rest of the leadership of the resistance and tell them so. I'll quit in a heartbeat." I used the deactivated torch as a pointer to motion around us. "You think I want this? You think I enjoy sending my friends, the people I love to maybe get killed over and over? That I don't look at Val and think it's my fault? That I should have done something different?"

I looked down at the torch and tossed it at the wall, taking my anger and frustration out on the tool. It clanged loudly, then thumped to a stop on the other side of the room, deep in the darkness. I let out a long breath, the anger leaving me as if I'd thrown it aside along with the torch.

"But until you all decide you want me out, I'm still in command, and I say that this is not who we are. This"—I motioned at the Anguilar prisoner—"is not what we do. Get out of here. Go be with Val. He needs the woman he married, not whoever this is that you've turned into. Go try to be her again."

Brandy said nothing, just stared at me with something that was not quite the hate or disdain of a few seconds before, but also wasn't the shame or realization I'd hoped for. Instead, it was… amusement? Satisfaction? I couldn't tell, and she wasn't about to enlighten me. Brandy turned and tapped out the code to unlock the door, then left it open behind her as she exited.

"Thank you," the Anguilar sobbed, reminding me he was still there, still strapped to the table. "Thank you…I swear, I don't know anything. There's nothing I can tell you that you don't already know."

"Shut up," I snapped, turning on him, finger jabbing toward him. "We don't torture people, not even Anguilar, though God knows you've earned it. Here's the situation, Jai-Latan. My first instinct is to just put a round between your eyes and toss you out the airlock. Clean, simple, better than you deserve. But then, I had a thought. You and your ilk are always so concerned about your bloodline, about your family status in the Emperor's court. Maybe you dying out here doing what you were ordered to do by the Emperor would elevate the status of your bloodline. And maybe that's enough incentive for you to just keep your mouth shut and take whatever comes."

The Anguilar goggled at me as if I'd slapped him, like he'd totally forgotten about the burn on his ear.

"How do you…" he began to ask but then clapped his mouth shut.

"Yeah, that's what I figured."

I circled around the table, and he cringed away from me, but I merely unbuckled all the restraints holding him down except the ones at his wrists and ankles. He couldn't sit up, but he shook himself like a dog crawling out of the hole it had dug.

"So, I'll tell you what I'm thinking," I went on, taking a seat on the edge of the gurney, clapping a hand down on his leg. Jai-Latan flinched away from the touch, and I grinned at him. Anguilar were such arrogant snobs, I liked it when they were afraid of us lesser beings. "Brandy, our overzealous intelligence chief who wanted to skin and gut you, has some great connections behind enemy lines in the Empire. It'd be child's play for her to plant a report that you told us everything we wanted to know, that you totally turned traitor and agreed to help us."

"They'd never believe that!" Jai-Latan insisted, though I thought his outrage was more feigned than real. "I would never have been trusted to come to this backward hovel if I wasn't trusted implicitly by the Emperor and General Zan-Tar!"

"Oh, I think they would," I assured him. "You remember the Nova Eclipse? Did your bosses tell you about that?"

"The Nova Eclipse suffered a major systems malfunction," he said, a hint of suspicion in his eyes, as if he was repeating the official story but had never really believed it. "It was lost during a hyperspace jump."

"No, Captain," I said, shaking my head. "Me and my crew infiltrated the Eclipse and blew her up. And you know how we managed it?" My smile grew broader. "We convinced one of your officers, a pilot from a distinguished bloodline, that it was in his best interest to screw over the old commander of your forces, Mok-La. He helped us destroy the planet-killer. So, don't try to give me your bullshit about how no one would believe you betrayed them. Hell, I wouldn't be surprised if good old Von-To was one of your superior officers by now."

The Anguilar's eyes went wide, his jaw dropping open.

"Von-To?" he gasped. "Colonel Von-To?"

Jackpot. Sorry, Von-To. I promised I'd let you escape. I never promised I wouldn't rat your ass out later.

"You know my good friend Von-To, then?" I asked him casually. "Nice to hear they promoted him to colonel after the whole

Nova Eclipse situation. But then, he always did seem like an Anguilar with an eye for the main chance."

"He's General Zan-Tar's first cousin," Jai-Latan blurted. "And his executive officer!"

Only the fact that I was already sitting down kept me from falling over, and I struggled to keep the shock out of my expression. Now, everything made sense. Too much damn sense. Swallowing hard, I collected my thoughts and pressed on, leaning toward the Anguilar and substituting aggression for the shock I felt.

"In that case, you know sure as hell that Von-To and Zan-Tar will believe you've worked for the resistance. Then, we'll push the idea by letting you loose on an Anguilar-controlled settlement with a pocket full of Trade Notes. And we'll make sure that one of Brandy's local contacts tells the Anguilar garrison you're in town."

As much as Jai-Latan had sweated and squirmed under Brandy's threats, it was nothing compared to the fear in his eyes now.

"What do you think the Emperor will do to your bloodline when he hears about this?" I wondered. "Maybe have it eradicated altogether. Maybe write your people out of the history books, wipe out every single member of your family." I laughed softly. "That's not even considering what he'll do to *you*, personally. Which would you think'd be worse, what Brandy had in mind, or what the imperial inquisitors will do to you?"

I bit back a curse. I might have been pushing things too far, because I wasn't sure if I'd heard the term *imperial inquisitor* from

Von-To or just in one of the science fiction movies I'd binged while I was on Earth. But from the way his face went pale, either way I must have called it right.

"What will you do to me if I cooperate?" he asked, his voice small and defeated. "If I tell you what you want to know?"

"You'll stay here until we find out if you're telling the truth, but you'll be given a more comfortable room with a bed and blankets, and enough food. Then, once we confirm you're not lying to us, we'll drop you off at a neutral trading world with enough money to get back to Anguilar space. Or, you know, go wherever you want. No one says you have to go back there. After all, the base you were stationed at got nuked. Everyone is going to assume you're dead."

He opened his mouth, but I silenced him with a raised finger.

"And don't forget," I went on, "that one of the ways we're going to check whether or not you're telling the truth is by offering this same deal to your buddy in the other cell. If he contradicts you, well…" I shrugged. "Then we go back to the hard way."

And I left it to his imagination to figure out whether I meant setting him up to be killed by his own people or turning him over to Brandy. And maybe leaving it to my imagination as well, because I really didn't know what I'd do if I found out he was lying…or if their stories were different.

"It's no good," he insisted, shaking his head violently. "I'll tell you, but I can't stay here. You have to get me out of here as soon as possible." The hair stood up on the back of my neck…he sounded more afraid of staying than he was of us.

"Whether you go anywhere or not," I said, "depends on whether I believe what you tell me. Start talking."

Jai-Latan squeezed his eyes shut for a moment, then nodded.

"Okay. We were sent here originally to recruit your enemies to be our"—he sneered—"cannon fodder. In the coming invasion. After the last time, it was decided that our ground forces were insufficient for a world of this population. The plan was for us to coordinate with the Russian military, to provide transport and air cover for them, to improve their weapons and armor as much as possible with their own manufacturing since there's no way for us to bring enough people here in secret to construct fabrication centers for them."

That made sense. Landing any kind of equipment would mean open warfare, and they weren't ready for that yet. On the other hand, they could give the Russians plans for improvements that they could build on their own equipment, which was probably why the Anguilar were still there and why they had engineers and scientists with them in the Siberia base.

"You said you were sent originally for that," I pointed out. "What changed?"

"One of the first things we built when we came here," Jai-Latan explained, "was a hyperspace communications antenna. The Russians constructed it according to our specifications." He shrugged. "Reception only, of course. They don't have the power cells to send, and we didn't bring any with us. We wanted them to be able to receive transmissions for the planned invasion. But we received a transmission a few days ago, which is why their scientists and engineers went back to Moscow. Events have been…

accelerated. The Empire received intelligence that you'd brought the remaining population from your world Sanctuary to Earth, that all your ships were here as well."

My stomach dropped as pieces began to fall into place.

"Oh, don't tell me…" I groaned.

"They're coming here," he confirmed, yanking against his restraints as if he wanted to run. "Soon. Days, maybe hours. The Empire is going to come here and kill all of us. You need to get me out of here!"

I didn't reply, mind working furiously, trying to come up with a coherent response, not to Jai-Latan, but to what he'd told me. I only knew one thing: it was too late to run. We were going to have to fight.

18

CHUCK BARNABY DID NOT LOOK happy to see me. Or happy about much of anything.

"You were supposed to call me the second you got out of the hospital," he chided, arms folded as he stood in the sweltering afternoon humidity of DC in summer.

I pushed the door of the Suburban shut and nodded to the driver. I had no idea if he was Secret Service, military, or some federal intelligence agency, just that his name was Bob and he'd driven me from Andrews to the White House the last four times I'd visited. Usually, we talked football, but this time I hadn't been in the mood. I'd just stared out the window at the traffic, the people walking the sidewalks, the tourists sightseeing, and wondered if any of them understood what was coming. If they did, would they run? Would they panic? Would they run back to their homes as if that would do any good?

"It was only a few hours ago," I reminded him. "Give a guy a break. I almost died pulling off that job for you guys."

He shushed me with a severe look and glanced around at the Secret Service guards stationed outside the entrance. None seemed to be paying us any mind, and he motioned for me to follow him. I did, gladly, ready to get from air conditioned car to air conditioned White House, and as we passed through the doorways, he leaned closer and whispered.

"You didn't pull off *any* job for the US government. That was purely on your own initiative and from your own intelligence sources. We had nothing to do with it."

I rolled my eyes, ignoring the stares from staffers passing by. They all knew who I was, and I had to figure they'd all seen the news stories. I'd watched a few myself on the shuttle ride down.

Sverdlov was a pasty-faced, jowly bulldog of a man, gray where he wasn't balding, his eyes hooded, his true thoughts perpetually concealed beneath thick eyelids and beetle brows. He could speak English, I was sure of it, but he never did in front of the cameras, making sure everyone knew that Russian was the only language he needed. His translator's voice was smooth and unaccented, almost drowning out Sverdlov's own gravelly growl as he'd stood at the podium in the UN.

"This American aggression is unconscionable, and it will not stand." He'd gesticulated wildly, as if trying to conduct an invisible orchestra. "Their government may claim that this was the doing of the so-called resistance, but we know that it is only a front for an American alliance with aliens who mean to conquer us all!"

"This was Russian President Anatoly Sverdlov," the network announcer had intoned gravely as the video had frozen with the Russian in mid-speech, "today during his address to the United Nations Security Council. Sverdlov has made repeated claims that the underground nuclear detonation detected last week in northern Siberia was the result of an American attack on a Russian scientific outpost that resulted in the deaths of several Russian scientists and workers."

The image of the announcer had been replaced with an orbital satellite view showing a thermal imaging video of the explosion. And of the Vanguards racing away from it.

"The aircraft you see above the underground nuclear blast have been confirmed to be the so-called Vanguard fighters of the resistance, led by American expatriate and supposed time-traveler from the 1980s, Charles Travers." I'd winced at the description. I wasn't any time traveler. "According to a press release from the Louis administration, the raid on the installation in Siberia was carried out independently by the resistance due to intelligence they received of the Russian government concealing representatives of the Anguilar Empire there. Images of the Anguilar prisoners have been released by the resistance."

After they'd both been cleaned up, of course. I might not have been raised in this century, but I'd learned enough about what they called optics to realize we needed to make this look as justified as possible. I'd also known what to expect when I arrived in DC, and if it was this bad with Chuck, who was my friend, I didn't want to think about how bad President Louis was going to take it.

"I figured we might go to the Pentagon first," I told Chuck as we walked. "Brief General Gavin and then head to the Oval Office…"

"General Gavin," he cut me off brusquely, "will meet us there. Donovan, too, along with Secretary of State Barret and the Central Intelligence director, Jeremy Garner."

"What happened to the other guy?" I asked, sure that the last time I'd met him, it was someone else, but wondering if I was mistaking him for the deputy director or something.

"Resigned to go work in the private sector." Chuck shot me a sidelong glare. "Which is looking more and more attractive every day."

"You were there," I hissed next to his shoulder. "You were in that office. You heard what they said. How is this my fault?"

"Because no one in that office said anything about setting off a nuclear weapon, Charlie," he whispered back.

I wanted to point out—again—that it wasn't *me* who'd set off the nuclear weapon, but we'd arrived at the Oval Office and the area outside it was populated by an entourage of staffers, Secret Service, and, to my surprise, press. A *lot* of press, standing behind a divider they'd brought in for them, though at least there weren't any camera flashes or bright lights shining in my face. Everyone pointed smart phones at me instead, shouting questions as we entered the hallway, like a gauntlet I had to run to get to meet with Louis.

"Mr. Travers!" a man wearing a brown suit and, for some inexplicable reason, a red bow tie, yelled at me. "Why did you launch a nuclear attack against Russia?"

"I didn't," I told him, finally giving voice to the explanation I'd kept trying to make over the phone with Chuck and General Gavin. A half a dozen other reporters tried to shout questions over me, but among the many things I'd picked up the last couple years was how to project my voice. "The Russians rigged their base with a nuclear self-destruct device to try to conceal the fact that they were conspiring with the Anguilar to support an alien invasion of this planet."

"Can you prove that?" someone yelled, I couldn't see who.

"Absolutely. I have recorded testimony from both the Anguilar we captured and a Russian survivor—a technician who was the only civilian on the base. He was the one who warned us about the bomb, which gave us time to evacuate, so naturally, we got him out before it blew."

It got wild then, of course, with the questions bellowed so loud and so close together that I couldn't hope to understand them, much less answer them. The door to the Oval Office opened, and a Secret Service agent—Gloria, I think her name was—waved for the two of us to enter. Chuck grabbed my arm and ushered me inside like I was an octogenarian grandma at a wedding, and I glared at him and pulled away just as we passed through the door.

The curtains were drawn over the windows, and the lights had been turned down below what I'd grown accustomed to in the room, as if no one really wanted to be here, or at least didn't want to have to look at the harsh, bright reality of what was going on.

I thought it had been crowded the last time I met with the

President, but this time, it was practically standing room only. Though that might just have been because there weren't enough chairs to go around. I recognized everyone this time, even the press secretary, a forty-something woman with a pinched face and absolutely no sense of humor. Except for one guy, middle-aged, with close-cropped gray hair and Coke-bottle glasses so thick I wondered if he could see past the end of his nose without them. He wore a suit that might have been in fashion around the time I got my commission and reminded me of one of my history professors.

I figured him for the new CIA director and wondered how this guy could be considered new blood when he had to be well into his sixties.

"Gentlemen," President Louis said, neither rising from his chair nor offering me one. "Thank you for coming."

"I hope you realize what a huge mess you've made here, Travers!" Parker Donovan snapped, not even looking at me. "We are on the brink of war with the Russians thanks to you!"

He stood, as did the press secretary and General Gavin, while the others kept their seats, and I couldn't help but think the whole arrangement was carefully calculated to make me feel like a grade-school kid called to the principal's office and told to wait for my parents to get there.

"Horseshit," I replied, eager to burst that bubble. Looks of outrage burst out like wildflowers in the spring, but I didn't give them time to bloom. "Everybody in this office with two brain cells to rub together for warmth knows I had nothing to do with setting off a nuclear warhead in Russia. If you don't understand that, you're too stupid to run the kiddy pool at the YMCA, much less the country. And if you're worried that Sverdlov is going to use this to start a war *after* I release the recordings of the Anguilar and the Russian survivor calling him a liar, then it's your own fault for pointing me in that direction to begin with. And don't even *bother* with that line about how you had nothing to do with it," I pushed on when Louis, Donovan, Gavin, Barret, and the CIA guy all opened their mouths at once. I pointed an accusatory finger at Barret. "You knew exactly who was coming into that office where you sent me and Chuck for lunch." I shifted the rude finger to the older guy with the glasses. "And assuming you're the new CIA director, so did you."

That shut them up, probably because none of them wanted to go into an in-depth discussion of the series of events in front of the Press Secretary. I shook my head, fingers curling into fists, wishing there was something or someone to hit.

"Shit like *this* is why I resigned my commission. You can get away with claiming plausible deniability, but you're not hanging me out to dry because *I don't work for you*. My job is to defeat the Anguilar, and I'll do that with or without your help and with or without your permission."

"All right," President Louis said, finally standing. Playing peacemaker as usual. More political maneuvering. "That's water under the bridge at this point. You said in your transmission this morning that you had other matters to discuss. Which is why we're all here."

I scowled at the president, very tired of his gamesmanship, tired of this whole relationship…but knowing we still needed it.

There was a chair across the room, shoved into a corner, unused. I walked over, picked the thing up, carried it to directly in front of the desk, and plopped down in it, ignoring a plethora of dirty looks.

"I captured two Anguilar prisoners," I told them, leaning my elbow on my knees, looking up at Louis and Gavin. "We interrogated them both separately and cross-checked what they said with what the Russian technician had witnessed, and the bottom line is, we can expect an all-out Anguilar attack on Earth within days."

President Louis gaped at me, stumbling back against his desk.

"How can you be sure they're telling the truth?" I would have expected the question in an outraged tone from Donovan, but it had come from the CIA guy...Garner, I recalled his name was. And it had been asked in an almost academic manner, as befitted his college professor vibe. "They might have been given this story as a fallback in case they were captured."

Which was not an unworthy question or idea, and I revised my estimate of Garner upward.

"I considered it. Zan-Tar is a smart son of a bitch, and I wouldn't put anything past him. But I had other intelligence, and they confirmed it as well. Plus, it wouldn't make any sense as a strategy. After all, we already have most of our forces here, so all this would do would be to get us on high alert."

"You have other bases," the CIA director reminded me. He moved around to the front of me, dragging his chair as he went so he could look me in the eye, and I had to repress a chuckle.

"Strada, this...Thalassia place. Perhaps they mean to strike one of them and want you to *keep* your forces here."

I considered what he'd said in silence for a moment, and no one else spoke, as if they held their breath, waiting for me to tell them that the dire threat I'd warned them of wasn't actually going to occur.

"Maybe," I allowed finally. "I can't say for sure you're wrong, but the problem is, if I assume it's a con and I'm wrong, you'll be the ones who pay the price. Not just our refugees, but everyone on this planet."

"They couldn't be trying a full-scale invasion," Gavin said, putting a hand on the back of Garner's chair to steady himself. "Surely they don't have the troops for that."

"No," I agreed. "And even if they did, they don't have enough ships to get them all here. Or enough landers to get them on the ground."

"Like the Chinese and Taiwan," Louis murmured, frowning thoughtfully. "That's why they were negotiating with the Russians."

"You're damned right it was," I agreed reflexively, then shut up when I realized the words meant he knew exactly what had happened in Siberia and all the reporters and this come-to-Jesus meeting had all been for show. "But they don't," I went on, shaking my head, both at the prospect we were discussing and the deception that seemed to come second-nature for him. "Which means when they hit here, they're going to be trying to take out our space assets, and if they can do that, they'll do as much damage on the ground as possible. But no, they won't be able to invade."

"Shit," Donovan said. His outrage, fake or not, vanished with these new revelations.

"This would seem to be a no-win situation," Jeremy Garner opined, pulling off his glasses and taking a lens cloth out of his pocket to clean them. He squinted at the lenses, trying to determine if he was doing the job. "If you're correct in your initial intelligence assessment and the Anguilar throw their entire might behind an attack on Earth, then we almost certainly lack the assets to defeat them without taking major damage, both to your space assets and our own."

"Not to mention," Gavin added dolorously, "they're almost certain to target the reactors we have under construction."

Louis pinched the bridge of his nose, looking as if he were close to either a panic attack or a migraine.

"In which case," he concluded, "I'm looking at impeachment almost certainly and maybe an indictment by the International Criminal Court."

"But if you're wrong," Garner went on, glancing aside with an irritated glare at Louis, seeming as annoyed as I was at the President of the United States trying to make an alien invasion all about his political future, "then the enemy will devastate yet another of your strongholds, and you'll not only lose the matériel support you would have gotten from that base, but…"

"…no one will ever trust us to protect them again," I finished for him, sounding as morose as Louis had about his reelection prospects.

I buried my face in my hands for just a moment and would have stayed that way longer if it hadn't been for the political sharks in the room, waiting for the smell of blood. And what the hell was *I* doing in the middle of this bunch?

"You knew all this before you came in here," Barret spoke up for the first time, the only one I'd seen who hadn't shown any signs of panic. She knew. "You didn't come in here without a plan of action."

"I have an idea," I told them. "Not exactly a plan, but the start of one. Our only hope to keep this from being an utter disaster is to get the Anguilar to do exactly what they don't *want* to do…to divide their forces."

"I assume you have an idea on how to do that," President Louis said, sounding suddenly enthusiastic at even the faintest strand of hope.

"I do. But to make this work, I'm going to have to pull some of our forces away from Earth."

"For how long?" Donovan asked sharply. "We can't defend ourselves against the Anguilar fleet with just two ships."

"You can't defend yourself against the entire Anguilar fleet even with every single ship we have added to yours," I pointed out. "That's the whole problem. We need to draw *them* away, too. They're not going to come after nothing."

Louis sighed and exchanged a look with Barret. She nodded.

"Sir," she said, "you know me. I'm not a woman given to overly trusting people. I know them too well. I'm also not fond of taking risks, and *definitely* not a fan of overly complicated plans, which are usually the hallmark of"—she eyed me sidelong—"amateurs."

Ouch.

"However," she went on, "I'm also a believer in results. Mr. Travers produces results." She offered me a lopsided grin. "Sometimes *sloppy* results, but for a young man with no formal military training past college ROTC, he's somehow managed to lead a resistance group against a far superior force for years now, while building his own military into a force capable of liberating planets. And most importantly, he has infinitely more experience than we do with the Anguilar. Bottom line, Mr. President, if you want to avoid both an impeachment hearing and the post-election lecture circuit, you should listen to him."

Louis's shoulders sagged in resignation.

"All right, Charlie. Tell me what you have in mind."

19

"This is not acceptable," Shindo grumbled, feet planted in solid stubbornness.

He waved a hand at the spread of canvas tents lined up across the grassy fields outside Minot Air Force Base, as if that should have made his argument for him, and his features screwed up in consternation when it didn't.

"I'm sorry," I told him, "but there's no other choice."

"The herd has not even completely settled into this new land. The tents are barely up, and the meeting place has yet to be fully assembled."

I followed his gesture to the timber structure going up slowly at the center of the massive cantonment. Adult females surrounded it, working with simple tools, hauling in lumber that they'd cut themselves from trees they'd felled by hand. The military had offered to have their engineers throw up a suitable hall for the Gan-Shi, but the Elder had refused. There was a ritual to erecting the meeting place, apparently, and it was a damn inconvenient one.

In fact, the Elder had taken the offer as something of an insult, and if she took what I'd just said as anything less, she sure as hell didn't show it. She stood behind Shindo and Warrin, not as if she feared Chuck and me or felt she needed the protection of the males but as if we outsiders were beneath her and the big bulls were a separation from the unclean. I knew she'd had a name back before the original Elder female had died back on Wraith Anchorage, but I couldn't for the life of me remember it.

"We have many young," she said, pawing at the ground with a bare foot, the nails thick enough that they could have passed for hooves. "They will not bear yet another voyage such as the one we just endured. And you say this one will be even longer…"

We'd drawn a crowd, mostly juvenile males who had nothing better to do. I assumed they taught them somehow, some sort of schooling, though I'd yet to encounter it, and having a bunch of bored teenaged boys hanging around looking for mischief didn't seem like the safest plan to me.

"It's my responsibility to keep you safe," I told the Elder. "I can't do that here. The Anguilar have found out where we evacuated to, and we have reason to believe they're going to attack. When they do, they're going to target our people first, both here and at the reactor construction sites. If you stay, you'll be out in the open, defenseless. We can either try to find underground shelters for all of you, which would mean splitting you up across three different states indefinitely, or we can evacuate you to somewhere more secure."

"What was the point of all this?" Shindo bellowed, his patience evidently at an end. He tossed his head in a motion not unlike the films I'd seen of a fighting bull trying to gore a matador. "We left our home for a better life on Sanctuary, then we were forced off Sanctuary to come to this place for what you claimed would be safety! Now, you say it isn't safe here! If you can't guarantee our safety on this planet, your homeworld, with billions of your people to defend it, why should we trust you to defend us somewhere else?"

"Calm down, young one," Warrin said with surprising gentleness, putting a hand on Shindo's arm, interposing himself between us. "Your anger is justified, but will it really help the herd? We had no choice other than to leave Wraith Anchorage. The entire station was drifting inexorably toward destruction. We all appreciated a life under the open sky on Sanctuary, but we live in a galaxy at war. We knew this, and we volunteered to be part of it so we could defend the herd."

"And how have we defended the herd?" Shindo demanded, pushing the older bull's hand aside. "We've run, and now these humans want us to keep running, to uproot our females, our children, and flee to yet another supposed shelter."

"This encampment here," Chuck said, making an expansive gesture around at the sea of tents, "was only ever supposed to be a temporary solution. We told you that from the beginning."

"And where would you have us go now?" Shindo snapped, taking a step forward until he loomed over Chuck, leaning down with their faces only inches apart. "What new false hope would you give us?"

"Thalassia," I answered for him, pushing Chuck back away from the Gan-Shi and taking his place. Shindo's breath reminded me of the golden retriever I'd had as a kid. "You'll be going to Thalassia, like we discussed originally. We need to start shipping you out within two days so you need to get your people ready."

"And what if we don't wish to leave?" Shindo asked, though not with the same outrage and indignation as before. His voice and his expression had sunken into a sullen funk. "What if we are tired of running?"

"I, too, am loath to run, Shindo," Warrin told him, his tone still soothing. "But our duty is to the herd, not to our ego." He offered a half-bow to the Elder. "With all respect, I believe we should do as Charlie Travers says. He has our best interests at heart, and if we can't trust him, then we may as well walk into the desert and starve, for we have no one else who will aid us."

I squinted at Warrin, wondering where all this trust had come from, but the Elder tossed her head and snorted softly.

"It shall be as you say," she told him, then nodded to me. "We will begin preparations immediately." Her expression hardened. "But be it known, Earthman, this will be the last time we run. Where we next set our feet will be our home, and any who tries to push us out will be our enemy, whether it be you or the Anguilar."

"Of course, Elder," I told her, but she'd already turned away, stomping back toward the construction site, no doubt to tell the females there not to bother.

Shindo offered us a scowl and followed her.

"That was pleasant," Chuck sighed, pulling off his beret and wiping sweat out of his eyes. "You'd better hope they like it on Thalassia."

"Our needs are simple," Warrin said, watching the young Gan-Shi males who had been our audience scatter as the show ended. "And Shindo will be fine. He is simply impatient, as all young males are." He glanced sidelong at us and his tone shifted. "Now that they've agreed to be sensible, I must ask you…how will you protect us on this new world? You've said you lack the resources to guard all the planets you control. How will this change if we simply move from one vulnerable place to another?"

A mosquito buzzed plaintively around my ear, and I smacked at it before attempting an answer. My palm came away red, and I cursed. The little bastard had already nailed me.

"It's a matter of risk vs reward," I explained. "The Anguilar will lose a lot of ships and people attacking Earth, whether we're here or not. They know that. It's only worth attacking Earth in force if they can finish us all at once. If we have all our ships and people here, it's worth whatever losses they have to take in order to wipe us out once and for all. If we have ships and troops here, ships and troops at Thalassia, ships and troops at Strada, then they're going to take hits to wipe out any one of those, and it'll still leave us with enough to fight them."

Warrin's eyes clouded in thought, and he stared unfocused at the tall grass at his feet for a long few moments before he spoke again.

"I believe I understand. Very well, Charlie. I can't say that I am happy with this, and I can guarantee that my people will be even less content than I am. But you have my support."

"Thank you, Warrin," I told him. My reflex was to offer a hand, but it wasn't their custom, and I had a feeling it made them uncomfortable. "We'll have people out here to help you pack up."

The old bull left us without another word, and I let out the breath I hadn't realized I'd been holding. Chuck fell in beside me as we aimed for the Hum-Vee that had dropped us off at the edge of the grass field.

"What now?" he wondered.

"Everything's in place," I said. "Now we wait."

WE DIDN'T HAVE to wait long.

"Charlie."

I blinked to wakefulness in a fraction of a second, though it took another beat before the fog parted across my thoughts and I remembered where I was. The Visiting Officer's Quarters at Minot Air Force Base reminded me of a discount hotel chain, but at least the room had blackout curtains. The darkness clung thick around me, and I might have wondered if I'd actually opened my eyes if it hadn't been for the faint, green glow of the comlink's screen.

I used the light as a beacon and slapped at the comlink like it was an alarm clock. I hadn't recognized the voice, just my own name.

"Yeah," I mumbled once I found the mic key. "Travers here."

"We received the signal." Lenny. I don't know who I expected, but Lenny wasn't it.

"Did it get transmitted?" Dumb question, I realized after I asked it. Letting the signal get transmitted had been the whole point of this exercise.

"The hyperspace comm antenna sent out a short burst less than five minutes ago." That was the great thing about Lenny. He didn't go much for snark, just the facts, ma'am. "I've sent the coordinates of the transmitter to your comlink."

"It might be disguised." I worried, sitting up in bed and switching on the light. There wasn't much to see. I'd brought a small backpack with toiletries and one change of clothes, and it still sat on the table by the air conditioning unit. "Are you sure I'll be able to find it?"

"It's not going to be small," Lenny told me. "It's not just a transmitter that can reach orbit, it's also a remote data penetration system capable of overriding our normal security protocols."

Knowing he wouldn't see it, I rolled my eyes as I pulled my fatigues on over my running shorts and tank top.

"So, would that be bigger than a breadbox?"

A long pause.

"Finding the item to which you referred required a complete search of your world's information network, but yes. It's going to be bigger than a breadbox. No smaller than three feet on each side."

"That should narrow it down," I said with a grunt, buckling on my gun belt. "Tell them to meet there."

I debated brushing my teeth but instead grabbed one of the

little sticks of gum Laranna had given me before the trip down. Not really gum, of course, but some kind of root from Strada. Her people chewed strips of it to kill germs in their mouth, and it worked pretty well since she had the whitest teeth I'd ever seen. It unfortunately tasted like ass or I could have made a fortune selling it in drug stores all around the world.

After chewing it for a few seconds on the way down to Chuck's room at the other end of the hall, I figured I had a suitably sour expression when I knocked on his door. A born Ranger, he didn't make me knock twice.

"Coming." Though muffled by the door, his voice sounded awake and alert.

When he opened the door a few seconds later, he stepped out into the brightly lit hallway completely dressed and even had his pistol belt and beret on.

"Did you sleep in your clothes?" I wondered, checking my watch. It was barely past three in the morning.

"Who sleeps?" he asked with a grim scowl. It cracked and he chuckled. "No, Lenny called me at the same time he called you."

"Figures." I motioned down the hall. "Come on, you're driving."

"You never drive," he complained, pulling his door shut. "Is it because you didn't have a car in college? Dad told me he had to drive you everywhere."

"I was a poor student getting by on scholarship and a job at a pizza restaurant," I admitted. "It's not like I've had a lot of chances since then. I'll tell you what," I continued, pushing the outer door open, the early morning air slapping me in the face with chill dampness, "you drive while we're here on Earth, and I'll drive whenever we're on another planet. Deal?"

Chuck didn't answer except to pull out his key fob and unlock the government SUV he'd left in the VOQ parking lot. Lots of sports cars and pickup trucks in that parking lot, but I figured that was from all the Air Force officers staying there. Our black Suburban seemed out of place among them, but I'd learned to appreciate the roomy interior and the comfortable seats.

"Skyros," I called into my comlink once I had the seat belt on. "You read me?"

"We're on our way down, sir," the Strada replied. "ETA twenty minutes. Where do you want us?"

"Touch down on the road beside the encampment. Stay there. I'll call your people in if I need you."

"What happened," Chuck asked once I'd ended the call, "to the whole spiel you gave about not knowing who the traitor was? That it could be anyone on Sanctuary, could have happened anytime in the last two years?"

I debated for just a beat whether to tell him the truth. I didn't like lying, but I could just blow the question off, let him know I didn't feel comfortable answering it, and I figured he'd respect that. But Chuck and I had been through the fire together.

"I thought it was one of the Gan-Shi from the beginning," I admitted, sinking into the seat, eyes on the passing buildings. "It didn't make any sense that it could be anyone else. The attack came right after they settled on Sanctuary, and I don't believe in coincidences."

"Then why all the kumbaya bullshit?" he asked, both hands off the wheel long enough to shrug.

"Because it couldn't be *all* of them, and I didn't want Brandy going off half-cocked and putting the thumb-screws on every Gan-Shi she could get her hands on. She's…a little unhinged since what happened to Val. I didn't want to come out and say anything until we had a way to find out who the spy was."

"Well, you do now." He drummed his fingers on the wheel. "Assuming this works."

"It already worked," I reminded him. "The message was sent."

"We have a location. That's not the same thing as having a name."

I didn't respond to that because there was nothing to say… and I didn't want to admit that he was right.

20

Between my freshman and sophomore year in high school, I'd snuck out of Poppa Chuck's house one night to go hang out with some of the kids from nearby farms, and we'd wound up going out to the cow pasture for a bonfire. The Gan-Shi encampment smelled a lot like that pasture, and sounded like it, too, right down to the gentle lowing.

The tents were dark, but a fire crackled in the center near where the meeting house had been going up. Lumber fed it, and a male sat beside a pile of the cut wood, ready to throw another piece on when it guttered low. He looked up as Chuck and I passed by, scowling at the intrusion.

"Where do the males sleep?" I asked him.

He pointed off to the left but said nothing, and I didn't press him on it, just checked the screen of my comlink again. The coordinates Lenny had sent me flashed brighter as we walked, and an arrow guided me in the same direction that the young male had pointed.

"Well, that's one guess confirmed," Chuck said, his hand resting on the butt of his gun as he glanced back at the fire tender. "You thought it was one of the males."

"It has to be." My gaze flickered up and down from the arrow on the comlink to the well-worn trail through the tents. "The females all live together, pretty much cheek by jowl." We'd passed by their communal tents on the way in, dozens of them, large enough to house hundreds of females and their children in each. "But the males are solitary."

Smaller tents, a fraction the size of the communal ones, the kind they sold for a family of four to six at the sporting goods store. Just big enough to be cozy for a Gan-Shi bull. None of them were out and about tonight besides the one feeding the fire, no sign of them other than a chorus of dull snoring. Boy, could these guys snore.

The arrow blinked faster as we approached the coordinates where the transmission had come from, and by the time we reached the flap doors of the correct tent, it had gone spastic, flashing so quickly it was barely visible.

"This is it," I told Chuck, switching the tracking function off. I tucked the comlink in the pocket of my fatigue jacket and drew my pulse pistol.

Chuck made a helpless gesture.

"Should we knock?" he asked.

I shook my head. "You got a flashlight?"

"On the end of my pistol." Chuck held up the SIG to show me what they called a tactical light nowadays.

"Good. Then you go first."

Chuck snorted a humorless laugh at that but brushed aside the flap and shone the light inside. The tent was roomy enough even with the seven-foot-tall Gan-Shi sleeping in the center of it, plenty of space for cloth shoulder bags filled with…well, with whatever one of these guys needed. I didn't feel like imagining what the bovines used for toiletries, but I supposed he had some spare loincloths in there.

Chuck scanned across the inside of the tent walls, past the cloth bags to what looked like crude blankets piled on the floor. The circle of light paused there, and he nodded to me. Looking harder, I spotted what he'd seen, a suspicious lump beneath the mound of cloth. I toed the blankets aside, revealing something definitely bigger than a breadbox.

Polished wood, the case was engraved with intricate designs that matched the etchings I'd seen on Gan-Shi jewelry and secured with a simple, copper latch. It fit right in with the style and culture of their society, something that wouldn't be noticed if you weren't looking for it.

I bent down and flipped the latch, and that gentle click was enough to wake him up. The Gan-Shi bull rolled over into a crouch, eyes flaring in the light from Chuck's SIG pistol. The play of harsh light and shadows across the alien face distorted the features, and I didn't recognize him until he spoke.

"Charlie Travers!" Shindo exclaimed. "What are you doing in my dwelling?"

I sighed. This was not how I'd wanted it to go down.

"Looking for this," I told him and pulled the case open.

Inside the simple, artistic elegance of the hand-carved wooden box was something centuries more advanced, intricate circuitry and a compact, fold-up dish antenna.

Shindo said nothing, his mouth dropping open, jaw slack as he stared at the satellite transmitter with dull incomprehension.

"The case…" he stuttered, and for the first time since we'd met, Shindo looked frightened. "The case belonged to my mother, but I have never seen that device inside it before. I swear on the souls of my ancestors."

"This," I told him, tapping the case with the muzzle of my pulse pistol, "is an orbital transmitter fitted with a hacking module to penetrate the security systems of our hyperspace comm satellite. The one we put in orbit here a couple months ago. The same kind that we had in orbit around Sanctuary." I shook my head, trying to feel anger but unable to work up anything harsher than a deep sadness. "It was sloppy pulling the same trick twice and thinking we wouldn't figure it out."

Shindo's eyes flickered back and forth between the two of us and the case, and something hardened behind them, a split-second's warning, but I took it the wrong way, rising to a crouch and readying for a charge straight at me. Shindo lowered his head…and turned away, ramming his horns through the side of the tent instead.

Nylon ripped but not fast enough. The entire structure collapsed, the support rods snapping, leaving me tangled in a sea of darkness, my pistol useless in my hand. The only thing

I'd have accomplished by trying to shoot the direction Shindo had run would be to set the damned tent on fire around my ears.

"Go after him, Chuck!" I yelled, my voice muffled by the tent material draped across my mouth as I struggled to free myself, thrashing like a drowning man in a riptide.

No answer, which was probably a good thing since it likely meant he'd already run after Shindo, so I concentrated on slowing down and finding a rational way out of this. The gun wouldn't help, and I couldn't get it safely holstered with all the folds of nylon, so I ripped open my fatigue shirt and jammed it into my belt.

A knife. I needed a knife. I had one clipped into my left pants pocket, a Zero-Tolerance lockblade George had given me as a birthday gift a couple months ago. Solid, durable, but most importantly to me right now, sharp as hell. I flicked it open, grabbed a handful of nylon, and slashed outward. The blade caught, ripped, and the stifling suffocation of the tent materials gave way, parting like the Red Sea before Moses's staff, the chill of the early morning air drying the sweat from my face in a second.

The darkness outside the tent was a lighter shade than being buried beneath it, but not by much, barely enough light filtering through from the bonfire to allow me to step out of the remains of the tent without tripping over the debris underfoot. While my eyes weren't helping much, my ears took up the burden. The undercurrent of raucous snores had faded away, replaced with alarmed and confused grunts, and somewhere off to my right, the shouts of Chuck Barnaby, yelling for Shindo to stop or he'd shoot.

No time for niceties like closing the lockblade and sticking it back in my pocket, so I whipped it blade-first into the dirt, leaving it sticking handle-up out of the ground. Grabbing the gun out of my waistband, I followed my ears. It wasn't as easy now as it had been on the way into the encampment because everyone else was following their ears as well, scores of Gan-Shi bulls stumbling out of their tents right into my way.

I slipped past the first few, cutting toward the center of the path, a kick returner trying to find the lane for a touchdown on a field full of offensive linemen. There was, however, a very good reason I'd run track instead of playing football, and that reason made itself very evident when I ran straight into the back of a Gan-Shi who inadvertently stepped in front of me.

I'd never actually run into a brick wall, but the saying sure took on new meaning as the wind went out of me and a lance of pain went through my upper back. Stumbling away from the older bull, I grabbed at him for balance, and the Gan-Shi turned on me, eyes flaring at the indignity.

"Sorry!" I yelled back to him, vacating the area rather than staying to try to explain.

No shots yet, despite Chuck's threat, and I understood why. This was a nightmare scenario, in the dark with innocent civilians all around, and Shindo was smart. He knew how we thought, and he'd take advantage of it. But where would he go? Where *could* he go? There was no way out of here for him, no possibility of stealing a lander, much less a starship. Maybe he'd just run in a panic, not thinking that far ahead…

"Charlie!"

Chuck's call from much closer than I'd figured, maybe two rows over to the right, and I cut between the tents, high-stepping to avoid tripping over tie-down wires. And there, finally, was light. Another fire, which made sense. The camp was huge, and the one bonfire wouldn't be enough, so they'd built another a few hundred yards away, at the edge of the tent city for the adult males.

I recognized the male tending it even in the flickering, unstable glow, from the scars on his chest and face, the remnants of old battles fought for the right to mate. Warrin stood ten feet from Shindo, the two bulls squared off in a confrontation that wouldn't have been out of place in the valleys of Yellowstone. They pawed at the ground, heads lowered, grunts and snorts their only conversation.

Off to the side, Chuck stood watching, his pistol held at the low ready. He glanced over at me and shook his head helplessly.

"Do you want me to shoot him?"

I held up a hand, watching the two bulls. What the hell was going on with them? How could this be Shindo's endgame?

"Shindo, you can't get away," I warned him, aiming my pulse pistol at center mass because there was a hell of a lot of mass at that center. "What do you think you're going to accomplish here? Just give it up. I promise we won't hurt you."

Well, Chuck and I wouldn't, but Brandy would likely want to turn him into a steer.

"The transmitter is not mine," Shindo said, though I could barely understand his guttural growl.

"Then you should surrender now, and we can get to the bottom of this without anyone getting hurt." I gestured with the pulse gun. "You saved my life, and I don't want to shoot you, but I will if I have to. We lost too many good people on Sanctuary, and it's my job to make that right."

"I require an explanation of what occurs here."

I realized tangentially that we'd developed an audience, but I didn't notice the Elder approaching until I heard her demand. She wasn't alone. Dozens of adult females accompanied her, as well as an honor guard of males, all of them surrounding us, making the two handguns we carried seem very, very small. I should have called in the Strada right then—actually, I should have done it the second Shindo had cut and run—but at this point, the Strada would have to shoot their way in and then back out, and it would be a slaughter. Knowing how tough the Gan-Shi were, it wasn't a given just who would get slaughtered.

"We detected someone from your camp hacking into the hyperspace comm satellite," I told her, keeping my eyes and my gun on Shindo. "They sent a message in the direction of an Anguilar outpost, informing them of our intention to evacuate our refugees to Thalassia. We traced it back to Shindo's tent and discovered a transmitter hidden there."

The Elder Mother walked through her crowd of would-be protectors to stand off to my side, eyeing Shindo and Warrin. Her son was with her, I realized. I'd met him back on Wraith Anchorage, though I couldn't remember his name. The kid didn't seem bothered by all this, as if this was just the sort of thing that happened on an average day in the herd. The Elder's expression was just as phlegmatic, though not as apathetic. She calculated behind that placid face, so much smarter than her cow-like appearance made her look.

"And you think Shindo was the one who gave away our location on Sanctuary as well," she deduced. "Causing the deaths of your friends."

"I'm sure the same transmitter was used in both cases. It was in Shindo's tent."

The Elder stepped in front of me, and I cursed softly, lowering my gun. She put a hand on Shindo's arm, her liquid, brown eyes meeting his.

"Shindo, you must tell me the truth."

"The device is not mine," he said, words clearer this time as he bowed his head to the leader of the herd. "I never saw it before this night."

The Elder turned to the old bull, who still squared off with Shindo, never taking his eyes off of him.

"And what of you, Warrin? Why do you seek to fight your brother when the time of matin has not yet arrived?"

He, I noticed, did *not* show the same level of deference, not bowing or relaxing from his combative stance.

"I was on the night watch, revered mother. I saw this one fleeing from our allies, and knew he must have done wrong else they would not chase him. I merely sought to…detain him so he could be put to the question."

"You merely sought this, did you?" she asked, sounding more

upset at him than she had at the notion that Shindo was a traitor. "And do you now owe loyalty to the humans over the herd?"

I shared a look with Chuck, his eyes going wide, his hand tensing on the grip of his pistol. I knew what he was thinking. This didn't sound good.

"I owe loyalty to the people who have sought to help us," Warrin snapped back at the Elder. "As should you. As should we all. Shindo has betrayed them and risked the lives of everyone. He should be turned over to the humans and forgotten by those who value the safety of the herd."

As for the herd, well…they didn't look happy. A low rumbling went through the gathered masses, what had to be thousands of the cows and hundreds of bulls, surrounding us in every direction except directly past the fire—no one wanted to be staring through it at the confrontation—for over a hundred yards. No one showed any signs of violence, but I thought of a stampede and how badly it would hurt to get trampled by a bunch of panicking Gan-Shi and reached into my pocket for the comlink. Maybe I could still get a lander in here to pull us out if things got bad.

"If you truly believe that the resistance is our ally," the Elder said to Warrin, her tone almost casual, conversational, "and that they mean for the good of the herd, I wonder why it is that my son saw you taking a large, wooden memory box into Shindo's tent when he went to take water to the male tending the fire not an hour ago."

Chuck's expression was a mirror for the one I felt, my head snapping around in shock. Warrin froze for a moment, a deer in the headlights, and I brought up my pistol. The old bull bellowed incoherently, feigned a charge at the elder…

…and dove headlong through the fire.

21

FLASHING embers scattered in every direction, obscuring my view, and I thought that the old bull had thrown himself into the flames as a particularly insane and painful form of suicide, like one of the Buddhist monks protesting the Vietnam War on the TV news when I was a kid.

"There!" Chuck yelled, pointing past the fire, out in the direction of the open field. "He's running."

Oh, shit. Not again.

But as loath as my mind was to engage in another foot pursuit, my body had other ideas. I don't know if I could say I *planned* to jump through the fire behind him, and I certainly hadn't thought the maneuver through, but I did it anyway, barely managing to get my arms over my face in time before the heat washed over me.

I had a brief rush of utter panic, the conviction that I'd made a huge mistake and was about to catch on fire, and at minimum look like an idiot and wind up spending another day in that damn tank. But then I was through, and the early morning air was a blast of sharp relief. Smoke trailed off the sleeves of my fatigue top, but the fabricators had done a good job, and I guess the thing was fireproof besides supposedly being stab-resistant and even bulletproof for smaller calibers.

Even the fancy material couldn't preserve my night vision after jumping face-first through a fire, though and I struggled just to find my way through the gate in the wire fence that separated the encampment from the road. Our car still sat there, gleaming black in the distant glow of the nearest street light…and Chuck, in pure Army fashion, had left the keys in it, figuring no one would mess with it way out here and either of us should be able to drive it if it came to that.

Warrin ran straight toward it, and if I didn't *think* the Gan-Shi could drive a Suburban, I didn't *know* he couldn't. One thing I was certain about was that I could outrun that old bastard, stampeding bull or no. His big legs pumped rhythmically, but he was twice my weight and probably twice my age as well, and I caught up with him a good twenty yards before he reached the car.

I should have shot him. It would have been the smart thing, but all I could think of was that I wanted to know why, and more than that, Brandy would want to know and she'd be very pissed at me if I didn't at least try. I shot less than a foot in front of him, blasting a crater out of the dirt road. Steam and debris shot up in a fountain. Warrin tumbled head over heels and crashed with all the grace of a felled redwood.

Trying to stop abruptly, I nearly tripped over him but caught myself against the hood of the SUV. My chest heaved as I caught my breath and pushed myself off the car, back toward Warrin. He rolled to the side, making a noise like a bull being castrated and tried to get up, but I kicked his arm out from beneath him. And nearly broke my foot in the process, even through my steel-toed boots.

"Stay down," I warned him, limping back a step, "or I'll blow your head off."

Chuck had caught up, and Shindo was right behind him, fury writ across his face. Warrin ignored my threat and tried to get up again, but this time, Shindo was on him. The younger bull slammed down onto Warrin's back and clubbed him across the jaw with a blow that would have killed a human, certainly would have killed me. It sent the older Gan-Shi sprawling, eyes glazed, and Shindo raised his arm to strike again, but I grabbed his wrist.

Not that I could have stopped him, but he looked up at me.

"Wait," I said. "We need to find out how much damage he's done." He looked doubtful, but he sighed and straightened, though he kept an eye on Warrin.

The Elder stepped through the gate, her son at her side, a few of the mothers of the elder council with her, all of them moving at a stately, sedate pace as if the danger was over.

"Warrin," I said, kicking at his side to rouse him. "I know you're awake. You need to tell me what you've done."

Warrin coughed and spat out a glob of blood, and the cough turned into a bitter laugh.

"You know what I've done, human. You told me as much."

"When did you start working for the Anguilar?" I demanded. "When did they give you the transmitter?"

"Answer him," the Elder ordered, her arms crossed, watching the fallen bull from a safe distance.

"I don't take your orders, you stupid cow," Warrin sneered, wiping a trickle of blood off his mouth from where Shindo had hit him. Gasps went up from the elder council, and Shindo kicked the older male in the side hard enough that I winced in sympathy.

"You will keep a respectful tongue in your head," Shindo warned, "or I'll reach in and yank it out."

Warrin moaned and wheezed, clutching at his side, face scrunched up with pain.

"I worked with them on Wraith Anchorage," he confessed, the words coming out in a resigned exhalation, as if he'd finally accepted his fate. "I wanted off. I'd had enough of living like a rat in the tunnels there, being subservient to the females according to customs from a dozen lifetimes ago." Warrin sent the Elder another ugly expression. "When you came to me with your plan to attack them, I went to General Zan-Tar, asking if he wanted me to sabotage your effort...and he told me to go ahead with it. He gave me the transmitter...said that you'd take us with you to Sanctuary and I should contact him then."

"Oh, son of a bitch," Chuck moaned, and the only reason I didn't echo his curse was that I was too stunned to speak.

A setup. It had all been a setup. He'd been willing to take all those losses just to get at us.

"Is…" I trailed off, slugging my brain into motion to fight through the shock. I'd screwed up. Badly. "Is there any special code you use when you transmit to them?"

"No. The device encodes the messages automatically."

"And what was your reward to be for this betrayal?" the Elder demanded, coming closer now that Warrin had been subdued. "I noticed that on Sanctuary, the Anguilar didn't attack us. Was this because of you? Did you at least try to protect us even in your treachery?"

"Of course I protected the herd," Warrin said, coming onto his hands and knees, still clutching at his side but recovered enough to project the maximum level of scorn into the reply. "You think that I would live what is left of my life as an exile? I would have treated our people well…under *my* rule."

"The mothers would never have accepted you!" one of the elder council gasped in outrage. "Or any male! That is an abomination!"

"They would have once you and the rest of the elders were dead or sold into servitude among the Anguilar." I'd never seen one of the Gan-Shi literally spitting mad before. It was impressive in a horrifying sort of way. Warrin clambered to his feet, and the elders retreated a step while Shindo moved between them and the older bull. "You would have had the rest of your miserable life breaking rocks in a mine or harvesting grain by hand on your Anguilar lord's farm to reflect on how utterly righteous and upright you were."

The females recoiled from the words, not in fear but in utter, religious horror. It was, I intuited, the equivalent of one of the Pope's senior cardinals coming out as a satanist. And I didn't need Brandy here to tell me that it was also an opportunity.

"You can see what the Anguilar have planned for you," I said, not shouting or projecting the words, just aiming them at the Elder and her council. "They don't make any secret of it. They'll find someone who'll betray you for the little bit of power they allow him, then kill or enslave your leaders and put your people to work for them." I put a hand on my chest. "I can't promise you all sweetness and light, and I won't tell you things will be easy. You'll have to fight, you may have to move. But you'll always be able to rule yourselves according to your own traditions, under the leaders you choose. And I swear that I will do all I can to protect you and give you a home where you can raise your young safely."

I wasn't much of a politician, though I'd definitely improved in that area over the last couple years. Maybe I'd even progressed to the point where old Colonel Danberg might have had to admit I would have made an adequate peacetime Army officer. The Elder regarded me with dark eyes gone totally unreadable in the darkness.

"If it is as you say, Charlie Travers," she said, "and we are to be allowed to rule ourselves as we wish, then shall we be left to deal with the traitor to the herd according to our own ways?"

Oh. Oh, *shit*. I'd walked right into that one.

I opened my mouth to tell her that we would need to question Warrin before we allowed her to punish him, but then closed it again. What could he really know, assuming he'd told us the truth? He'd explained how he got the transmitter, and if he'd gotten it earlier or later, would it affect our strategy? If I was being honest, the only reason to bring Warrin in for interrogation was so Brandy could have her vengeance.

"Yes," I told her. "I'll allow you to have your justice for Warrin. But," I felt compelled to point out, "if you choose exile as your punishment, bear in mind that he can't stay on this planet or go to Thalassia with your herd. No one on either world would have him."

"That is fair," she acknowledged, then cocked her head to the side, looking at Warrin with thoughtful eyes. "However, it is not our way to impose death as a punishment. The only alternative to exile would be if one of our males would agree to act as our champion and challenge Warrin to a trial by combat."

"I'll do it," Shindo said immediately.

The young bull still didn't look happy with Chuck and me for accusing him of being the spy, but his real anger focused like a laser on Warrin.

"Trial by combat?" Chuck repeated, disgust dripping off the words. "You mean like…to the death?"

"Of course," Shindo said, snorting in amusement, like only an idiot wouldn't already know that. "How else would the gods show who've they've favored?"

"What happens if he wins?" I asked, my objection to the idea more practical than ethical. "If Warrin kills you?"

"Then I would be allowed to rejoin the herd as if none of this had ever happened," Warrin answered for him, an evil smile spreading across his face. He cracked his knuckles, as loud as distant firecrackers on July Fourth. "I accept."

"And when is this fight going to happen?" I wanted to know.

"There is no better place than here," the Elder declared as if the words were part of some ancient ritual. "There is no better time than now."

"Commander Travers, this is Skyros," my comlink chirped in muted insistence in my pocket. "Do you copy?"

"Yeah, I'm here," I told him, fishing the device out of my pocket.

"Do you need any support, sir?"

"No," I told him, watching the Gan-Shi filter out through the gate, forming a circle around the prospective combatants right there in the middle of the road. "I need a drink."

"IF WARRIN WINS," Chuck asked in a low murmur, shoulder to shoulder with me, "are you really going to let him just walk back into the camp and act like everything's copacetic?"

"No," I assured him, keeping my tone just as subdued, not wanting the scores of Gan-Shi in the circle to hear me. "He'll wander off on his own one night, and one of Brandy's people will take him out. He's responsible for over two thousand deaths." I looked across the circle at the Elder, who watched me just as carefully as she did the two circling bulls in the ring. "But that'll probably be the end of our alliance with the Gan-Shi, so I'm rooting for Shindo pretty hard."

I was also rooting for a quick fight. False dawn glowed gray at the edge of the horizon, and we still had a hell of a lot to do and probably not much time left to do it. The two Gan-Shi bulls didn't seem too concerned with how long things were taking. They circled each other, hands wide, eyes locked. That was a mistake, I thought. I'd always been taught *not* to watch the other guy's eyes, to concentrate on his hips, his center of gravity. When he moved, it would show there first. But I didn't think this was the sort of situation where Shindo would welcome a ringside trainer so I kept my mouth shut.

I wondered if either of them was actually going to launch an attack, but Shindo was the first to lose patience. He charged straight into Warrin, swinging a wide left at his head, but the older Gan-Shi was ready for it and ducked the punch, then slammed his fist into Shindo's side with the sound of a hammer striking a side of beef. Shindo rebounded, air gushing out of him like a steam engine clearing its throat.

Chuck and I groaned in unison, both of us likely thinking the same thing, that Warrin would follow up with the attack and pound Shindo to pulp. But Shindo set his feet, prepared for it, and Warrin fell back into a fighting stance. The older Gan-Shi was a seasoned fighter, the scars showing he'd done this sort of thing before, and he wasn't going to be suckered into an easy kill.

My own breath came as quick and labored as Shindo's, my hands clenched into fists in sympathy. I'd like to have said I wished it were me in the ring instead of Shindo because it would have made me sound very honorable and brave, but the fact was,

Warrin would have broken me like a twig, and the only way I'd face him one on one was if I had a gun.

Shindo wasn't as quick to charge this go-around, staying on the move. They both maneuvered flat-footed enough that my old Taekwondo master would have made them do push-ups until they remembered to stay on the balls of their feet. Which would have been easy for him to say, since a five-eight, 150-pound Korean was a good deal more agile than a 300-plus-pound Gan-Shi. Their sidesteps left an eldritch pattern of concentric circles in the surface of the dirt road, like some pagan cult had performed a ritual here, and I wondered if it would wind up being a blood ritual at the end.

And whose blood.

A chant rose from the females watching the fight, low and unintelligible at first but rising to a crescendo before crashing down again. It was probably something poetic in their own language, something that rhymed, but translated by the goo inside my ear, it came out simpler, like a cheer at a boxing match.

"Fight! Fight! Fight! To the death! To the death! To the death!"

Shindo darted in as fast as a snake, putting more care and precision into this attack, and Warrin wasn't able to easily dodge this one. He managed to shift backwards just enough for the blow to take him in the shoulder instead of the chin, but it landed hard enough to push him back a step, and Shindo, younger and bolder, pressed his luck. A kick, though not the sort I would have tried, more like a mule with the upper half of his body leaning forward and his foot pistoning backward.

That was a mistake, and I winced even before it failed spectacularly. Warrin slid aside a half step, then caught Shindo's leg, levered it upward, and shoved the younger bull to the ground, before falling on top of him. Warrin's fists pounded like sledgehammers, raining blows down on Shindo as he struggled to cover up, and any one of the punches would have killed the average human. I thought Shindo was done, that this was all going to wind up in the nightmare scenario Chuck and I had discussed, but he whipped his leg up and hooked it around Warrin's arm, then straightened it and threw the older Gan-Shi off of him.

Warrin flopped onto his back, and Shindo used his youth and resilience to his advantage, jumping to his feet before the other bull could roll into a defensive position. And Shindo finally showed some savvy rather than just enthusiasm. The easy thing to do, likely his first instinct, would have been to stomp on Warrin while the other bull was down, followed by an urge to pound hammer blows onto his opponent just like the older fighter had done to him, but he resisted both temptations.

Instead, he fell down with both knees into Warrin's chest, all of his considerable weight going into the blow. Ribs cracked, and Warrin bellowed in pain, doubling up, his chin coming forward directly into Shindo's devastating punch. I'd been in fights before, more so recently, and heard a lot of punches hit a lot of jaws, but none had been as loud or brutal as this one. It was a major league hitter smacking a home run ball out of the park, and Warrin was definitely out of the park.

His head snapped backward, eyes rolling into his head, and he slumped to the ground, snoring as loud as one of those males sleeping alone in their tent. I'd heard of people snoring when they were knocked unconscious but had never actually seen it before. Shindo took his time getting back to his feet, standing over the traitor, fists clenched.

"To the death!" the females chanted. "To the death! To the death!"

22

I winced in expectation, prepared to look away, but Shindo hesitated.

"It does not feel right."

The chant ceased and the Elder fixed Shindo with a glare.

"It is a trial by combat, Shindo. You knew it was to the death when you issued the challenge."

"To the death!" Just the one iteration this time, though filled with accusatory disapproval.

"But he is helpless," Shindo said, frowning at the unconscious Warrin. He looked back up to the Elder. "Is it not wrong to kill those who could not fight back?" His nostrils flared in anger. "Is it not what you and the other mothers teach? That killing is wrong?"

"If you fail to kill him," the Elder warned, "then he will win by default. He will take his place among us, and you will be exiled."

Dammit. That complicated matters. I knew what I should have done. I'd killed Mok-La once, when he'd been helpless, though that was more a matter of putting him out of his misery, and had felt nothing about it, but I knew how the Gan-Shi felt. I should have told him it was okay, that Warrin deserved it, which was the truth, but that didn't matter. It wasn't about what Warrin deserved, it was about what Shindo deserved.

And maybe he deserved not to have to consider himself a murderer.

"Shindo," I blurted, "don't do it. If you think it's wrong, don't do it."

Chuck goggled at me.

"Are you nuts?"

I ignored the question and the likely answer, instead meeting Shindo's startled gaze.

"You have more reason than I to want him dead," he pointed out.

"I do. But you still have to live with yourself. Don't do it if you feel like it's wrong."

Shindo took a step away from Warrin, shaking his head.

"I won't kill him. I don't care what the punishment is."

The females keened loudly enough to drown out Warrin's snoring, and the Elder pounded her fist into her chest, her expression agonized.

"Shindo, son of Mardo," she intoned, raising her hands high, "you may no longer be part of the herd. You may no longer live among our people, may no longer make your tent among our encampment, may no longer compete for the affections of our females during the rut. You are exiled from our midst and may not return. May the gods have mercy on you."

Shindo bellowed a sorrowful moan, went down on all fours, and beat his head against the dirt, though I had the feeling this, too, was ritual. It was joined by the others, the females adding their own, mournful cries to the chorus, so loud they nearly drowned out the alert from my comlink.

"What?" I asked, holding it up to my ear. "I couldn't hear."

"Charlie, it's me." Laranna's voice, and she sounded worried…and not just worried about me confronting Warrin.

"I copy, Laranna. What's going on? Is there a problem?"

"It's the Anguilar," she said urgently. "They've arrived just outside Lunar orbit. You need to get up here."

I suppose I should have been surprised, but we'd been expecting it. The timing was inconvenient, but wasn't it always?

"Copy. We're heading up." I waved at the Elder, trying to cut through the wailing to get her attention. "Elder, the Anguilar have arrived in orbit."

The keening shut off as if someone had flipped a switch, and the Elder speared me with a hard and accusatory stare.

"You said we would be away from this place before they came."

"I'd hoped we would be," I told her, "but all we can do now is hope that they got Warrin's message. It's what we were counting on."

"I don't understand," the Elder snapped. "What have you not told us?"

"Get your people away from the tents. Get into the woods." I pointed off to the north, to the lines of trees there. "No matter what, don't come out of them until we give you the all-clear."

"And what about me?" Shindo wondered. I would have expected the words to be sullen, resentful, but the young Gan-Shi seemed at peace with his decision. "I have nowhere to go."

"Yes, you do," I told him. "You're coming with us. I don't care if your people don't want you, we do. You're officially on the team...*my* team. Chuck," I said aside to the man, "get the car started. We have to get back to the lander."

He nodded and jogged over to the Suburban, while Shindo followed me dutifully, as if he'd simply replaced his loyalty to the Elder mother with me. There was something we'd all forgotten about, though.

Warrin.

I noticed the movement out of the corner of my eye, the old bull clambering to his feet, rushing forward. It didn't make any sense. He'd won, he was back in the herd and could go back to living as if no one knew he was a traitor...but he didn't know that. He'd been unconscious for the entire exchange, and as far as he knew, he'd lost the fight and was as good as dead. Which was the only way it had made sense for him to charge straight at Shindo, head lowered, ready to gore the younger Gan-Shi right through the back.

I acted without thinking, following an instinct learned the last two years, one I'd never thought I'd developed. The pulse pistol leapt into my hand, extended behind me as I turned, and when the shot came, it surprised me. Not as much as it surprised Warrin. The last thing that went through his mind before he died was about a hundred kilojoules of scalar energy.

Warrin toppled backward into the midst of the females, and a gasp went up from the gathered crowd. I blew out a breath and reholstered the pistol. Shindo regarded the smoking corpse with what might have been regret…or maybe relief. Me, I thought of Val and Nareena and all those bodies back on Sanctuary and felt not one shred of guilt.

"I suppose," the Elder told me with a chilling equanimity, "that solves both of our problems."

I had to remind myself very forcefully that I was dealing with an alien culture, not human, and that I couldn't judge her by the standards of Twentieth or even Twenty-First-Century human civilization. It wasn't fair.

And I didn't care. I did it anyway. I didn't like her at all.

"Get your people to safety," I reiterated. "The Air Force personnel from the base will help you move supplies out to the forest."

Chuck had the car going, and the backup lights threw long shadows from Shindo and me as we waited for him to stop and let us in. I put the Gan-Shi herd out of my mind. I had a battle to fight.

"What's the situation?" I transmitted to Laranna even before the lander had cleared the airfield at Minot. "What's the size of the incursion force?"

All around us, Starblades took flight, rising like a flock of waterbirds into the gentle glow of dawn, passing in front of the rising Sun on their way to orbit. Other fighters were up as well, the conventional ones—conventional in the here and now, though the F-22s and F-35s looked nearly as futuristic to me as the Starblades. They left the runway at a rate of one every few seconds, and I whispered a prayer for the pilots since they had no hope of surviving a one-on-one confrontation with an enemy plane. A few months ago, they also wouldn't have had any chance of even damaging an Anguilar troop lander, but the same sort of tech the Russians had gotten from the Anguilar, the Americans had gotten from Lenny.

"Not as bad as it could be," she said, "but worse than we'd hoped for. I'm sending you the sensor readings."

I cursed softly at the red icons popping up on the sensor screen, way too far for the lander to detect on its own, relayed to our shuttle via the feed from the *Marauder*. I tried to count them, but the icons were too close together, the screen too small.

"Twenty-one cruisers," Laranna told me, saving me the trouble of finding the count on the display. "Probably carrying at least thirty or forty squadrons of fighters, depending on whether they've replaced some of them with landers."

"Zan-Tar wouldn't bother with landers," I judged. "He knows he can't hold ground here, not without laying waste to the entire infrastructure. This…this is a probe. He's trying to attrit us again. We could take them easy if we had the Liberators here."

"If?" Shindo repeated, speaking for the first time since we'd gotten into the Suburban outside Minot. "Why are the Liberators not here?"

That was a question I wouldn't have answered a couple hours ago, back when we weren't sure who the traitor was, and it still wasn't one I was completely comfortable revealing the answer to even now. Shindo wasn't a turncoat, but he also wasn't someone I trusted implicitly yet.

"It was part of the plan to smoke out the traitor," I explained as completely as I was prepared to at the moment.

"How are you going to evacuate the herd without the Liberators?" he persisted, but Laranna's voice over the cockpit speakers spared me from having to answer.

"Gib and I have our squadrons deployed, but yours is waiting for you to dock with the *Marauder* before they launch. At their current acceleration, ETA to orbit for the Anguilar ships is forty-two minutes."

I took my eyes off the controls long enough for a careful scan of the sensor screen, and the object of my search was conspicuous by its absence.

"Where are the *Victory* and the *Endeavor*?" I wanted to know.

"Just where you told them to be," she said, a gentle chiding in the words. And yeah, maybe I was showing my doubt, but it wasn't as if they hadn't given me reason for it. "You said we needed to draw them in."

"Yeah, I know," I acknowledged. "Thanks for reminding me this was all my idea."

"It's why I'm here," she told me, laughing softly. But her next words were sober, sincere. "Don't worry, he is *not* smarter than us. He's not smarter than *you*. Get your ass in that fighter, and let's show these bastards that they're messing with the wrong people."

"Love you," I told her. "I'll see you up there."

"Love you too."

Silence as the transmission ended, and I realized Chuck was staring at me.

"What?" I asked.

"How the hell do I find myself someone like that?" he lamented, shaking his head.

"It's not the first time you've asked me that," I reminded him. "But the answer's still the same. There *is* no one else like Laranna. And if I could figure out how the hell I got lucky enough to have her fall in love with me, I'd write a book on the subject."

"Oh, dude," Chuck said, laughing. "A book? When this is all over, you could make a fortune on the talk show circuit. Maybe you could have your own YouTube channel…talk about monetization! And of course there's gonna be a movie deal, whether or not you sign off on it. I'd be shocked if one isn't already in production."

"You humans are very strange," Shindo interjected from behind me. He looked ridiculous jammed into a seat built for someone a lot smaller than a Gan-Shi, but I was getting used to that…and he'd better get used to it, too, since he was going to be hanging out with us a lot more. "I suppose that's inevitable since you have to spend so much time with the female of your species, when it would be so much more sensible to only live together when it's necessary for procreation."

"I think it's just as well we got you off Earth, buddy," Chuck said, "before you talked to some reporter. You'd be hell on PR."

I shut out their banter as the cruiser grew larger in the main screen, her docking bay yawning wide, waiting for us. The *Marauder* didn't look as much as the Anguilar cruiser it had once been, not since Lenny and the other Liberator ships had unleashed their construction 'bots on it. They'd done more than just give it a new paint job, though there were shaded stripes across its silver hull now that gave it a camouflage effect, as well as the new symbol of the resistance, one I'd developed as an homage to Poppa Chuck. It was the US Air Force roundel with star and stripes, like the ones on the wings of the old fighters and bombers from World War Two.

Flags and symbols on ships were something else most societies out in the galaxy didn't do, just like giving the spacecraft names, and I figured anything that set us apart from the Anguilar would be better for recruiting allies. Plus, it was fun, kind of like painting a model airplane, though I hadn't shared that thought with anyone else because Chuck would have made way too much fun of me for it.

"Captain Calabro," I transmitted, "this is Charlie. I'll be on board in five minutes. Tell Lt. Dagon to get the squadron ready for launch."

"I was wondering when you'd get your butt up here, sir,"

Calabro replied, in a remarkably good mood given the circumstances. Brazzo and Mallarna had never struck me as the upbeat, sanguine types, but then they'd both seen the death of their planet while Calabro had grown up on a far-off colony world. "I mean, I'm damn good at my job, but there *are* twenty-one of those bastards out there, and it'd be nice to have a little help."

Docking in a shuttle used to scare the crap out of me, the equivalent of driving KITT into the back of a moving semi-trailer on Knight Rider, but time and practice had made it old hat, and I barely thought about the maneuver as I took us through the airlock field and touched the shuttle down gently between two others just like it.

"What am I supposed to do while you fight the Anguilar?" Shindo asked, a little resentment in his voice. I suppose I understood that, since he sure as hell couldn't fit in the gunner's chair of a Vanguard.

"You're with the resistance infantry now, Shindo," I told him, leaping up and yanking open the hatch. "Go report to Skyros and tell him you need to get outfitted with weapons and armor."

"And what good will that do now?" he demanded, following Chuck and me out of the shuttle.

A small team of hangar bay crew waited for us there, delivering flight suits and helmets for Chuck and me. I grabbed mine, then kicked off my boots and pulled the suit on right there beside the shuttle.

"You'll get your chance, Shindo," I told him, just before I settled the helmet onto its collar and jogged toward my Vanguard.

Right now, it was our turn.

23

"This wasn't the plan, was it?" Chuck asked quietly.

"Sort of," I lied, staring at the cloud of Starblades advancing on us like a swarm of army ants in the jungle, ready to devour everything in their sight.

I had, to my recollection, never seen so many of the things in one place. This was a new tactic for the Anguilar, another innovation we doubtless had Zan-Tar to thank for. Every other battle I'd fought with them, they'd treated the cruisers as the main attack force with their Starblades used as distractions to keep our ships busy while they maneuvered into firing position. It had been a winning strategy likely for centuries for them because they'd usually fought enemies who had the same setup, their only interstellar fighting spacecraft large capital ships.

But all that had changed when we got the Vanguard wing. They'd taken months to adjust to the new weapons, and we'd kicked their asses ever since, but that was the problem with evolution on the micro scale. I'd heard about it from Dani, how the antibiotics that used to work on everything weren't as effective anymore because all the bacteria that had survived the onslaught of penicillin and amoxicillin and doxycycline were the ones who were resistant to them.

Zan-Tar was our version of antibiotic-resistant bacteria. And now that bacteria spread out before us in a cloud of Starblades, forming a particulate barrier between us and the cruisers. And they'd been smart enough not to launch until they were inside minimum safe jump distance, where we couldn't hop in and out of hyperspace the way the Vanguards specialized in. Which meant we'd have to wade through a couple hundred of the things just to get to their cruisers.

It was brilliant, and I hated that bastard for it. They weren't even hurrying, advancing at about half a gravity acceleration, knowing we didn't have any choice but to attack them before they reached orbit and started wreaking havoc on the planet's surface.

"Vanguard One, this is *Marauder*," Calabro transmitted. "I admit, I'm fairly new to this game, but I've never been in this particular situation before. You're the boss. How do we handle it?"

"They're a cheese grater, and we're a block of cheddar," I murmured. "But only if we play their game. And they don't know about the *Victory* and the *Endeavor*."

"You're talking to yourself again, Charlie," Chuck sighed. "It's a bad habit."

"Add it to the list," I told him in the same quiet tone, before I spoke up. "Vanguard Wing, swing wide, on the axes I'm sending you."

Again, that handy software the Air Force had given us proved useful, and I traced out three approaches through the Starblade formation, north, south, and west, relative. I know, I know, the cardinal directions didn't mean anything in space, and Chuck kept telling me that every time I used them, but it was the easiest way to describe things, and it meant translating a bunch of numerical coordinates into one word.

"*Marauder*, you punch straight through the center," I added.

"Like I said," Calabro replied, an edge of skepticism in her voice, "you're the boss. But that many Starblades can take out a cruiser."

"Trust me, Captain."

I would have explained in detail, but we were accelerating at half a *g* ourselves, which meant we'd be in firing range of the Starblades in about a minute. Less, once we started the ball rolling. And I had another call to make.

"Space Command, this is Vanguard One." I couldn't speak directly to the American cruisers, but I still had a direct line to the planet, and all those handy communications satellites surrounding it. "You copy?"

"Copy, Vanguard One." Wow, it was General Gavin himself, not some Space Force colonel they'd assigned as a go-between. I felt honored. "We're monitoring the situation. Do we need to amend the op order?"

"Yes, sir. We need the Starblades on a protective patrol in low orbit just in case any of their birds get past us. That's their fallback to keep us from bypassing the fighter screen."

"Already done." He sounded pleased about that, as if he'd proved that the Joint Chiefs actually knew how to prosecute a war even without the help of a twenty-five-year-old ROTC grad who'd never served a day in the active military and wouldn't have even if I hadn't been abducted by aliens. "What about the cruisers? Same schedule?"

"No, I don't think we can wait quite that long. Ten minutes."

A whistle over a radio, even one as sophisticated as the communications systems on a Vanguard, is a painful burst of static, and Gavin damn well knew it.

"That's cutting things close. I'm not sure if they'll make it."

"Yeah, well," I said curtly, "you said you're monitoring the situation. I'm not sure *we'll* make it ten minutes. So tell them not to be late. Vanguard One out."

"Good luck, Charlie." Leave it to a general, always had to get the last word.

"Vanguard Wing," I said, fingers hovering over the throttle, "tally ho."

Which sounded more professional than my first impulse, which was to tell them to lock s-foils in attack position. Chuckling, I opened the throttle and rode hot plasma into the fight.

I DECIDED I liked the fact that the inertial dampeners weren't perfect.

If they'd done their job completely, then none of the boost would have slipped past them, and I would have felt nothing other than the artificial pull of the grav plates securing us to the floor. That was convenient in that it kept us from having to worry about motion sickness, and the lack of any sense of acceleration would have made it easier to concentrate on technical tasks like reading the sensors.

But I liked the feel of the boost leaking through, the push back into the seat. It focused everything, made it more real. Helped me not to worry. That part was the most important because my wife was in one of the lead fighters in our three formations, and my best friend was in the other, and God knows, that was enough to worry about without adding the fate of my home planet and the whole galaxy into the mix.

The boost pushed all that into the background. Every single gleaming pinpoint of light that was a Starblade fighter streaking toward us cohered into sharp contrast, and the pattern of their movement became predictable. I knew which ones were going to break off and follow my squadron, which were going to go after Gib and Laranna, and which would be shocked enough by the *Marauder* barreling right through the middle of the formation that they'd pull up willy-nilly just to get out of her way.

It might have seemed like a game, otherwise, and I needed it to not feel that way. I needed it to be real, needed to know if I screwed up, that there'd be no second life, no popping another quarter into the slot, that the stream of blue dots that represented my squadron passing to the relative left of the enemy formation each held the lives of two real people who would die if I didn't do my job. That the red dots that were the Starblade swarm each contained two very real enemy pilots who wanted to kill us because the Anguilar had conned them into believing this was their only way out of subservience and misery, serving the ones who'd imposed those fates on their people.

Except for the Krin, of course, who were just assholes.

"Bandits coming into pulse cannon range in five," Chuck told me, and I tried not to roll my eyes at his use of the Air Force terminology, failed miserably. For some reason, it sounded silly coming out of the mouth of an Army Ranger. Silli*er*, anyway.

"First squadron," I said, the words breathy with the strain against acceleration, "fire as you bear."

"That's Navy talk," Chuck mocked, and I didn't feel so bad about rolling my eyes.

I didn't have a straight shot with the particle cannons before Chuck opened fire. The discharge of the pulse turret thudded softly through the hull of the fighter, a rhythmic sound like cards in a bicycle's spokes, unworthy of the light show it produced. Red streaks in the dark, and not the only ones. The rest of the squadron opened up less than a second later, and the Starblades responded in kind, the entire view in the front screens layers of interlocking crimson energy, spiderwebs that stretched for tens or hundreds of miles in every direction.

I don't recall ever before envying the gunner while I flew the Vanguard. I mean, *I* controlled the particle cannon, a massively powerful weapons system that could take out a cruiser, while the right-seater only had the pulse turret, which was mostly useful for taking out small spacecraft. But he could aim the damn thing without reorientating the whole ship, which meant he could sweep streams of scalar energy across the entire line of oncoming Starblades while all I could do was drive.

It was maddening, like a theater showing Star Wars on one of those huge new iMax screens just out of view, only the sounds and flashes hinted to the drama going on nearly within arm's reach. And I couldn't even spare a glance off to the side to watch the show because the main attraction loomed ahead of us, a twenty-one screen diorama. The Anguilar cruisers had reduced acceleration, giving their fighters time to winnow our numbers or at least distract us, leaving us open for their first barrage when we got into range. And it would work.

A trio of enemy fighters drifted into my targeting frame, forcing my attention to the nearer distance, only a few hundred miles away instead of the ten thousand or so where the cruisers lurked, just the way they intended. A nudge against the steering yoke, a pull of the trigger, and I finally had the chance to shoot back. The enemy fighters disintegrated, but it didn't produce any sense of satisfaction, just honed my impatience to a finer edge.

The shields glowed, not bright—not yet—but a reminder of what would happen to any of us who slipped up and got themselves surrounded, and I allowed myself the sin of a quick look to the side and rear camera views, hoping to check on the others, but it was useless. All the displays revealed was incoherent energy drowning out all other sensor readings in a wave of heat and electromagnetic fury. Particle cannons, pulse turrets, plasma drives and the fiery deaths of Starblade fighters conspired to leave us blind.

The *Marauder* was plain enough, though, too big to be hidden. And her shields didn't have the golden glow of a mother-to-be who'd just discovered her pregnancy…they raged with the holy fire of the ark of the covenant after the Nazis had dared to touch it, absorbing not just multiple barrages of pulse gun rounds from the Starblades but plowing straight through several of the fighters physically. Now *that* would have been satisfying, and I'm sure Calabro loved it. I could imagine the Peboktan captain whooping like one of the Duke boys jumping the General Lee over a moving train to escape Sheriff Roscoe P. Coltrane.

But it was also disturbing, since even a cruiser's shields could only absorb so much energy before they overloaded and we were plowing through the cloud of fighters on the way to a much bigger fight with nearly two dozen Anguilar capital ships.

"It must suck to be an Anguilar fighter pilot," Chuck said tightly, squeezing off another burst, then pumping a fist when the target came apart. "Ha! I mean, they're expendable like British infantry in World War One."

"I wonder if they know it," I mused, the idea worming its way past all the other crap I had to offer my concentration. "I mean…" Biting the words off, I rolled the Vanguard away from converging streams of scalar energy, lateral acceleration kicking me in the gut as the fighter's drive pods spun at my command. The Starblades trying to flank me managed to clip each other's wings and spun away, glittering bits of wreckage bursting away from the collision like a fireworks display.

It would have been a perfect opportunity to finish them off, and I hoped one of the other fighters took it because we were already dozens of miles past the damaged spacecraft by the time I got the Vanguard back on track.

"I mean," I continued as if the interruption hadn't happened, "it must have been a pretty sweet gig before we came along. First the Liberators, then the Vanguards, and now, these last two battles, Zan-Tar is throwing the planes at us like a distraction. That's gotta piss some of those guys off."

"What?" Chuck barked a laugh that ended in a grunt as he leaned to the right, as if his body weight would help the external turret adjust quicker. Another burst rattled the hull before he slapped his palm on the control panel in exultation. "You gonna organize them into a union or something? Get them to strike for better working conditions?"

"Just something to think about," I said, tilting us to the left and aiming a bolt of atomic lightning into the center of a cluster of the luckless fighters. These guys were poorly trained, not maintaining the proper separation. The blast swallowed up two of them, and the third spun away, either out of control or just panicked.

Poorly trained meant something, too. Maybe they were running out of good pilots.

I'd run out of time for thinking, though. We were only a couple hundred miles from the edge of the fighter screen, less than a thousand from the cruisers, seconds from the effective range of their main guns. They'd open up on us when the midpoint of our formations were within that range, and when they did, all the Vanguards with overstrained and overloading shields would burn away like ash.

Or would have, if something else hadn't gotten their attention first.

The rainbow rings opened at the extreme edge of minimum safe jump distance, only a few hundred meters from the line where the gravitational pull of our planet would have torn the wormhole to shreds, and the ship trying to come through it as well. Through those twin holes in space emerged a pair of cruisers that could have been first cousins of the *Marauder*, might have been identical triplets but for the American flags in the place of the World War Two roundels.

The *Victory* and the *Endeavor* weren't nearly as patient as the Anguilar cruisers—they opened fire less than a second after emerging from hyperspace, a micro-jump from the asteroid belt, where they'd hidden, powered down and waiting. Twin lances of coruscating power connected each of the American cruisers to an Anguilar counterpart for a fraction of a second, and the enemy warships both expanded to miniature suns.

"Space Command," I said, a fierce grin splitting my face, "send up the Starblades and keep these fleas off our backs. We have work to do."

24

This was the plan.

Tapping out the tactical designations took all of five seconds, and by the time I looked up from the touch pad, half the surviving Anguilar cruisers were in the midst of a 180-degree turn, trying to face the rear attack. Too slow. The gravity-resist and inertial dampeners and artificial gravity were very high-tech, but what they weren't, it had been explained to me at length by Brazzo two years ago, were an honest-to-God gravity drive.

The difference had been lost on me at first, but he'd taken the time to give me the details. A gravity drive, which everyone had been trying to develop since Lenny's people had been biological, would have allowed those cruisers to spin like the proverbial bottle, telling each of us who a particle cannon was about to kiss. But even the inertial dampeners, though they could make high acceleration easier to endure, couldn't make a starship that big any less massive. Turning around took time. Time they didn't have.

The particle cannons took a few seconds to recycle, something about superconductive capacitors recharging, and it seemed forever in a fight, I knew from hard experience. But it wasn't as long as that interminable wait for the forward cannons to come to bear. Two more Anguilar cruisers died in helpless panic and in the space of less than a minute, the enemy numbers had been cut to seventeen, and the resistance forces hadn't even engaged the capitol ships yet.

If they were working from the same playbook Zan-Tar had been running, it wouldn't take many more losses before they cut and ran. But that wasn't good enough. Not after Sanctuary. Some people didn't get taught a lesson unless their nose was rubbed in it.

Not *all* of the Anguilar had panicked of course. If they were perhaps short on competent fighter pilots, Zan-Tar wouldn't put idiots in charge of cruisers, but even professionals got caught with their pants down, and with every cruiser that vanished in a bubble of vaporized metal, another decided to turn and face the more pressing foe.

Their formation had gone to crap, of course, but the closest would be in particle cannon range in seconds, and my hand tightened on the stick, ready to trigger the main gun…when a pattern struck me. The Anguilar cruisers had drifted into a chaotic mélange, but there, even in the disorder, was still some semblance of purpose. Of the seventeen…no, another of them went up while I pondered. Of the *sixteen* cruisers remaining, ten of them had at least tried to fall back into a formation to meet the threat from both sides while the other six adjusted their maneuvering jets, turning away from both us and the American ships.

They were running.

"Vanguard Two and Three," I said, "go after target designations Gamma, Delta, Chi, Rho, and Epsilon. Take them out. *Marauder*, fall in beside my squadron."

The shift split us up and also cleared us from the cloud of Starblades, giving me my first chance to check on our numbers. I grunted, feeling like I'd been kicked by a mule. We'd lost a Vanguard. I hadn't even seen it. One of Laranna's birds, Vanguard Two-Seven. The pilot was Copperell, a female named Palla, with a Strada gunner whose name I couldn't recall. She'd been with the wing since Thalassia, and now she and the gunner and that irreplaceable Vanguard were all just gone.

"Vanguard Three, I copy," Giblet responded, for once sticking with comm protocols.

"*Marauder* copies," Calabro chimed in. Laranna took another half-second, and I knew why.

"Vanguard Two copies. We've..." Her voice broke. "We've lost Two-Seven. We lost Palla."

"I saw. Go blow those assholes to hell."

There was nothing else to say. We knew it would happen again eventually. The starfighters were tough birds, but they weren't magic, and we'd been hemmed in by the Anguilar strategy. If this war went on, they'd all die. *We'd* all die.

As if to punctuate the thought, the enemy cruisers had finally brought their guns to bear on the American ships and particle cannons fired back for the first time. The *Endeavor*'s shields lit up bright at a glancing blow, but before that Anguilar could fire again, the *Victory* cored her amidships, and she tumbled at the sudden escape of pressurized and heated gas, drifting off her trajectory, her engine dead.

My squadron fell in behind me, with our cruiser just off my right shoulder and a few thousand miles back, the curve of the dark side of the Earth on the left. What was left of the Anguilar Starblade squadron fell behind us, turning to try to decelerate. They wouldn't make it before the American birds caught them. Nothing to do but what I said, kill them all.

Or maybe not.

Not thinking it through much more than a second before my actions, I flicked the comm frequency to the one I knew to be the general Anguilar network and touched the transmit key.

"This is Charlie Travers, the commander of the resistance. You're not going to survive this battle. We'll be on you before you reach minimum jump distance, and that'll be it. We may lose ships in the process, but every single one of you will be dead. Unless you surrender."

Chuck's jaw dropped open and he stared at me like I'd grown a third head. Anguilar didn't surrender. But maybe that was because no one had ever put them in a position where they didn't have any choice.

"Listen to me," I went on. "General Zan-Tar is throwing your lives away. He sent you here as a sacrifice, hoping to bounce us around and keep us guessing, hoping enough of you would get away to keep his fleet intact. But he screwed up. He tried the same trick one time too many, and you're going to pay the price for it. Unless you heave to and turn over your ships. You have my word of honor that all of you will be treated humanely and repatriated to a neutral planet of your choice with every opportunity to catch a ship from there to wherever you want. I don't want you, don't care about killing you. I want your ships and your fighters, and if you turn them over, your lives will be spared. If you want the deal, power down your drives, shields, and weapons and open your hangar bays and prepare for boarding. You have five minutes to decide, and anyone who fires on us will be destroyed immediately."

I let off the transmit key and shared a look with Chuck.

"Assuming the close," he observed, and I knew what he meant.

The Anguilar still had enough ships to win this fight if they pulled together, got back into formation, and broke through our lines until they could make the jump. But if I distracted enough of them by offering surrender terms…

"We've been told you'll execute us."

I blinked. I hadn't expected them to answer, hadn't expected anything more than to get them busy arguing with each other. The voice was Anguilar—the species, not just the Empire—and much more tentative than I would have expected.

"We've never executed any prisoners," I told them. "In fact, we have two Anguilar and a Krin in holding right now, getting ready to drop them off on a neutral world. The only reason we don't take more prisoners is because most of you never give us a chance. We don't want you dead. We don't want you at *all*. You can go home. You can make up whatever story you like about how this happened, you can blame the whole thing on General Zan-Tar. We just want your ships. The offer is open to any of your cruisers, any of your fighters that wishes to give up."

"Charlie, look!" Chuck said over our private channel, pointing at the feed from Earth-based satellites.

One after another, Anguilar fighters were decelerating into a stable high orbit, powering off their drives. I switched frequencies to Space Command.

"Don't fire on them!" I yelled at Gavin, forgetting my own callsigns in desperation. "Tell the Starblades not to fire on the surrendering fighters. This is important. Do *not* fire on them."

"Got it," Gavin said. "I've been following your comms. We're on top of it."

And thank God *he* was the one on the line, not some functionary because we didn't have time for a colonel to be calling up the chain right now. The American fighters had only been a few dozen miles below their Anguilar counterparts and burning upward, but now, they leveled off and waited.

Not everyone waited, of course. The six ships making a run for it had reduced thrust, their trajectory not taking them toward jump distance…or toward my squadron and the *Marauder*, which had moved into position to block their retreat. But the other ten ships, the ones that had turned into the attack, showed no such hesitation, and I wasn't about to tell the American cruisers or the Vanguard squadrons to hold off shooting back.

They were distant now, tens of thousands of miles away, far enough that I couldn't see much on optical other than the flash of particle cannons and the occasional explosion, but long-range sensors told a more complete story. One by one, the Anguilar cruisers flared, and were extinguished until only four of them were left, limping away from the American and resistance forces. A tipping point, I think that was what it was called.

Three of the last four Anguilar cruisers shut down their drives almost simultaneously, their shields going down. I wished I could listen in on the intership comms between the Anguilar, but all I could do was watch as that fourth ship turned on one of their own, one of the three that had surrendered and opened fire.

"Kill that ship!" I yelled at our Vanguards, not caring which one of them heard.

Laranna did, as it turned out. Her squadron darted toward the lone belligerent in an arrowhead formation, approaching broadside, well into particle cannon range, before the cruiser could maneuver her main guns toward them. The squadron fired nearly simultaneously, splitting the Anguilar starship in half, the two jagged, glowing sections of the cruiser tumbling wildly apart.

"We surrender! Don't destroy us!"

I don't know who said it. It might have been the Anguilar captain who'd replied earlier or it might not, I could barely tell the difference between them up close and personal much less over the radio. And I had no idea what ship the transmission came from, but it didn't matter. All of the remaining cruisers had shut down their drives and shields, not even trying to decelerate.

I stared at them for a moment, realizing this was a situation I'd never encountered before.

"What the hell do we do now?" Chuck blurted in disbelief.

"I have no idea," I had to admit. But it was my job to figure it out. "Eight cruisers," I murmured. And we needed to board them all before any of their captains got bright ideas about trying to bolt. I adjusted frequencies to the *Marauder*. "Captain Calabro, I need Skyros and the Strada infantry armored up and ready to board those cruisers in ten minutes. You have enough landers for all the cruisers?"

"Yeah, if we use the troop transports," she said.

"Get them launched and get our people on those ships before someone changes their mind. And make sure Skyros knows we're using the minimum force necessary. Assign whatever backup bridge crews you have available to run the cruisers until we can get their weapons locked down and their personnel locked *up*."

"I'll do what I can. Don't know if we have enough qualified bridge crew to run eight cruisers, though."

"We'll figure something out," I assured her. "Do what you can."

"We have spare crews on the *Victory* and the *Endeavor*," Chuck reminded me, sounding like a kid on a carnival runway with a fistful of cash.

"Yeah, I know," I told him. "But I'm kind of worried about how easily they'll give the ships up once they get them."

His mouth formed an "O" of realization, and following close

on the heels of that was another expression I recognized as ambivalence. He knew what I'd meant, that if I let Space Force troops onto the cruisers, they'd probably wind up claiming them for the government. I had different plans for the ships.

"I'm not hanging anyone out to dry," I promised Chuck. "But I want to be the one making the calls, not some politician trying to get reelected."

"I still work for the US government, Charlie," he said with a quiet firmness in the words. I closed my eyes and made some silent calculations.

"I'll give them two of the cruisers. The other six go to us."

Chuck nodded, then chuckled softly.

"I wonder what the President would think about an Army major negotiating how many star cruisers the Space Force is going to get."

"Yeah, well, let's not get ahead of ourselves. We don't have any of them yet." I switched to the American frequency. "Space Command, I'm going to need troops and bridge crews from the *Victory* and the *Endeavor* on cruisers Delta and Gamma. Advise that these are surrendering EPWs from a uniformed military and should be treated according to the Geneva Convention."

Chuck glanced at me sharply, probably remembering the long discussion we'd had about the war on terror and the difference between an Enemy Prisoner of War, or EPW, versus an Unlawful Combatant.

"I copy, Vanguard One," Gavin said, and I thought I heard the same hesitance in his tone that I saw in Chuck's expression. "But I don't know…"

"Sir," I cut him off, "I don't give a damn about the Anguilar, and if some spook wanted to take them off to Guantanamo Bay and waterboard them, I would usually volunteer to be a towel boy. But if we want this whole surrender thing to work so we can all get a lot of really cool armed starships, then the crews on those ships need to believe they'll be well-treated. So, we *are* going to treat them well, both because it's the right thing to do and, more importantly, because *I* promised it, and I don't lie. I have a reputation out here for being straight with everyone, no matter who it is, friend or enemy. It's not much but it's all I've got."

Chuck winced, as if anticipating General Gavin's response to my tirade, but when Gavin spoke again, I didn't detect any anger. Acceptance, maybe.

"I copy, Vanguard One," Gavin sighed. "We'll do it your way."

And it'll be on your head if it goes wrong, he didn't say but I heard just as clearly.

"First squadron," I said, reversing my drive pods for a braking burn, trying to match trajectories with the cluster of ships as we approached their high orbit, "I want you in a patrol orbit that can cover each of these six cruisers. Dagon, you're acting squadron leader for the moment."

"What are we gonna be doing?" Chuck wondered.

"We're going aboard one of these ships," I told him, my voice distant and distracted as I concentrated on bringing us closer to one of the cruisers. "I need to talk to one of the Anguilar captains."

"Why?" he asked and I shrugged.

"Because I just had the horrible thought that it's not impossible Zan-Tar might be on one of these cruisers and this could all be a huge con just to catch us with our guard down."

I barely heard Chuck's soft moan over the roar of the drives and the insistent bangs of the maneuvering jets as I brought us closer to the cruiser's hangar bay.

"I really wish," he muttered, "that you hadn't said that."

25

I HADN'T BROUGHT a rifle along. Chuck had one slung across his chest, and I'd advised him to keep his helmet on as well, visor down, both to look more intimidating and to deemphasize the fact he was human like me. I wanted them to think he could be any resistance fighter from any world.

My face was bare, my helmet back on the Vanguard, and my only weapon was the heavy pulse pistol at my waist. If the crew of the Anguilar warship decided they wanted to kill me, one extra rifle wouldn't stop them. But the image, the confidence, the *legend* might.

I walked with the legend in mind, striding purposefully, ignoring the stares of the Anguilar and Krin and Copperell lined up in the corridors of the cruiser just past the hangar bay, like it was a July Fourth parade and they wanted to see the show. None were openly armed, but I wouldn't have favored them with a glance even if they had been. I kept my expression neutral, unworried, all business. Totally calm, on the outside.

I was, of course, scared shitless. Every fiber of my being screamed at me, demanding what I thought I was doing here, why I'd risk everything to walk about this ship and give some patriotic Imperial the opportunity to be a big hero, be the one who assassinated Charlie Travers.

I'd picked the ship at random. That didn't make it any less likely that there'd be a potential hero on it, but I was hoping it would, at least, keep anyone from making a plan before I showed up. They certainly *seemed* surprised. Not a one of them said a word to me, not one got in my way, they just watched. And out of the corner of my eye, I watched them.

There was something different about this bunch that was hard to put my finger on at first. I'd encountered Anguilar ship crews before, usually under less calm circumstances since we'd been trying to kill each other, but there'd been a couple times when I'd been in disguise and seen them at work without the added stress of attempted homicide. What had struck me then had been the undercurrent of fear keeping everyone in line. Not just discipline, not the way the Army Rangers were precise and diligent from training and pride, but an unmistakable sense of paranoia of a superior looking over their shoulder, ready to pounce if they faltered.

I didn't see that in the faces of the crew lined up in these passageways. Not that they looked relaxed or secure. To the contrary, they still shared a ragged edge of panic, but not the sort a worker might get from having an intrusive boss checking for screwups. No, this was the look of someone deathly afraid the entire company was about to go out of business. And they stared at me like I was the corporate raider walking in to buy the place out and fire them all.

Luckily, I already knew where the bridge was because it would have disrupted the whole mystique I'd gone to so much trouble setting up. I also knew who the captain was without asking. Anguilar starship masters decorated their uniforms like a North Korean general, the gold rings and medals wrapped around their chests and down their sleeves, and this one was no different. His grooming didn't match the decoration, his feathery, graying hair grown thick and sloppy in a comb at the back of his head and down from his chin in a wobbling beard like a Tom turkey.

"You are Charlie Travers," he said, keeping his hands at his sides, far away from the handgun holstered across his chest. He bowed slightly at the waist. "I am Captain Cham-Ven of the Anguilar Imperial Fleet."

He reached for his pistol, and mine leapt into my hand without thought, the muzzle inches away from his nose. Cham-Ven's eyes went wide and his hand shook, but he grasped the butt of his gun anyway with thumb and forefinger and pulled it out slowly and carefully. He reversed it and handed it to me, grip first.

"I offer you my surrender," he said, "on the terms you guaranteed, that all of us will be released on a planet where we can gain passage back to our worlds."

I took his weapon and reholstered mine. The gun was a pulse pistol but not the plain, unadorned tool carried by everyone else I'd encountered on both sides of this conflict. Instead, it was gold plated and inscribed with patterns I didn't recognize, which meant they weren't a language or the translation goo would have let me read them.

"We'll hold to our word," I assured him. "We have crews on their way to fly the ships, and we're going to need to confine everyone to quarters until we can arrange transport. We'll also need all weapons locked up in the ship's armory. Do you have any self-contained rations your crew can take with them into their rooms until we're ready to transfer them off the ship?"

"We do," Cham-Ven confirmed, brusque and dismissive as if the well-being of the crew was irrelevant to him. "I'll see to it that they're distributed. We'll cooperate."

I frowned, bothered by the words...by his attitude.

"Why?" I asked him, and kept on before he could feign ignorance of what I was questioning. "Why did you surrender? I've fought more battles with the Anguilar than I can count, Captain Cham-Ven. And every single time before now, your people fought to the last man." I shook my head. "Even the four officers you left talking to the Russians tried to go down shooting. Why did you surrender?"

The bridge crew was all Anguilar like their captain, no Krin or Copperell or any other subject people trusted for a job like that, and none of them could meet my eye when I scanned around the compartment.

"You don't *have* to tell me," I admitted. "We'll still going to live by the deal we made. But believe it or not, I don't especially like killing people...not even you Anguilar who keep trying to kill me and my friends. So, if there's a way we can do this without killing you, I'm all for it."

Cham-Ven's sneer told me what he thought of my attempt at altruism.

"I do what I do for the Empire," he said stiffly. Then gritted his teeth in a grimace. "Though some may not see it that way. But I do not share information with the enemy."

"Only warships," I observed, cocking an eyebrow at him.

"The ships will do you no good in the long run," Cham-Ven insisted. "We are more valuable than the cruisers."

I grunted skeptically…but noticed when he spoke that Cham-Ven kept an eye on the others in his crew, wary as if he worried they would report what he said.

"Okay then, keep your secret," I told him. "For now, I want you to come show me your security systems so I can arrange to have the compartments locked once your crew is in place." I nodded to Chuck. "You stay here and keep an eye on the control room."

I put a hand on Cham-Zen's shoulder and pushed him off the bridge ahead of me. He stiffened at the touch but kept walking, and I guided him away from the crowd gathered in the hallways, off into a side door leading into a maintenance access compartment. He frowned as I pushed the hatch shut.

"All right, we're alone," I told him. "What couldn't you tell me in front of the others?"

"What makes you think I would tell you now?" he demanded, not acting afraid of me at all here in private. So, as much as I'd wanted to think that it was the intimidation of my presence that had caused him and the others to surrender, that obviously wasn't the case.

"I meant what I said," I assured him. "I don't want to kill any more of you than I have to. I don't have any interest in wiping out your people, I just want you gone from this galaxy. If I can do that without another death, I'd do it." I offered him a feral baring of teeth, hoping it meant something similar to his people. "On the other hand, if I have to kill each and every one of you to accomplish the same goal, well…let's just say there are those in the resistance who don't share my feelings on the sanctity of life."

And I left it at that because any overt threat would have been a statement that he couldn't trust my word and I hadn't been overstating things to General Gavin when I'd told him how important that was to me. Cham-Zen stared at me through narrowed eyes, licked his hard, beak-like lips.

"It's the bloodlines," he said as if that explained everything. I made a come-along gesture, and he sighed in apparent exasperation. "You know of the bloodlines?"

"I've had it explained to me by one of your own. Von-To, actually. I think you probably know him."

Cham-Zen's eyes widened.

"How do you know Colonel Von-To?"

"He sold out General Tok-Ma and smuggled me on board the Nova Eclipse so I could blow it up. All for the good of his bloodline, of course."

Of all the reactions I expected from Cham-Zen, throwing his head back and laughing wasn't among them.

"Brilliant!" he said, unable to keep himself from a chortle

halfway through the word. "That's something I'd think worthy of General Zan-To himself. I knew someone had to have helped you, but I had no idea it was Colonel Von-To…though that makes perfect sense given how quickly he rose afterward." The chuckling died off and he grew serious again. "So, you do know of the bloodlines, and you know how the actions of one can benefit an entire family. But for the bloodlines to benefit, then there must be males serving the Empire in the Fleet. And you and your resistance are making it more difficult for that to happen. There is pressure from the First Families—the ones who hold the real power in the Empire, far more than the Emperor himself—for General Zan-Tar to avoid unnecessary casualties."

"I noticed," I told him, nodding slowly. "I figured it was because you guys were running low on ships."

"That's what the cannon fodder believe," Cham-Zen snorted derisively. "To tell them the truth would make them more hesitant to fight for us. But the truth is, we are shorter of senior officers than we are of capitol ships. Our orders from the General are to retreat rather than risk losing senior officers…but we have other orders from our bloodline leaders. We are to preserve our lives at all costs."

Finally, something that made sense.

"All right, then I only have one other question. Is General Zan-To on one of these ships?"

He looked over at me sharply.

"The General would never risk himself on such a venture as this," he told me.

Now, I've never been that great at poker, and it was even

harder reading a tell when the player wasn't even human, but I thought I'd been around the Anguilar enough to know when one of them was lying to me.

Shit.

I grabbed the comlink off my belt, wishing I'd kept my helmet. The device wouldn't reach the others while I was inside the ship, not by itself, but the signal would be relayed by the Vanguard back in the hangar bay.

"This is Vanguard One," I said urgently into the general channel, half-turning away from the Anguilar captain, "General Zan-Tar is on one of these ships..."

I underestimated Cham-Zen, misjudged him because of all the fruit salad on his uniform and the ease with which he'd surrendered. I didn't expect the punch, wasn't prepared for it, and when it struck, I was in mid-step back to the door.

I'd been punched before, so much harder than this douchebag could manage, slugged by a Kamerian who *really* didn't like me, but the surprise blossom of pain in my jaw and the fact I was off-balance sent me sprawling, the comlink flying out of my hand... along with Cham-Zen's fancy golden gun.

Stars erupted in my vision and I didn't have the time to wait for them to clear, not with the Anguilar right on top of me. I kicked out blindly and connected with what felt like a shin, and was rewarded with a yelp of pain...and a body falling right on top of me. He wasn't heavy enough to drive the wind out of me, but he did his damage on the way down, his shoulder striking me in the chest, making my ribs creak in protest.

I couldn't see well enough to be sure of grabbing his wrists, but I sure as hell didn't want to let him hammer at me even at close range where he couldn't get up any momentum. I grabbed him around the arms and dug my head into his shoulder, a tactic I'd learned from the MMA stuff Chuck had taught me.

Cham-Zen cursed and spat and yelled and tried to headbutt me but couldn't manage more than a harmless bump against the back of my skull because of how tightly I held him. Unfortunately, neither could I, and of the two of us, I was the one running out of time. I had the weight advantage on him, and I used it, rocking back and forth until I was able to roll him off me and throw him to the side.

We both raced to be the first to scramble to our feet, and unfortunately, that weight advantage worked against me, particularly with me weighed down by the armored flight suit. Cham-Zen sprinted across the room, making a beeline for his fallen pistol, and I gave up on trying to stand, instead spinning into a leg sweep. The back of my feet thumped solidly into his ankle, pain flaring even through my boot at the impact. It hurt him worse.

Cham-Zen squawked, went down face-first, and I winced at the crunch of his aquiline nose against the unyielding deck, but to his credit, he kept crawling toward the gun, blood dripping from his upper lip. I rolled to one knee, drew my pulse pistol, and held it extended in both hands.

I came within about an ounce of pressure of shooting him in the back of the head, but I remembered the whole business about them not surrendering if they thought I'd kill them, so I shifted my aim and blasted his fancy pistol instead. The golden gun sparked and smoked, the flare spattering up into Cham-Zen's face. The Anguilar captain screamed, clutching at his eyes, and I spared a brief look to make sure his gun had been destroyed by the shot before retrieving my comlink from where it had dropped beside the door.

Cham-Zen clawed blindly at my boot, but I kicked him aside and dashed out of the compartment, heading back to the bridge.

"Vanguard Wing," I snapped, "*Marauder*, all resistance and American units, this is Vanguard One. General Zan-Tar is aboard one of the Anguilar cruisers."

Skidding to a halt on the bridge, I faced a dozen Anguilar, suddenly not too hesitant to meet my eyes, one or two already edging out of their seats, hands drifting toward holstered pistols. I raised my pulse gun and aimed it between two of the bridge crew, cocking my head to the side in a warning.

"Be on the lookout, and if any of those ships attempts to break orbit, take out her drives," I went on. "Including the one I'm on. Warn the boarding parties to expect opposition because I'm fairly certain this whole thing was a trap."

"Vanguard One, this is Two," Gib replied, urgency in his voice, "I think we're a little too late for that..."

Movement on the main screen caught my eye, one of the Anguilar cruisers from the cluster of six that had first surrendered powering up, boosting toward jump distance and freedom.

"Take him out, Gib," I said.

The Anguilar crewman who'd been reaching for his gun took that as a cue to do something stupid, probably figuring that I was too caught up in the events out there to notice. I could have shot him, but I sensed that would be the match to light this whole thing on fire and I was close enough for something less lethal. Not pleasant, but not lethal either.

The bad part about chest holsters is, your hand is right there on your chest, across your body, exposed. Just begging for a spinning back kick. His ulna snapped like a twig breaking, and he gasped, falling back into his chair, arm pinned to his chest. Only one other crewman wore a holster, and I preemptively smashed him across the face with the barrel of my pulse pistol, sending him sprawling out of his chair, head lolling, semiconscious.

I snatched the pistol from the holster of the guy with the broken arm, then pushed him away across the bridge before retrieving the last weapon.

"Everyone over there now!" I yelled, motioning with a gun in each hand at the other side of the bridge, near the entrance. "Get out of your seats and up against the wall. Anyone takes a single step toward me, and I lose my patience and put a round through your chest. Move."

Hard glares followed me, but the Anguilar crew slowly got out of their seats and shuffled across the bridge. It was hard watching them and keeping an eye on the screen at the same time, but I had to know. A single Vanguard closed with the cruiser, firing off a barrage from the particle cannon even as I watched, and the capitol ship lurched from the blow, her shields glowing fiercely, but she didn't stop.

Just a couple seconds…that's all it would take for the Vanguard's weapon to recycle or for another of the fighters to approach effective range. A couple seconds too long. A rainbow ring appeared in the vastness of space, and the cruiser elongated like a rubber band being stretched, then whiplashed through and was gone.

"Charlie...." Gib said, the hopelessness of the word coming through even the tiny speaker of the comlink.

"Yeah, I saw," I sighed.

I was about to tell him to fall into position to cover the other cruisers when the snap-crack-*BANG* of pulse fire echoed off the bulkheads on the other side of the bridge entrance. The Anguilar crew glared at me with hatred and the promise of violent death, and suddenly the two pistols I held seemed totally inadequate.

"Gib, I think I have a bigger problem."

26

"Chuck, do you copy?"

Holding the comlink against my ear while holding the guns on the Anguilar was like juggling live squid, and I wound up tucking the device against my chin. All that was missing was the elastic phone cord holding it to the receiver and I could be back in high school.

"Chuck, we got trouble…"

"Don't you freaking think I *know* that?" The reply didn't come through the speaker of the comlink…it came from Chuck as he backed into the bridge, rifle at his shoulder, helmet visor up. I wondered why until I saw the scorch marks on his armored flight suit, the cracks in his visor. "It was like someone flipped a damned switch! What the hell did you do?"

A burst of pulse gun fire streamed through the entrance corridor, and the Anguilar bridge crew ducked away, covering their heads, forgetting all about their hatred and resentment for the stupid humans. Chuck cursed and leaned around the edge of the bridge emergency seal, firing off a long burst in response, though I couldn't see if he'd hit anything.

"Zan-Tar's on one of these ships," I explained, back against the wall beside him. "Probably the one that just managed to shoot her way out of here a few seconds ago. This was all a damn trap to let that bastard get away."

"Gosh, y'think?" he asked, then flinched at another burst of scalar energy spalling shrapnel from the opposite wall.

"I need to lower the emergency seal," I decided. I'd been holding off on it, hoping there was some way we could make it back to the hangar bay before things got too crazy, but that obviously wasn't going to happen. "Cover me."

"We'll be stuck in here," he reminded me, grunting the warning as he fired off another barrage at our attackers. "They have engineering…they can cut us out of the control loop."

"Yeah, I'm well aware." I kept a gun and one eye on the bridge crew while I hunted for the right button to push. I kind of sort of knew where it was, but I hadn't spent a lot of time on cruisers, and the control setup on an Anguilar ship was totally different than the one on a Liberator. "But if we don't seal up, we're going to run out of ammo and then they can just rush us. If we can get the door closed, we might be able to hold up in here until help arrives."

"Are we sure help *is* going to arrive?" he asked.

I didn't answer him, but something did. Shouts, alarmed yells, screams, running steps, and the unmistakable sound of pulse rifles spitting out full-auto fire. Then another sound, one almost familiar yet also qualitatively different. A fist smashing into flesh, yet so much louder and harder than any fist I'd heard before, and every impact was followed by the clatter and thump of a body hitting the wall or the floor.

"Whatever the hell that is," Chuck gulped. "I hope it's on our side."

"Sir!" a familiar voice called from outside the entrance. "Are you on the bridge?"

"Skyros!" I exclaimed. "Yeah, we're in here!" I could have rushed around the corner, but I had to keep the prisoners covered.

Skyros wasn't the first one through the doorway. They all wore the same sort of sealed combat armor, but there was no mistaking this soldier for the Strada warrior. For one thing, he was a full head taller and probably a hundred pounds heavier, and the rifle he carried tucked into his right arm looked more like a pistol relative to his size. He also wore no helmet, probably because they hadn't been able to construct one that would fit over his horns.

"Are you well, Charlie Travers?" Shindo asked, eyeing the Anguilar balefully.

"Better now," I assured him, sighing heavily, finally lowering the handguns with which I'd been covering the prisoners. "Skyros," I said as the smaller Strada followed the Gan-Shi onto the bridge, "do our people control engineering?"

"And the hangar bay," he confirmed, tilting back his visor so we could talk without using the comlink. "And the auxiliary control room, and the armory. It's only a matter of time before the Imperial troops surrender. They could still reach the escape pods, but there's nowhere to escape to."

"Charlie," Shindo asked, jerking a thumb at the prisoners, "what do you want to do with these?"

"What do you want to do with *all* of them?" Skyros elaborated. "We have teams going aboard every ship, and none of the others got away. We're gonna have over a thousand prisoners."

"That's a damn good question," I admitted. "But I'm not going to answer it standing here." I waved at Chuck. "Come on, we need to get back to the fighter…and back to the *Marauder*. We have somewhere else to be."

"That could have gone better," Giblet said, sprawled out on the captain's chair of the *Marauder*, letting his head tilt backwards over the armrest.

Calabro kicked his leg, and Giblet yelped, glaring at her.

"Get out of my chair, Varnell," she growled, her antennae wagging at him. Giblet sighed and moved out of the seat.

"I'm tired," he confessed. "I've been chasing around Anguilar cruisers all day."

"It wasn't that bad," Calabro reasoned, sitting down. "We have six more cruisers than we had before."

I winced at the pronouncement. We *would* have had eight if one hadn't escaped and another hadn't been destroyed in an attempt to disable her drives.

"Palla and Titus might disagree," Laranna said, arms crossed as she leaned against the bridge railing, her brows knitted. I slipped an arm around her, and she leaned into my chest.

"We lost two good people and an irreplaceable starfighter." It hurt putting that into words, but it was necessary. "In return, we got six cruisers, two of which we owe to the American military, and several hundred prisoners. Which…I have to figure out what to do with, and fast."

"I thought we were going to let them off at an inhabited world," Chuck said, shaking his head. "That's what you promised them."

"I did," I admitted. "But that was if they actually surrendered. This whole thing was a ploy to give Zan-Tar time to get away, which means I don't know if anything that captain told me was true or not."

"It would make sense," Calabro said. "The bloodlines are very important to the Anguilar. We know the bloodline families wield a great deal of power in the Empire."

"Which means," Gib put in, "that if you let the officers go, it might mean trouble for Zan-Tar. He may be this strategic wunderkind you think he is, but he still has to keep his job."

He was right. And the bottom line was, I didn't have any more time to think about it.

"We have flight and engineering crews on board the ships?" I asked Calabro.

"We do." She shrugged. "Some of them are just Strada warriors who've been cross-trained, but they can get the ships from point A to point B so long as they don't have to fight any battles along the way."

"And the Anguilar are all sealed in their quarters?"

"The survivors," she confirmed. "Quite a few of them didn't give up easy. Krin mostly, of course. The Anguilar officers mostly just let the Krin die for them. I don't know if our skeleton crews are going to be able to keep an eye on them for long."

"Leave the infantry troops on board. I'll leave a message with Space Command to transfer their prisoners over, and we'll use the cruisers to take them to…" I snapped my fingers, trying to come up with a name. "What was that place where we infiltrated to find the Anguilar espionage station?"

"Keystone," Laranna said immediately, nodding. "They can hire transport there." Her lip curled in a sneer. "Though I'm not sure we should be letting them go. The only good Anguilar is a dead one."

"I agree in principle," I told her. "But this is war."

"You think I don't know that?" she shot back, pulling away from me. "It's a war I was fighting before we were taken."

"What he means," Chuck said, coming to my rescue as only a West Pointer could, "is that if you want to win a war, you need to have an endgame. You need to have a strategy beyond just killing your enemy. We learned that the hard way in Vietnam and Afghanistan. We killed the crap out of the VC, the NVA, the Taliban for years, and there were always more. We thought we could kill them until they were all gone, but there are always more people willing to be cannon fodder out there. Particularly when the Anguilar have whole planets to draft new recruits. You have to find a way to make things too expensive for the enemy to keep fighting…or find a way to make it impossible for them to get resupplied."

"That had been what I was hoping for," I admitted. "I thought we could keep taking out their ships until they couldn't make enough to keep fighting. But if that Captain Cham-Zen was telling the truth, they still have enough ships not to worry about it and plenty of foot soldiers…but not plenty of high-ranking officers."

"Then why are we giving them back their high-ranking officers?" Laranna insisted.

I knew why she was angry, knew what the death of her parents and Jax and Nareena meant for her. It was something I couldn't completely understand even though I'd lost friends to the Anguilar.

"If they keep losing battles," I said, "if we keep showing them that their best and brightest are vulnerable because of Zan-Tar, they'll replace him. And if we send these guys back to let them know how badly Zan-Tar screwed up, that he was willing to sacrifice all those high-ranking officers from the bloodline families, then they'll be even more pissed off."

I sagged against the chair behind me and felt suddenly very tired.

"If any of that was true. If I'm not screwing this up again."

"You didn't screw up anything," Laranna told me. "You're the one who knew they'd come here and knew how to split their forces. When Warrin sent that message, they had to have sent off at least half their ships to Thalassia."

"If they hadn't," Gib added, nodding, "we would have been totally hosed. I mean, if this group hadn't been overconfident because they figured there wouldn't be much resistance here, we still could have been totally hosed."

I didn't want to admit they were right, maybe because I felt guilty about Palla's death, but self-flagellation, while it might have felt good, accomplished nothing. And there'd be plenty of time for it in hyperspace. I nodded.

"Then there's only one thing left to do," I said. "And we're already a few hours behind them. Captain Calabro, send off the orders to get the cruisers under way and then we have to get to Thalassia. And hope we haven't wasted too much time already."

27

"I wish we'd had a chance to check in with Brandy and Val before we left," Laranna said softly.

I blinked fully awake in the darkness. I wasn't sure how long I'd been asleep or how long she'd been talking, but a sudden chill told me she'd turned down the air conditioning since I'd been out. I pulled the blanket up and rubbed at my eyes.

"You still up?" I murmured. "Everything okay?"

I could barely see her in the low light of the security panel on the wall, just the outline of her hair and the hint of bare skin at her shoulder. She shook her head.

"No. I can't stop thinking about them."

Realizing I wasn't going back to sleep anytime soon, I sat up, then felt around for my shirt on the table beside the bed. It wasn't much shelter against the cold out of the overhead vents, but now would be a very petty time to go adjusting the climate control.

"Val's going to be okay," I told her. "You've seen Constantine. He's got...replacement parts and you can't even tell. He'll still be able to raise that baby with her. It's not how anyone wanted things to go, but he's still there for her."

"But is *she* there?" Laranna insisted, shifting around to look at me. I knew she had better night vision than I did so she could probably see how out of it I looked. "You told me what she wanted to do with that Anguilar prisoner. I hate them, you know that, but I wouldn't do that, and neither would Brandy before what happened at Sanctuary. She's about to have a baby...and I'm not sure she's in the right place for that."

"They both knew the risks. Just like you and I do." I ran a hand down her arm, warmth radiating from her skin. "This a war without any safe places, without any front lines you can hide behind. And if anyone didn't know before, they do now."

"We have to help her somehow," Laranna insisted. "We have to get her back to where she was."

"I don't know if that's possible," I admitted. "Neither of us is the same person we were before this all started. The only thing we could do for her and Val is leave them on Earth. It's not a hundred percent safe, but it's as close to safe as it gets. But that'd mean giving up her position, and I don't know who the hell else could fill it."

Maybe that was being cold and selfish, but I wasn't sure what the resistance would do without its intelligence chief. We'd all have been dead a dozen times over without the information she'd given us. Laranna stiffened, and I thought she was angry at the way I'd phrased that, but when she punched the bed, it was with frustration instead.

"It's not fair. They deserved to be happy. This shouldn't have happened to them."

"It's my fault," I told her, looking into the darkness. It mirrored what was in my heart. "I brought the Gan-Shi to Sanctuary. I'm the reason they found us."

"They would have eventually anyhow," she said, wrapping me up in an embrace. "You said it yourself more than once. They'd been bringing refugees there for years, and the Anguilar had to have been looking for it. If it hadn't been the Gan-Shi, it would have been someone else. You can't blame yourself."

"I'm the commander. If it's not my fault, who else can I blame it on?"

"You always told me that the enemy gets a say." Laranna backed out of the hug, holding me at arm's length, her eyes glowing green in the darkness. "No one expects you to know everything. No one else blames you for this. You've always put yourself right at the front, taken as many chances as any of the people serving under you."

"Yeah, and maybe that's the problem." I rubbed at my chin. I needed a shave. "Maybe I should worry less about kicking in doors and more about thinking. Maybe if I wasn't a twenty-five-year-old ROTC grad, if Lenny had picked someone with more experience, like Chuck, we wouldn't be in this position."

Laranna laughed, and I looked up in surprise.

"I like Chuck," she said. "He's a good man and a good officer. But do you really think if Chuck had been stolen away by Lenny and shoved into the same situation you were that he'd even be alive right now? I've met a lot of your people since we first visited Earth. Some of them were brave and intelligent and honorable, like Chuck and Dani, others…not so much. But even Dani wouldn't have been able to survive without the help you gave her adjusting. You didn't get any of that. You were thrown head-first into the deep end and expected to swim."

"Even if you're right," I said carefully, not really willing to grant that much but not wanting to argue about, "I can't just live off what happened then. I'm not just running around with a handful of outlaws anymore. I have to lead what's turning into an entire government." I shrugged. "And that's something else that's starting to bother me. We're not just an army anymore. With the Gan-Shi, we have about three or four times as many civilians as we have soldiers now. We've been letting everyone run themselves according to the laws and customs of the cultures they came from. I thought that was okay because the end goal was always to take back their worlds and let them resettle once the war was over. But the war's been going on for years now, and eventually, if this stretches on much longer, we're going to have to figure out a way to live with each other, and that means laws. It means some kind of vote."

"Charlie, not everyone comes from the sort of democratic tradition as your country," Laranna said gently, as if treading on dangerous territory. "Even on your planet, the Russians and Chinese and others are not governed the same way as your United States."

"We'll have to figure something out," I insisted. "However

each group wants to select a representative, we need to have someone who can speak for them. Let me ask you, though…what do you think the endgame is here? Are we just going to let everything go back to the way it was before the Anguilar came along? With everyone separate, isolated on their worlds? Because that's exactly the setup that left you vulnerable to them in the first place." I spread my hands demonstratively, as if taking in all of creation from my vantage point here in hyperspace. "And before that, before the Centennial War, you had the Kamerians running everything like a dictatorship. That couldn't last, and it didn't. And before that, you had Lenny and his"—I struggled for the right word to use for a robotic hive mind—"*people* guiding you like you were children and they were your teachers. And that's not going to happen again since they learned their lesson with the Centennial War and the Anguilar."

"What are you suggesting, then?" Laranna wondered, and this time, there was genuine curiosity in the question.

"I don't know. I'm not an expert on government. I think we need to have some kind of conference with representatives from every people and planet in the resistance and see what they have to say."

"And you don't think that's premature?" she asked, cocking an eyebrow at me. "You mentioned a saying about not counting chickens before they're hatched."

"You're not wrong. But I also know that the surest way to guarantee another war after this one is over is to not have a plan in place for how things are going to be run." My head hurt, probably from lack of sleep, but I tugged at memories to make my point. "When the French overthrew their king, they wound up replacing him with a bunch of fanatics who killed everyone who'd ever been loyal to the king and then started killing each other. Then they were replaced by a military dictator who got all of Europe at war with France and wound up getting about six million people killed. When the Russians overthrew their czar, the oligarchy that replaced him wound up killing in the hundreds of millions over the next few decades, and the mess left there today is still a result of that. We can't get rid of one dictator just to replace them with another. Too many people have died on my watch for me to let that happen."

"And maybe there wouldn't be the temptation to do something like Brandy tried to do to those prisoners if we had laws against it?" she deduced.

"That too. Not that a law would stop Brandy right now. The only thing that would stop her is Val." I shook my head. "And I don't know if he's in the mood to do anything. Back when we were on Earth, I tried to get down to see him, but he never answers the comm."

"He's not there now," she reminded me. "He stayed on the *Liberator*."

"And God only knows why." I threw up my hands. "He knows what's going to happen at Thalassia. Why the hell would he and Brandy both go into that right now? She's about to pop in a month."

"They left Maxx behind with her friends at one of the reactor sites." Laranna said it like it made the action more reasonable, and I goggled at her.

"Which just means that if anything *does* go wrong, Maxx will lose his mother, stepfather, and unborn baby brother all at once. It's nuts, and the only thing I can think is that Brandy…"

I bit down on the words, unwilling to say them.

"She doesn't care about living anymore," Laranna finished for me. "I've thought the same thing. But how do we change that?"

"I'm still thinking. I hope I have a solution by the time we reach Thalassia."

Laranna snorted a humorless laugh.

"That reminds me of another saying you've taught me, Charlie. Hope in one hand and shit in the other and see which one fills up faster."

I'VE OFTEN HAD the thought that my life was like some science fiction movie, and not without justification, but there was one big difference between fact and fiction. While a movie could bend the rules it had created for dramatic effect, real life had to live by them. Maybe I had hyperdrives and blasters and aliens, but everything still had its own rules, and as much as it would have been dramatic and oh-so-convenient for Thalassia to suddenly be a few hours away in hyperspace, the reality was, we spent over a week and a half in transit.

I don't know if it's possible to convey just how utterly frustrating that was. Not just because of the constant tension bordering on paranoia, convincing myself that Zan-Tar had figured out my plan and this was all for nothing, that he'd doubled back with his force and attacked Earth again without the Vanguards and the *Marauder* there to turn him back, that we'd return to the Solar System to find the planet's cities a smoking ruin. Not just from the worry that he'd sent more ships and troops than we'd anticipated to Thalassia and we'd get there only to be overwhelmed, basically the entire resistance fleet destroyed.

Those were bad enough. But the worst part was the questions.

"What happens if we get there and it's all over with?" Chuck asked, looking up from the stripped-down pulse rifle on the table.

The things didn't need *much* cleaning but there wasn't anything else to do, and I figured Chuck Barnaby, being a Ranger, would feel comfortable wasting a few hours disassembling and oiling every pulse rifle and pistol we had in the armory. That had been, as it turned out, a mistake.

"Lenny knows the deal," I assured him. "He's going to scout the system out and wait until we give him the signal before he tries to land with the transports."

"But what if the Anguilar just show up and wipe out the settlement there before we arrive?" he insisted. "Even if they don't get the Liberators, they could still destroy everything on the ground."

I counted to ten and concentrated on putting the slide assembly back on my heavy pulse pistol before I answered.

"What would the point be?" I asked, forcefully wrangling down the edge of annoyance from the last couple words of the reply. "They're not coming to kill some colonists, they're coming to wipe out our fleet."

Chuck nodded, then took a swig of coffee from the mug on the table, too close to the internal parts of his rifle if you asked me. I mean, I didn't *know* what coffee would do to the innards of the gun, but I couldn't imagine it would be anything good.

"Okay, that makes sense," he acknowledged and I sighed, thinking perhaps I'd addressed all of his worries by now, after an hour of random questions. No such luck. "Why couldn't we just time it so that we all came out at once? I mean, the Liberators could have gone slower and waited for us to catch up…"

"Because that's not how the hyperdrive works." My exasperation wasn't so much from the fact that it was a dumb question this time as it was that I had no idea of the why, only the how. "You don't go faster or slower in hyperspace. It's not like the Autobahn where there're no speed limits, it's like…a tunnel through a mountain. Or maybe an elevator through a tunnel through a mountain. Anyway, it's a shortcut but it always takes the same amount of time to go from one place to another." I closed my eyes and hissed in exasperation. "Well, it feels like the same amount of time to anyone going through, anyway. But it's not exact, not like down to the second, for reasons I don't completely understand. It's like…if you went into hyperspace right next to each other, at the same time, going to the same place, you'd come out close to the same time, within a few seconds or a minute apart at most. But if you're like over here…" I took the trigger assembly of my pistol and set it off to the side. "And your friend is in a system over *here*…" I set the barrel a few inches away. "And you're both going *here*…" The empty magazine stood in for the destination system. "Even if you both leave at the same time and the systems are the same distance apart, you won't arrive at the same time. It could be a few minutes' difference, it could be hours. There's no way to tell."

"That's pretty confusing," he complained, nudging the pieces of the pulse weapon around the table. "How does anyone ever get anything done?"

"Well, it's not like things back home. There's no way to keep in constant communications, there's no way for the Pentagon to look over anyone's shoulder. There's no way to get everything timed down to the last second, either, which means you're mostly on your own. It's like the 17th-Century sea captains, they're the master of their fates."

He nodded, though he didn't look happy about it. I couldn't blame him. He'd been born and raised with the instant communications and new orders coming in for every different situation, and this was some outlaw stuff that he'd never been trained for. I wasn't sure anybody had. Maybe Laranna was right, maybe Chuck couldn't have handled the whole abduction thing.

"Okay, but there's one other thing I was thinking about last night," he said, raising the cooling jacket of his rifle like it was a conductor's baton. "Let's say we get there and the Liberators send down the transports and the Anguilar just…blow them up? I mean, why wouldn't they? They're gonna think it's the Gan-Shi, and I thought part of this whole deal was to wipe out our refugees."

At least this one I could answer, even if I wasn't entirely sanguine about that answer.

"Warrin. Zan-Tar still thinks Warrin is his agent in place. There's no way he can know that we rooted him out. And he promised Warrin the Gan-Shi as his own private fiefdom. We have to believe he's going to keep his word."

Chuck squinted at me skeptically.

"And why would we believe that, exactly? The guy's a first-class douchebag."

"But he's a douchebag who thinks about the long game," I said. "So far, he's used that against us. I'm hoping this is the one time we can use it against him. Make him realize the short game is important, too."

"Do we *have* a long game?" Chuck asked, not looking up at me, concentrating on his rifle.

Which was uncomfortably close to the conversation Laranna and I had a couple nights ago. And the answer was the same.

"I guess we'll find out in a couple days."

28

It had been a while since I'd visited Thalassia.

I'd meant to, and I'd sent patrols out here more than once, supply runs from Sanctuary, administrators to help the Copperell here get their local government and economy set up, but things kept coming up, getting in the way of my plans to come back and check on the place.

Flying my Vanguard well out into the system's asteroid belt, the planet felt just as far away as it had back on Earth for all that I could see the blue and green sphere clearly in my cockpit optics.

"No ships in orbit," Chuck said, and I glanced over at him, wondering if he thought I couldn't read the sensor display myself or if the Copperell who'd trained him for the right seat had told him he needed to announce everything aloud just in case. "No weird energy readings on the surface. I guess we made it in time."

"You're a major, right?" I asked, tapping a command into the communications console.

"You know I am. You were there when I got promoted." I couldn't see his face with his visor down, but I heard the irritation in the reply.

"If you're not a captain anymore," I went on, adjusting the transmission antenna toward the outer system, "then you shouldn't be captain obvious."

"Oh, you're a barrel of laughs, Travers," he sneered. "I'm a Ranger, not an Air Force zoomie. I'm doing the best I can."

I waved an apology, blaming my short temper on tension. There was a lot to be tense about. The rest of Vanguard Wing floated as if in a long, slow orbit around the system's sun, matching the path of the rocks that, theoretically, shielded us from sensors. Until I sent this signal. If the Anguilar picked it up, they'd know we were in the system and this whole thing might come apart at the seams.

I touched the transmit control. No words, no images, just a short burst of data, and I didn't expect a reply. Transmitting outward was a gamble. Sending a signal back inward toward the planet would be suicide.

"Signal is out," I told Chuck. "All we can do is wait."

"Who's Captain Obvious now?" Chuck murmured. "How long do you think it'll take for them to show up?"

"Assuming they're somewhere in the outer system," I said, ignoring the verbal jab, "just a few minutes. They have to clear the gravity well of whatever they're hiding behind, then micro-jump in."

"Where do you think the Anguilar are hiding?"

As if I knew.

"If I had to guess, they're probably toward the inner part of the system, using the sun to drown out the sensors from the Liberators."

"That means we won't see them, either, until it's too late," Chuck worried. Chuck constantly worried whenever we were in a ship or a fighter, I suppose because he was out of his element. Dani had been the same way at first. The memory of her took the bite out of my reflexive reaction to Chuck's kvetching.

"We know they're here, and hopefully, they won't know we know." Which sounded more confusing than I'd intended. "What I'm counting on, other than surprise, is that Zan-Tar is pissed. This whole time, since he took over, he's been one step ahead of us, and part of that is he doesn't get emotional. The last Anguilar general was a diva, thought he was God's gift to the universe and made it personal when we got in his way. Zan-Tar has been a professional up till now. I want to make him mad."

"You've got a real gift for pissing off our own generals," Chuck admitted. "Hopefully, it works on both sides."

I had a very snide comeback ready about how the Anguilar Empire would never have conquered the galaxy if they had their own version of the Pentagon, but never got the chance to use it. Chuck waved frantically at the sensor screen, but I'd already seen the eruption of blue icons flashing into existence off the shoulder of Thalassia. Four of them, massive and monolithic, each capable of carrying thousands of refugees to their new home here on this isolated colony.

"How long do you think they'll wait?" Chuck asked, leaning closer to the screen as if he could get more details that way.

"Till they think it's too late," I told him. "Once the transports are in the atmosphere."

And thankfully, that satisfied him. At least long enough for the Liberators to head planetward, inserting into a high orbit. I badly wanted to radio the rest of the wing, or at least my squadron, and warn them to be on the lookout for the Anguilar fleet, but that was just as much an attack of nerves as Chuck's ceaseless questions. Everyone knew what to do. We'd spent the last eleven days rehearsing it over and over.

Still, I couldn't resist a glance at Dagon's Vanguard, nestled into a close orbit around the same rock we circled, shrouded in the darkness of the asteroid's shadow, barely a blip even on thermal. I'd had an idea of asteroids based on movies and TV shows as jagged and oddly shaped, but the truth was, they were mostly round, drawn into the same shape as a planet or moon by the same force—gravity. It was a little disillusioning, taking away some of the mystery of the things, revealing them as just small planets, or planetoids, which was another sort-of-scientific name for them. No giant space worms burrowed into bottomless caves, ready to leap out and try to eat spaceships. Just a handy little planet getting in the way of the enemy's sensors.

The Liberators maintained a tight formation on their way to orbit, just blue dots on the sensor screen, much too far away for us to even see a glint of reflected light from them. Everything was far away. That was another illusion of space combat that reality had disabused me of the idea that you could see all those ships floating in space like World War Two fighters and bombers in a 1950s war movie. At anything past a hundred miles or so, they weren't even glowing dots, just simulated shapes on the sensors, and we were lucky to have those. Forget the video games I'd played in the arcade, this was more like the old asteroids game with a little white triangle on a flat screen.

It created an artificial distance on top of the real one, which was dangerous because a pilot could easily forget how quickly a hyperdrive starship could close that gap. I tried to keep that in mind as I watched the Liberators drop into high planetary orbit. It was barely a few seconds later that the transports launched, a swarm of tinier dots against the curve of the planet. No details were visible on the screen, but if I closed my eyes, I could envision the bulbous, portly cargo landers waddling their way out of the hangar bays, dropping with casual abandon into the atmosphere, just like a welcome visitor heading down to friendly territory.

This would be about the same time that Lenny would broadcast the warning to the colonists, sending them into their shelters. It sucked for them, and guilt stabbed at my chest at the thought of Wendra and Maya having to hide in fear again after we'd promised them we'd defend their people against the Anguilar.

And we would. But that didn't mean we'd be able to prevent the collateral damage from this fight. All I could think to console myself was that we'd pay to rebuild any destruction we brought to them.

"There!" Chuck said. "Hyperspace windows on the opposite side of the planet.

The threat alert did a better job of warning us, but I hadn't needed either of them to tell me what I could already see. Not just a single formation of red icons, but a sea of blue, like someone had emptied out one of those ball pits for kids at a Chuck E. Cheese's. For a moment, I thought every one of them was a cruiser and we were totally screwed, but the panic dissipated when the sensors reported back that only twenty-one of them were cruisers, the rest the Starblades and troop landers they'd launched almost immediately after coming out of hyperspace.

"Go!" I transmitted, powering up my reactor before anyone else had the chance. "Everyone jump!"

The great thing about asteroids, despite their appalling lack of giant space worms, was how little gravitational pull they had and how little they disrupted the formation of a wormhole into hyperspace. Drive pods down, add a little thrust to clear the rock, tap the preprogrammed coordinates for the hyperdrive, and I pushed the jump levers forward hard enough to bruise the heel of my hand.

The Vanguard surged into the roiling nothingness, snapping my thoughts like the business end of a bullwhip, and it took every bit of willpower and concentration I had to keep my eyes on the timer telling me when to yank the levers back the opposite direction. Coming out of hyperspace after a micro-jump toward a planet was how I imagined it was like being born, emerging from the utter darkness into the glaring light of Thalassia.

Unbelievably close, yet too far away, a baseball glowing in the night, and I shoved the throttles open, heading not straight at the planet but straight for the Anguilar cruisers. They were visible with the optical cameras, silver wedges cutting through the ether, and around them were clouds of Starblades, though not as many as they'd launched at Earth. Maybe they'd made a strategic decision that they'd need more of them for that battle.

Chuck made a strangled sound deep in his throat that he'd probably rather I hadn't heard, an instinctive fear that I was about to commit suicide by throwing the two of us alone against an enemy fleet, but I noticed the IFF board lighting up as the rest of the wing emerged behind me…and behind them, the massive slab of metal that was the *Marauder*.

The Anguilar cruisers were backlit by the flare of their sublight drives, shrieking toward the Liberators like wolves on a flock of sheep, but the second the *Marauder* jumped out behind us, their drives went dark almost as one. If they had been wolves, they were the cartoon version surprised by the sheepdog, digging in their heels and trying in vain to stop their forward motion.

They'd been accelerating too fast, though, and so were we. The red range line on the targeting screen intersected the lead cruiser before any of them even had the chance to hit their maneuvering jets, and I jammed down the firing stud without bothering to designate targets. No time for such tactical niceties now.

The blast of atomic lightning didn't destroy the enemy ship, not this far away, but her shield glowed in a crackling, static arc, and she shuddered upward with the jolt of kinetic energy. On the heels of my shot, a barrage from the rest of the wing as well as the *Marauder* tore into the Anguilar ships, half a dozen of them erupting in gouts of vaporized metal. And that was before the Liberators got involved.

The Anguilar thought they could handle four of the giant ships with twenty-one cruisers, and maybe they could have, but the combat crews aboard the former Zoo Ships proved that it would still have been a near thing. Particle cannons were fearsome weapons—I'd been on the ground in the open way too close to one of them striking home, and I'd been ready to believe it was the planet exploding around me. Out here, they crisscrossed in a galactic spiderweb, our beams passing theirs along the way.

Some of theirs hit. The Liberators were big targets, hard to miss. But they also had some badass shielding, more than a cruiser, *much* stronger than a fighter, and while all four of the Zoo Ships were quickly surrounded by the white globes of their defensive fields being taxed to their maximum, they held. The Anguilar cruisers did not.

Supernovas burst like fireworks, each taking with them hundreds of Anguilar and Krin and Copperell, and for some reason, I felt each of those deaths more than I had before. Maybe because I'd just seen all those crewmen on the enemy ship, seen the fear and resentment and desperation in their faces.

This time, the Starblades stayed out of it, following the landers down to provide air cover, which worried me. I counted the number of remaining Anguilar and made a decision.

"Vanguard Two and Three, stay on the cruisers. My guess is they're going to make a run for it once their losses approach one-third. First squadron, we're going down to cover the landers."

"Vanguard One, this is One-Two," Dagon called immediately, almost stepping on my transmission. "Shouldn't you let me take point?"

"Two-One," I replied, grunting with the effort of speaking against the lateral acceleration of the drive pods swinging around and pushing us back toward the planet, "the day I let someone else take point is the day I'm ready to retire from the field. Follow me in."

29

THE TEMPTATION TO keep checking the rear sensors was nearly irresistible, not just to make sure that my people were okay but because I had a paranoid suspicion that the cruiser Zan-Tar had escaped in was coming here. Just one extra enemy ship might or might not make a difference in the fight, but if it did, I'd blame myself. And I'd need to take my squadron back up to deal with him.

Right now, though, the biggest worry was four squadrons of Starblades riding cover on two dozen troop carriers. They descended through layers of cumulus clouds on the day side of the planet, fading from view on the optical cameras but still shining bright on thermal from their drives. They were diving fast but not as fast as we could since they didn't have shields, a factor I hadn't completely understood at first, thinking of the shields as something that only blocked energy weapons. Gib had explained it to me, snide and snarky as usual.

"Whaddya think heat from friction with the air *is*, you big dummy?" he'd said. "It's energy! We can't just zoom straight down like a brick, of course, because the shields have their limits and we'd burn up eventually, but yeah, the shields work against friction!"

I hadn't exactly been embarrassed because how the hell would I know? But any discomfort I felt then was well balanced by how useful that information was right now. It wasn't natural, boosting straight down into the atmosphere, not even trying to orbit the planet a few times to slow the descent, and my stomach tried to claw its way out through my mouth in protest. The only thing that kept me from panic was a complete focus on those fighters, on the rangefinder reading telling me how far out of the range of my particle cannon they were.

Too far. They were going to get too close to the troop transports who'd already landed, and I couldn't have them firing on those ships or the people in them. A feral grin accompanied the thought that the particle cannons might not be able to shoot those Starblades down from this range...but they could sure as hell make things uncomfortable for them.

After shifting the reticle to a spot at the center of the rearmost squadron, I pulled the trigger.

"Shit!" Chuck blurted as the blast shook us like a bone in a dog's teeth, turbulence from the sudden spike in heat and static electricity washing back over us and sending the shields glowing a dull orange.

The effects on the other side of the weapon were a good deal worse. The cumulus clouds crackled with lightning, a wash of heat turning them into a wave of plasma pushing a wall of hot air in front of them. Into the rear of the Starblade squadron. The Van de Graaf generator effect of static electricity slicing through the fighters probably did nothing to the pilots inside, didn't affect their drives, but it sure as hell affected their trajectory. The little spacecraft tumbled out of control, two of them slamming into each other and coming apart in a spray of debris and white-hot plasma.

The others managed to get back under control, but I'd achieved my goal. All four squadrons broke from their formation into long, arcing curves, turning to meet us. Leaving their troop transports to fend for themselves. That was all I'd wanted.

Be careful what you wish for, I'd always heard, and God chose that moment to illustrate the point. Over a dozen pulse guns converged on our Vanguard, and I rolled away from the blast with the shields glowing white hot around us, another roll of thunderous turbulence hitting hard enough that I almost lost control. The drive pods whirled on their gimbals, and one elephant stood on my chest while another planted a foot directly in the family jewels, forcing the air out of me in a wordless moan.

"Shoot back!" I wheezed at Chuck, spinning the fighter end for end and getting our nose lined up with the wedge formation of seven Starblades coming straight at us.

"I have been," he insisted. "It's hard to aim when you're spinning us around like that."

"I'm sorry, I'll just sit here and take all those hits, and we can have a congratulatory celebration of how well you can aim from a stationary base...in the afterlife."

At least the rest of the squadron wasn't sitting on their laurels. Dagon spun and feathered and rolled like the pro he was, his gunner laying out a blood-red rope of scalar energy that flared an angry white when it touched enemy fighters. I knew the Copperell could make a Vanguard stand up and beg, but the other five pilots showed me what I'd been too busy to see when I'd been off on my own, trusting Dagon to run the squadron while I did commander stuff.

Starblades burned and tumbled out of the sky, and I did my part, circling around the individual clashes and cluster attacks until one of the enemy fighters filled my sights. The pulse turrets might take a couple dozen shots to put down the bad guys, but a particle cannon wiped them out of existence with a single pull of the trigger.

Yet as I patrolled the perimeter of the conflict, I kept an eye on the one below. The Anguilar transports touched down in a ring surrounding the landers from the Liberators, their boarding ramps falling open before the landing gear had completely settled into the soft earth of the grass fields outside Philos.

The city watched, barren and resolute behind its walls, not a single civilian to be seen but their hopes and fears hanging over the towers and domes, the knowledge that once the armored Anguilar soldiers pouring off the ramps finished with the people inside the resistance cargo ships, they'd be next. Gray and black, the ground troops were Krin, Copperell, and a mishmash of other conquered peoples, maybe some of the officers even

Anguilar, and they all carried with them a confidence born of thousands of battles won.

And out of the boats from the Liberator...poured hundreds of United States Army Rangers, a full battalion, clomping stolidly off their own boarding ramps in brown-and-green-camouflaged armor seven feet tall, each weighing in at 300 pounds counting the new battery packs Lenny had helped them build. Armored exo-suits, that was what Chuck had called them. I'd seen the experimental samples, but these were off the rack, production models, designed to bring the pain to Anguilar soldiers in any terrain.

The Anguilar troops fired at extreme range, spooked by this new weapon, their pulse gun discharges barely visible even at extreme magnification on the optical cameras. Some of the shots hit, leaving charred, blackened stains on the camouflage coating of the armor and not doing a damn thing otherwise.

Trails of smoke shot away from the backpacks of the Onyx powered armor and missiles arced high above them before streaking back down at high speed and impacting in the midst of the charging Anguilar. The explosions at the center of the enemy formation weren't the typical puff of dark smoke I'd expect from a hand grenade or even the larger fountain of black with an orange flash at the center of a mortar round.

The blasts were more like the warheads the Russians had used against us in Siberia, sun-bright starbursts of plasma at the heart of a shock wave of concussive force. At the heart of the blast zones, pieces of armored soldiers were all that was left of the Anguilar forces, and even twenty yards away, the enemy troops collapsed, either knocked over by the heat and concussion or speared through the vitals by shrapnel.

Dozens of the Anguilar went down, and for all that their infantry had a reputation for being more brutal than smart, someone down there made the right call. When the opposition has a weapon that can blow the crap out of you at long range, shorten the range. The Anguilar charged, probably banking on their rifles being more effective against the thicker armor of the Rangers at a closer distance.

They were likely right about that, but they'd forgotten that the mechanical muscle that allowed carrying all that extra armor also allowed the Onyx suits to carry heavier weapons. I'd seen the prototypes for those, too, though I couldn't remember if they had a cool code name like the armor. The concept was simple enough. Just take six pulse rifles, pull out the guts, and build them into a rotary frame and you had yourself a minigun that fired scalar pulses at a faster rate than anything except the turret on a fighter.

It wasn't perfect. The things went through ammo like it was going out of style, and even with the mechanical muscle, there was only so much of the stuff they could carry. That, and those missile launchers on their backpacks took help to reload and you wouldn't be doing it under fire. They wouldn't be ideal for an extended battle that took them on foot over long distances, but for this kind of combat, they were ideal.

Swathes of energy sliced the Anguilar troops apart, stacking them up like cordwood, and from 1,000 feet up, the tipping point of the battle was as obvious as the last cut on a tree before it fell.

The enemy recoiled backward from the Rangers' withering fusillade, turned around, and fled back toward their landers first in ones and twos, then in squad-sized clusters before finally devolving into a panicked route.

Shifting my attention back to the battle in the air, I noted that the Starblades, too, were done with this fight, and the last handful of fighters had turned tail, making a run for cruisers that had probably already fled the system. I gave them little thought. Either they'd turn around and surrender or fall afoul of the Vanguard squadrons still patrolling in orbit. But I didn't want these ground troops trying to take off. There was too big of a chance that they'd try hiding in an unpopulated area and force us to root them out at the cost of high casualties.

"Take out the Anguilar troop transports," I ordered, reducing the power to the drives, sending our Vanguard downward so precipitously that my stomach stayed up there at 1,000 feet.

Swiveling the drive pods downward, I kicked the throttle again, and my spine shrank by a couple inches as we braked hard into a hover at the perimeter of the landing field. Chuck didn't need me to tell him what to do, his pulse gun chattering in excitement at the opportunity to take out sitting targets.

Red dashes chewed through the hulls of the grounded transports, blasting ragged holes through their engine compartments, and the other fighters in the squadron got in on the party, making sure the boats would never fly again. I refrained from joining in on the fun with the particle cannon. The Anguilar transports were parked way too close to our own landers, and I didn't want to risk collateral damage that would leave our own troops stranded on the planet.

Caught between the Scylla and Charybdis, the Anguilar soldiers looked back at the rows of their people still being chopped down by the Rangers and forward at the rain of fire disabling their landers…and surrendered. It started at the front, the ranks of the infantry who'd watched their escape plan go up in smoke, then moved backward until it reached the ones still engaged with the Rangers. Weapons were thrown down, hands thrown up.

I thought for a second I was going to have to radio Colonel Chapman and order him to start taking prisoners instead of just mowing the enemy down rank by rank, but the man surprised me, getting his troops in line with admirable alacrity. Rangers swiveled their rotary guns up on motorized gimbals and herded prisoners ahead of them, laying each out flat with their hands on the backs of their heads.

"Two-One," I radioed Dagon, "this is Vanguard One. I'm touching down. Keep a multi-level patrol of the airspace and send someone wide to make sure none of these guys got away."

"One, this is Two-One," he said dutifully. "I copy."

"Damn," Chuck said, drawing the word out into three syllables. "Those Rangers kicked some serious ass."

"That's what happens when the enemy is expecting to find a bunch of unarmed cows and gets Onyx powered armor instead," I agreed, the words emerging grim rather than exultant. That the plan had worked and we'd managed to pull it off without major casualties was reason enough to be happy, but worry still nagged at my guts, a conviction that there was a variable I hadn't yet accounted for, something I'd forgotten.

I pushed the thought aside and focused on landing safely amidst the wreckage of the smoldering troop transports. There was a narrow gap at one side, and I managed to squeeze the Vanguard into it, ignoring the painful crunching of debris under the fighter's landing gear. We sat there in silence for a moment, both of us catching our breath. Fighting a battle in a Vanguard and running a marathon had way too much in common.

My helmet suddenly felt claustrophobic, and at first I tried pushing up my visor, but then I just yanked the whole thing off. Maybe I'd regret it, but I had a sense that it was more important right now to be seen than to be protected. The helmet hit the floor with a metallic clunk, and I opened the hatch.

Crisp fall air struck me in the face like a splash of cold water, drying the sweat matted in my hair, and I sighed in relief. Before the stench hit hard on its heels. Burning metal, an uncanny chemical smell, acrid and sulfurous, enough to make me gag. Other things burning, not acrid or unpleasant but uncomfortably similar to a pork roast, and the knowledge of what I was really smelling turned my stomach more than the smoldering wreckage of the landers.

"Stay down!" a Ranger yelled, pushing a Krin back into the prone position. "Everyone take off your helmets and keep your hands behind your heads. Do *not* touch a weapon! If you have a handgun or a knife, we'll take it off you ourselves. Keep your hands away from them."

The prisoners seemed to be complying, and the few who

didn't received a painful thump from an armored gauntlet in the back of the shoulder to remind them. This close, the Onyx suits towered over me by a foot, the hum-whirr of their servomotors giving the Rangers a vaguely robotic feel. Heat radiated off their weapons still even a few minutes after the last shot had been fired, and I was sure if I had marshmallows, graham crackers, and chocolate bars I could have made s'mores by holding the combination over the rotary barrels of their pulse guns.

They were, as Chuck had noted, badass, and they knew it. That much was obvious from their gait, their swagger, the grins visible through their visors. They'd learn to get over that. Either Colonel Chapman would teach them the lesson or reality would. For now, though, they'd won a battle, and I wasn't going to be the one to rain on their victory parade.

"Your Rangers did a great job," I told Chapman as he clomped up to me with stiff, mechanical motions, his visor pushed up, his smile saying he agreed with me.

"Surprise is a hell of a force multiplier," he admitted, then tapped his chest. "Not that the Onyx didn't help." Chapman jerked a thumb behind him. "But it wasn't just us. We had one of your guys along for company, and he didn't even need a suit."

I hadn't noticed before, though I should have. I blamed it on the smoke and choking fumes and my stubborn refusal to keep my helmet on. He stood tall…taller than he had been before, nearly as tall as the Rangers in their Onyx suits. That was what had thrown me. It was the metal legs. And broader at the shoulders because those, too, were bulkier, gleaming silver. I didn't know how far into his torso the shoulders and hips extended because he wore a sleeveless leather duster over what looked like leather chaps and a vest, crisscrossing gunbelts at his waist.

What I should have noticed, though, was the cowboy hat. It was unmistakable, as was the face beneath it. The beard had grown back, but it stopped just short of his left ear and more metal stretched from where the ear had been to the eye on that side, which had been replaced with a glowing red ocular.

"Howdy, Charlie," Valentine McKee said, tipping his hat.

"Val," I stuttered, unable to keep the shock out of my expression. "What the hell did you do to yourself, man?"

He shrugged, a more mechanical motion than it had been once.

"Oh, you know me, ol' buddy. Just couldn't wait to get back in the fight."

30

"Shut your mouth before something flies into it," I advised Gib in a whisper, nudging him in the side.

It wasn't entirely his fault, of course. I'd had hours to get used to the new RoboVal, while Gib had just jogged onto the bridge after the last of the Vanguards had docked with the *Liberator*. He'd been presented with a *fait accompli* and was handling it about as well as I had.

"Dude," he blurted. "Why'd you do it? I mean, Lenny told us you could get replacements that looked just like your old parts, that you could feel just like before and everything. You look just like Brazzo, but he only had bare metal because that was all his people had to give him."

And wasn't *that* just awkward as hell? Laranna put a hand over her eyes as if she was embarrassed just to watch the reaction to Gib's clumsy commentary and the only reason I didn't was I couldn't look away from Brandy. I'd expected her to either lose her shit with Giblet for what he'd said or lose her shit with Val over what he'd done. She did neither. She simply rested her hands on her belly, a handy place for it as pregnant as she was, and looked at Val with utter adoration.

"I certainly offered him the other alternative," Lenny asserted, his voice as close to outrage as I'd ever heard it. "Despite my recommendations, he insisted on the option that offered the maximum protection and strength."

"It's his decision," I said with what I hoped was a note of finality, wanting to put an end to the conversation. "We're not going to sit here and try to talk him out of it. Do you all understand that?"

Giblet nodded with obvious reluctance, while Laranna said not a word. Luckily, we'd kicked the crew off the bridge, which just left Chuck as the only outsider present for the discussion. If I could still call him an outsider after everything we'd been through. I decided that was fair, since the rest of us had been together from the beginning and Chuck's first loyalty was still to the Army and the President.

He sort of half-nodded, as if he was very aware of that outsider status and didn't want to push his luck.

"Okay, what's the sitrep with the prisoners?"

"They're being locked up in what used to be the holding facilities for the miners when the Anguilar ran the operations," Brandy reported, clinical and casual as if the entire subject hadn't come up. "That's only a temporary solution, of course." She sneered. "I could think of a few more satisfying and *permanent* ones, but since we're committed to trying to end this conflict as bloodlessly as possible, we can't leave them in those ratholes. Not if we're going to make people think we're any better than they were."

Gib snorted derision.

"Shit, most of the people we recruit are just as happy forcing the Anguilar to live the way they had to when those bastards were in charge. They'd be just as happy killing them all."

"And that's the problem," I snapped, unable to hold the annoyance back, not with Gib but with the attitude he'd described. I looked around at the others. "I know we haven't talked much about this, but what happens if we win this war?"

"We go home and get drunk!" Gib said, spreading his hands. "I mean, I didn't sign up to be a traffic cop or a politician. What do I care what happens when we beat the Anguilar?"

"Do you intend to *live* in this galaxy after we free it from the Anguilar?" Laranna asked him before I had the chance, stepping nose to nose with Gib. "Because if you do, then you *should* care. What do you think is gonna happen if we just slaughter prisoners and don't give them the chance to surrender?"

"We'll kill every single one of the bastards?" he asked with a shrug. "And maybe most of the Krin, too."

"And then what?" she demanded. "Who do you think is going to run things? How are they going to get things done? Who's going to choose them? What if we wind up with someone as bad as the Anguilar? Or the Kamerians?"

"And who would that be?" he scoffed. "The Copperell? No offense"—he waved at Brandy—"but you guys couldn't organize a shore leave, and if you did, half of you would wind up turning in the other half to the cops. And the Strada, well, you guys are great fighters, but do you really think any Strada would even *want* to rule the galaxy?"

Chuck snorted a laugh, having the same thought that I was, but I didn't want to say it.

"And what about humans, Gib?" Chuck, apparently, wasn't afraid to say it. And Gib wasn't afraid to laugh at it.

"Are you serious? You guys didn't even have fusion until we gave it to you! You're too busy fighting each other to think about conquering anyone else."

"Gib," I said softly, "*I'm* a human, and I led the first successful uprising against the Anguilar. With me in charge, the resistance has gone from five unarmed Zoo Ships and a barely trained militia hiding away on a planet a thousand light-years from nowhere to a fleet worthy of the name and tens of thousands of troops. And there's a whole planet filled with people just as aggressive as me who we just gave starships and weapons to. If we don't take charge of trying to organize the galaxy, you can bet your ass that some Russian or Chinese or even American politician is going to do it for us. Do you want to be a second-class citizen in a *human* galaxy?"

Gib was used to talking people into things, into being the persuasive one, the smartest one in the room. His frown wasn't so much displeasure at what I'd said, I thought, as it was disappointment he hadn't come up with the answer himself.

"All right," he acknowledged quietly. "So we need to find a

new place for the Anguilar prisoners. Do you want to release them on someplace they can get transport back to the Empire?"

"No," I decided, an idea coming to me. "In fact, I think what I want to do is let the Anguilar pure-bloods out on a world like that and put all the non-Anguilar on…Sanctuary."

"What?" Laranna exclaimed, blinking in confusion. I hadn't talked with her about this because it had just come to me.

"Sanctuary was our home," Val protested, his red eye and his natural one both gleaming in disapproval. "You want to give it to them?"

"The Anguilar know about it," I pointed out, pacing across the bridge. "They'll be checking it to see if we come back. And we'll make sure to tell the ground troops and tech workers and fighter pilots about it, that all they have to do if they want to go back to being cannon fodder for the Anguilar is to wait until the Empire drops by and ask for a ride."

Laranna's confused frown morphed into a knowing grin…as did Brandy's.

"The Krin will want to do it anyway," she warned.

"So maybe we force the Copperell and the others to make a choice. They can either go back to being sacrificial lambs…or they can rise up against the Krin."

"And maybe wipe them out," Giblet said hopefully. "Then we get the bad guys dead and our hands are clean. I like this plan."

I shrugged.

"Yeah, there is that possibility, and if it happens, it's not my problem. I'm trying to teach them to take responsibility for their lives, that they have a say in their fate. If that means hanging their bosses from the highest tree and hoisting the black flag, well, that works, too."

"It's good to know we aren't getting *too* goody-two-shoes," Gib said, barking a laugh. "I don't think I could handle it."

"Then it's settled. Lenny, I don't suppose moving around EPWs is something that violates your Prime Directive shit about not engaging in combat?"

"I believe it would be allowed," Lenny told me, and if the machine had a tongue, it would have been planted firmly in his cheek.

"Then I'm counting on you to take the lead in this and organize the transport of prisoners to Sanctuary. Chuck, I need you to get with Colonel Chapman and see to having his Rangers guard the shipment back to Earth to pick up the prisoners from the cruisers and Starblades. Once they're back to the Solar System, we can switch the Rangers out for Skyros and the Strada and take them the rest of the way to Sanctuary."

"And what happens if there's a bunch of Anguilar cruisers hanging out at Sanctuary waiting for us?" Gib wondered.

"That's why we'll be going with them in the Vanguards," I told him. "But I think if I'm being honest, if there were enough enemy cruisers ready to go, Zan-Tar would have showed up here with more of them." A scowl showed up unwelcome on my face. "I would have sworn he'd come here, that he would have known what was coming after what happened back in the Solar System, that he'd outsmart us again here."

Chuck laughed and clapped me on the arm.

"Come on, Charlie. I know you think this guy is the Anguilar version of Napoleon or something, but there's a limit to how much he can anticipate. He's not psychic. He got caught with his pants down. He's probably off somewhere licking his wounds."

"Maybe," I grunted, unconvinced, "but I feel like if he was on that cruiser that got away, there's no way he wouldn't have at least shown up here."

"If he wasn't on that ship," Laranna pointed out, "that would have to mean he's dead, that he was on one of the cruisers that got destroyed."

"And then all of our problems would be over," Gib enthused, laughing. "The only other alternative is that he surrendered and he's stuck in a prison camp with the other Anguilar waiting to be repatriated. And that's impossible because there's no way those idiots could keep quiet about it."

"And on that cheerful note," I said, offering him a baleful glare, "we have work to do. Let's get to it."

The group scattered to their various tasks, but before I could clear the bridge, a touch on my arm stopped me. Brandy's eyes were the scanners from a warship, picking out every detail, every weakness inside me.

"I respect you, Charlie."

I blinked. It hadn't been my first guess of what she was going to say.

"Thanks," I said, turning the word into a question.

"I wanted you to know that," she expanded, eyes darting off to the side as if checking to see if Lenny was listening. He always was, of course. Lenny was the ship. Lenny heard all and saw all and said next to nothing. "Because of how we last left things."

"You mean the Anguilar prisoners," I guessed. I did my best to keep the anger and disapproval out of my tone, and it was easier now than it would have been a couple weeks ago. "Look, I understand what you were going through. Val had just been hurt, and you're pregnant…"

Brandy chuckled, not the reaction I'd expected.

"Charlie, I was never going to torture the prisoners. But I badly needed them to *believe* I would. Which meant *you* had to believe it, because for all your many strengths, you're a horrible liar."

"Um…thanks, I guess." I wasn't sure I believed her. It might have been true, but it also sounded a lot like someone trying to excuse their bad behavior. But she seemed to sense my suspicions and rolled her eyes.

"Come on. Do you think that I would somehow lose my self-control because I was pregnant and my husband was injured? This was not the first time I've been in that situation. Many years ago, my husband, Maxx's father, was killed by the Anguilar, leaving me alone on a strange world with no friends and no family. I don't panic, and I don't lose my composure. Unless I want people to *think* I've lost my composure."

I don't know why that pissed me off so much, but it certainly did, and if Brandy never lost her composure, I'd never made that claim. I leaned closer to her, determined to keep the words private from the bridge crew even if Lenny would hear them.

"Yeah? Then what about Val? How could you let him go through with that? You're turning him into a damn killing machine." I jabbed a finger in the direction Val had left the bridge. "He could have a normal life…as close to normal as any of us could have."

I suppose I'd been trying to provoke her, but as if she were trying to prove the point that she couldn't be pushed into losing temper, Brandy remained calm.

"Val knows as well as I do…as well as *you* do that there's no normal life for any of us until we drive the Anguilar out of this galaxy. We were kidding ourselves to think there was, and now we're paying the price for it. That's why Val made the choice he did. He wants to end this as quickly as possible, and he'll sacrifice a chance to be normal to finish the job. For us." Brandy put a hand on her stomach. "For our son."

She walked past me off the bridge, leaving me staring after her. I still didn't want to believe her, but maybe that was because I didn't like being played. Because if Brandy was telling the truth, she'd played me big time, and she was my friend. What the hell could Zan-Tar have done?

31

Angular faces filed by me, each of them a sullen study in defeat.

"Why the hell are we doing this again?" Skyros asked quietly from beside my shoulder, his rifle clasped across his chest. Neither he nor the other Strada overseeing the prisoner transfer appeared comfortable with the process, and I couldn't blame them. "Why do we have to move the prisoners to one of the Liberators? I thought the plan was to use the cruiser we captured."

I nodded, distracted, not playing complete attention to him, concentrating on checking each of the faces passing by me, searching for something familiar.

"It was. But that was before we captured all those ground troops on Thalassia. We made the decision to send them to Sanctuary, which means we have to send the Vanguards to cover their approach and we can't afford to send them with these guys. The captured cruisers don't have complete crews yet, so that leaves a Liberty ship."

I wasn't being completely truthful with Skyros and I felt bad about that, but he should have known better than to ask me a question like that in front of the enemy prisoners of war. Chuck would have known, and I considered that in light of our new strategy, maybe I should consider running classes on military procedure for the Strada…and the Gan-Shi. A few of them were scattered through the Strada guards, their pure bulk and innate nastiness more of a deterrent toward any misbehavior from the Anguilar than the rifles.

The real reason was much scarier, one I didn't feel like sharing with Skyros or anyone else. It was stupid, unrealistic, and probably unprofessional of me, but I'd given into paranoia and used—possibly abused—my position of ultimate authority to make sure I got the chance to see the face of every single Anguilar before they were shipped off to repatriate back to their people. As crazy as it sounded, I had to make sure Zan-Tar wasn't hiding among the prisoners.

It was insane, a waste of time and resources, and I still didn't look away from each of those faces as they passed by. They looked back, each and every one of them. A few looked like they wanted to come at me, but none did. I wanted to think that it was because they were intimidated by me, but it was likelier the Gan-Shi.

Hundreds of them shuffled by through the airlock connecting the captured cruiser to the *Liberator*, and after a couple hours of watching, they all seemed to run together. One dirty look after another, wishing me death in so many unpleasant ways. I wondered if I'd made a mistake allowing them to repatriate. I'd expected at least a modicum of doubt among them, maybe planting a seed that this war wasn't worth fighting, but only open hatred and resentment greeted me. Maybe Gib was right and we should have just killed them all.

I'd just about given up on the whole thing and begun to invent excuses to give everyone except Laranna. She knew. I could never keep anything from her. Before I could come up with any ideas beyond admitting I was a paranoid loon, an Anguilar caught my eye.

By trying not to. Not one of them had attempted to disguise their feelings, much less their faces, but this one had found a formal dress cap somewhere. I'd seen them before, on Copperell, but only among garrison troops trying to impress their underlings with how important they were. The thing resembled a cross between a Robin Hood hat from that Erroll Flynn movie—or maybe the cartoon one—and a Russian *ushanka*, that fur thing with the ear flaps. And if that sounds inexact, I can't help it. They were aliens, and they wore funny hats.

This guy had his pulled down over his eyes with his chin tucked down into his chest for good measure, and he kept his shoulder against the far bulkhead, as if he was trying to use the Anguilar crewman ahead of him to block my view. It was clumsy, doomed to failure, but what else could he have done? There was nowhere to hide, nowhere to run.

I didn't say anything immediately, worried he might try something violent, but I did pull out my comlink and whisper a command to one of the Strada across the airlock umbilical. Just in case. The guard moved slowly, naturally through the crowd, as if going off shift or simply taking up a new position.

Good soldier. Her name was Shonna, and I only knew her because she and Laranna had talked at the memorial service for the fallen Strada on Sanctuary. It was an uncomfortable feeling leading so many people I could never hope to remember all their names, so I made a note of those who stood out, creating a mental list of who I could trust with responsibility. The list was depressingly short.

The Anguilar in the hat did his best to fade into the background, and I let him think it had worked, not focusing my gaze on him, just following a long scan up and down the ranks. I kept track of him in my peripheral vision using a trick Laranna had taught me, one her people taught to hunters. They shared the same superstition as human soldiers, that staring at a person even from hiding, even from behind, would alert them to the fact they were being watched.

We just had to wait until the guy in the hat made his way close enough to my position that he wouldn't be able to bolt and then….

He bolted.

"Shit!" I blurted, pointing at the shadowy figure as he turned and made a run back into the cruiser. "Stop him!"

But the Anguilar had stopped being sullenly cooperative like the shadowy figure had flipped a switch, all of them throwing themselves at the guards, pounding fists futilely into hard body armor…except *I* wasn't wearing hard body armor or a helmet, and they were coming after me, as well.

I'd never been a big fan of zombie movies, and this was a lot like being trapped inside one, ravening expressions, gnashing teeth and grasping hands everywhere. Except these zombies weren't the silent kind. The Anguilar yelled obscenities, some of which made no sense even running through the translator, or just screamed incoherently, determined to block our way even if they couldn't harm us.

And because I was the only one not wearing combat armor, a whole bunch of them took a special interest in me, taking out their frustration over not being able to hurt the guards. There was neither the time nor the space to draw my handgun, pressed as I was on every side by enemy, and a dozen blows rained down on me in as many seconds, the impacts dull and blunted by how packed together they all were.

Panic surged in my gut, and I lashed out instinctively, forgetting everything from Taekwondo, from Laranna's Strada self-defense classes, from the MMA Chuck had practiced with me and resorting to the tactics of the playground when I was eight. Elbows and knees and stamping on feet and shins and God only knew who I hit or how much good it did, but gradually, an envelope opened around me, giving room for me to put force into the blows.

It reminded me of *poomse* practice in Taekwondo, fighting multiple faceless opponents at once in a series of choreographed kicks and punches. I'd always thought they were silly, artsy, and impractical and mostly just good for practicing balance and precision, but I recalled them in this moment. Block, elbow, punch, kick, turn, kick again, just like the forms except that each blow found a target, sank deep into a solar plexus, or cracked against a jaw, each block pushed aside a wild strike.

The guards waded in behind me, rifle butts flashing like reapers among the sheaths of wheat, and behind them, Shindo swept backhanded blows that sent Anguilar tumbling in his wake. Between their efforts and mine, a hole opened through the throng of enemy, a gap back into the cruiser, and I took it, ducking my head and guarding my face as I raced back through the docking umbilical.

Then I was through, past the end of the crowd of enemy prisoners and the guards trying to get them back under control, into the empty corridors of the captured cruiser. And lost. I had no idea where this guy would run to. Engineering was occupied, and so was the bridge, and if the escaped prisoner was crazy enough to go there anyway, they'd at least call for help if they didn't just shoot him.

Hangar bay. There were shuttles there, but we didn't have enough people for a permanent crew yet. He'd be heading for the shuttles. None of them were capable of interstellar flight, but if he got one, he could fly anywhere in the Solar System, and if he was smart, he could make a pretty big mess with just a lander. He'd definitely force us to waste a lot of time and resources looking for him.

I had to get there first.

Running through a basically empty ship felt surreal, like one of those weird dreams where you were lost in a strange city and couldn't find your way home, and there was no one to ask for directions. Not quite a dream though. The weight of my pulse pistol gave a grim sense of reality to it.

It had to be Zan-Tar, I figured. He'd been on one of the ships, and his hadn't been the one that escaped so he'd hidden among the crews. Maybe he'd thought he could pass for just another officer, that we'd miss him, repatriate him along with the rest of the Anguilar, and he could go back with a treasure trove of intelligence. And maybe I wasn't nearly as paranoid as I thought.

What was the old saying? If everyone's out to get you, being paranoid is just good sense.

Pushing aside the worry that he might be lurking in some niche or doorway, ready to ambush me, I sprinted through the corridors, the empty echoes of my footsteps hollow and haunting. He wouldn't be thinking about attacking anyone, just getting out before the warning could be sent ahead to intercept him.

Maybe that was what I should have been doing, getting on the comlink and letting Gib and Laranna know to launch the Vanguards, or telling the crew of the *Liberator* to blast any shuttles they saw launching from the captured cruiser. I didn't. Maybe because I sucked at delegation or maybe because I had to know. I had to see his face and know for sure that it was him, that he was out of the picture and we didn't have to worry about him anymore.

The hangar bay wasn't far from the utility airlock where we'd hooked up for the transfer, just a few levels down. No gravity chutes on Anguilar cruisers, not even an elevator, just simple ramps between floors, and I picked up speed as I descended until I was nearly out of control. Maybe that was why I blundered straight into the back of the escaped Anguilar, ran into him hard enough that it knocked the breath out of me, sent me tumbling off to the side with stars busting across my vision and my pistol spinning across the deck out of sight.

Stupid. I'd been stupid and careless, and I wanted to waste time chiding myself for it, but above the self-recriminations was the gut-level fear of letting Zan-Tar get the best of me again. I could barely see him, was only vaguely aware of his presence from a darker figure among the starbursts floating in my eyes, but that was enough.

He tried to jump to his feet, and I intercepted the move with a roundhouse kick to his knee. A squawk of pain rose up, and the Anguilar went the opposite direction, collapsing onto his back, clutching at his knee. His hat had fallen off in the struggle, but his face was still a blur behind the afterimages. I determined to make it even blurrier with an elbow strike. The screeching ended abruptly in a grunt, and his head slapped against the deck before he went motionless.

Heaving a sigh, I blinked the last of the lights out of my eyes, the details of the hangar bay finally coming into focus. The shuttles watched from the other side of the bay, their cockpit screens staring in disapproval at the show we'd put on for them. My gun had clattered up against the wall, and I rolled toward it, scooped the weapon up, and rose to cover the semi-conscious Anguilar.

A low moan came from beneath his hands, covering his broken nose, blood trailing down his chin, and it took a moment for his eyes to focus on me. I expected hatred, resentment, anger. What I got was…recognition.

"Hi again, Charlie," he said, pulling his hands away.

Suddenly, it was over a year ago, and I was back on the Nova Eclipse, making a deal with a very ambitious, self-serving junior officer in the Anguilar fleet. He'd made a deal to betray his own people in order to advance his career, and I'd let him do it. I'd let him get away because I'd given him my word, because the fate of multiple planets was more important than giving the low-life scumbag his just desserts. That would, I reflected grimly, teach me to ignore the bitch that was karma.

"Von-To," I sighed. "Fancy meeting you here."

EPILOGUE

"You're sure about this?" Gavin said, staring through the one-way glass at the interrogation room.

Colonel Von-To sat shackled to the metal table at the center of it, his expression glum, his nose swollen and red. I'd whacked him pretty good, plus his knee still wouldn't bend right, but he didn't seem put out by the whole thing. For all his moral and ethical failings, the Anguilar was smart.

"How do you know we can trust anything he says?" Parker Donovan added. Now he, unlike Von-To, *did* seem put out. If he'd had his way, the Americans would have all the Anguilar prisoners, and I had no doubt what he'd be doing with them.

Which was one reason we were up on one of the captured cruisers—*our* captured cruisers, not the four I'd given to the US Space Force. I'd decided provisionally to name her the *Flying Fortress*, though I was still open to suggestions. Lenny's construction bots had done a number on her before he'd taken the Anguilar to a non-aligned world for repatriation, and now her interior was more suited to the resistance crews who would be flying her. Or sailing her, or whatever the correct term was. Opinions varied.

"We made a deal with him once before," I pointed out, "and he kept up his end of it. I think if Von-To believed there'd be a personal advantage in it for him, he'd sell out his own mother."

"And we already saw how ready he was to sacrifice the other Anguilar to facilitate his own possible escape," Laranna added. The rest of the Vanguard Wing had gone ahead with one of the other captured ships to watch over the transfer of the non-Anguilar Imperial soldiers to Sanctuary, but I'd asked her and Gib to stay behind with me.

Gib…he was in the interrogation room, though I couldn't see him at the moment. He stood in a corner, arms crossed, silently watching Van-To. Neither Gavin nor Donovan seemed convinced, but before they could give voice to any further objections, Gib spoke up.

"Tell me something, Von-To, old buddy." There was a qualitative difference to Gib's voice, something only those who knew him or knew of the Varnell would have picked up. A smooth, lullaby lilt that made my ears prick up, drew me toward the window with eyes wide, like I was listening to Albert Einstein discuss physics. "How the hell did a guy like you wind up second-in-command for a straight shooter like General Zan-Tar."

Giblet shrugged expressively as he moved out of the corner

and stood above Von-To. He leaned toward the Anguilar, palms flat on the table.

"I mean, he's as straight a shooter as you guys get, I should say. He wants to get the job done and doesn't seem too interested in all the political bullshit like your old boss, Mok-La. So, how did an ambitious bullshitter like you wind up working hand-in-glove with him?"

Von-To smirked confidently, though I couldn't be sure that was because he'd fallen prey to Giblet's Varnell charms or just from the Anguilar's innate smugness.

"You're right, General Zan-Tar only cares about getting the job done," he admitted. "And he doesn't much care how. He also doesn't have any use for the bloodline families." Von-To raised an eyebrow. "Calls us a bunch of back-stabbing bastards, which is surprisingly accurate. Which is why he needed someone like me. Someone on the rise in the families, someone with something to gain by hitching their wagon to a rising star. Someone who could smooth things over with the other bloodlines."

"Someone who has a secret he could hold over their head," Gib finished for him, cocking an eyebrow. "For example, the junior officer who made a deal with the enemy to sabotage a rival bloodline."

"Yes," Von-To said, pleasantly agreeable, not seeming bothered by the accusation at all. He spread his hands, the shackles clanking against the loop holding them to the table. "Someone exactly like that."

"And he isn't worried you'll betray him just like you betrayed Mok-La?"

"I'd be stupid to do that," Von-To scoffed. "He promoted me to colonel in a fraction of the time it would usually have taken and made me his second-in-command. Under one of the traditional officers of the old bloodline, I'd have languished away as a captain for another ten years and never been trusted with so high a position."

"Sure," Gib allowed, falling into the chair opposite Von-To's. "As long as his position is secure. But is it anymore?"

"Why wouldn't it be?" The Anguilar seemed genuinely puzzled.

"He just lost two battles in a row. Lost a bunch of cruisers. Won't that piss off all those traditional bloodline families?"

"Naw." Von-To waved the idea away in casual dismissal. "They don't give a damn about battles fought out here at the edges of the Empire. Dying out in the periphery is the military's *job*, after all. So long as the core worlds of the Empire remain untouched, no one cares."

"Well, *that* sounds very familiar," Gavin murmured cynically.

"So, what if we…*touched* them?" Gib suggested. "What if we were to hit Copperell, for example? Would the Emperor and the bloodline families be so blasé about it all then?"

Von-To laughed, not scornfully like some movie villain, but with genuine amusement.

"And how, pray tell, would you do that? I know *exactly* how many capitol ships you possess, and even considering the ones you captured from us and the effectiveness of your Vanguard fighters, there's no way in hell you could launch a successful raid on Copperell, much less hope to take the planet. After your boss, Charlie Travers, snuck onto the world for just a day and stole the secure ID processor, planetary defenses were doubled and internal security measures were beefed up to the point that *I* can barely get into the military headquarters." The Anguilar shook his head. "No, you're dreaming. You'd have a better chance of attacking the Imperial Redoubt itself than taking Copperell."

Frowning, I reached back and touched the comm control beside the one-way mirror.

"The Imperial Redoubt?" I repeated. "Where is that located? What do you know about it?"

Von-To looked around as if trying to figure out where I was hiding.

"Oh, hello again, Charlie. Why don't you come in and talk to me in person? It's so nice seeing an old friend pop up unexpected."

"Why don't you just tell us what you know about the Imperial Redoubt," Gib suggested, reengaging that smooth, convincing voice.

"I've heard rumors of this," Laranna told me, speaking quietly beside my ear. "But just wild tales from traders and smugglers, nothing I would have trusted."

"Who can *know* anything about the Imperial Redoubt?" Von-To replied. "The General has been there to receive his commission, but I certainly never have."

"What star system is it located in?" Giblet pressed him. "Surely you know that much."

"It was in the Copperell system when General Zan-Tar was

invited to meet with the Emperor," Von-To answered readily. "But I wouldn't look for it there now. It's long gone."

Gib's frown probably matched my own, and Laranna's mouth dropped open at the revelation we'd all received at approximately the same moment.

"It's mobile," Gib said. "This Redoubt thing is a ship?"

"No," Von-To said through a guffaw, his chains rattling as his shoulders shook with laughter. "To call it a ship is to call the polar caps of your world down there an ice cube. The Imperial Redoubt is the vessel that brought our people to this galaxy. It's a hollowed-out *world*, with dozens of hyperdrives, each of them the size of a cruiser, and it takes thousands of power cells to move it." He smiled, and his expression changed from narcissistic confidence to something approaching pride or patriotism. "It's magnificent. It's the reason we'll never be truly defeated. It's why I had no qualms selling you Mok-La, why I'd even consider betraying General Zan-Tar if you work hard enough to make it worth my while. Because no matter what you do, the Emperor and the bloodlines will be safe on the Redoubt."

"It's heavily defended, of course," Gib said, turning the question into a statement of the obvious in a way that might have been disarming even if it hadn't been delivered by a Varnell.

"Not as well defended as Copperell," Von-To told him. "As I said. But it doesn't need to be. It's a *planet*. A world the size of the fourth planet in this system. What do you call it again?"

"Mars," I supplied into the speaker, and Von-To nodded.

"Yes, that. It's an odd name. What is it in aid of?"

"An ancient god of war," I said.

"Well, your god of war would be at home on the Redoubt. The bloodlines each have a house guard to keep the other families from wiping them out. And of course, the Emperor's Own keeps the families from replacing him with one of their own choosing. Let's just say you could get past the patrols and the orbital defenses—that's very possible." He shrugged. "What would you do then? Would you lay waste to the planet's surface? It wouldn't matter. Our civilization is inside this hollow world, and all you'd accomplish would be to quash all the internecine fighting between our houses—and there is *so* much of that, as you've already guessed—and focus that hatred and resentment against you. If you attempted to land troops and go in on foot, you'd have to bring hundreds of thousands of them to get through the family guards and the Emperor's Own."

My hand crept toward the speaker control to give voice to a question I wanted to ask, but Giblet beat me to it.

"I suppose no non-Anguilar troops are allowed on the Redoubt." Another question couched in the form of a statement.

"Oh, a few," Von-To allowed. His eyes had taken on a glaze, like he was drunk or stoned, and I'd seen it before when the Varnell magic got to working on someone. "Some of the bloodlines don't trust other Anguilar to guard their families, fearing they would be too easily bribed into disloyalty to allow for an assassination attempt. They prefer Krin, of course, because those bastards are too mean to be bought. They're loyal not out of any sense of honor but just because disloyalty would require too much thinking. But I suppose there are a few other lesser peoples among them as well."

"Lesser peoples," Laranna snarled, surging forward a step as if she wanted to jump through the mirror and strangle Von-To.

"You've got something on your mind, Travers," General Gavin judged, watching me through narrowed eyes.

"I do," I confirmed, a smile spreading across my face of its own will. "And I'm happier than ever that I resigned my commission."

"I don't like the sound of that," Parker Donovan said.

"I'm not sure I do, either," Laranna admitted, eyeing me sidelong.

I turned away from the mirror, shaking my head.

"Then you're definitely not going to like *this*." Leaning in like I was the quarterback in the huddle for a fourth and long hail Mary at the end of the championship game, I sketched out my plan.

I was right. They didn't like it.

Amazon won't always tell you about the next release. To stay updated on this series, be sure to sign up for our spam-free email list at jnchaney.com.

Charlie and the rest of the crew return in Citadel's Fall, available on Amazon.

CONNECT WITH J.N. CHANEY

Don't miss out on these exclusive perks:

- Instant access to free short stories from series like *Backyard Starship*, *Sentenced to War*, and more.
- Receive email updates for new releases and other news.
- Get notified when we run special deals on books and audiobooks.

So, what are you waiting for? Enter your email address at the link below to stay in the loop.

https://www.jnchaney.com/taken-to-the-stars-subscribe

CONNECT WITH RICK PARTLOW

Check out his website
https://rickpartlow.com

Connect on Facebook
https://www.facebook.com/DutyHonorPlanet

Follow him on Amazon
https://www.amazon.com/Rick-Partlow/e/B00B1GNL4E/

ABOUT THE AUTHORS

J. N. Chaney is a USA Today Bestselling author and has a Master's of Fine Arts in Creative Writing. He fancies himself quite the Super Mario Bros. fan. When he isn't writing or gaming, you can find him online at **jnchaney.com**.

He migrates often, but was last seen in Las Vegas, NV. Any sightings should be reported, as they are rare.

Rick Partlow is that rarest of species, a native Floridian. Born in Tampa, he attended Florida Southern College and graduated with a degree in History and a commission in the US Army as an Infantry officer.

He has written over 40 books in a dozen different series, and his short stories have been included in twelve different anthologies. Visit his website at **rickpartlow.com** for more.

Printed in Great Britain
by Amazon